Meridian

BOOK & CANDLE

AURELIA T. EVANS

ENTWINED PUBLISHING

Book & Candle
ISBN # 978-1-80250-243-5
©Copyright Aurelia T. Evans 2025
Cover Art by Kelly Martin ©Copyright March 2025
Interior text design by Entwined Publishing
Published by Eternal, an Entwined Publishing imprint

Published in 2025 by Entwined Publishing, United Kingdom.

Entwined Publishing is a division of Totally Entwined Group Limited.

BOOK & CANDLE

Chapter One

Violet didn't even smell the incense anymore. People walked in and wrinkled their noses from the strength of sandalwood, cinnamon, lavender, whatever happened to be burning that day. The smoke got into her clothes, her hair, her skin. It rose up through the building to permeate the apartment above. But she'd gone almost completely nose-blind to it by now. Every morning, before turning the 'Closed' sign to 'Open', she lit the incense, closed her eyes, lifted prayers and blessings to the pantheon, then sent a text to Clive to come down when he was done fiddling with the coffee machine.

Her loose sleeves brushed against inventory like fingertips as she inspected the merchandise, mentally determining what she needed Clive to pull out from storage and what she needed to replace. Some—like the *Blessed Be* keychains, her stock of incense and candles, as well as cheaper altars and common tools and ingredients for rituals—were regularly reordered through wholesale vendors. No one *needed* a hand-crafted altar or a knife plated with real sterling silver to celebrate their spirituality. She had products for all kinds of budgets.

But she had to keep an eye on the rarer and more esoteric products, and twice a week, Father Bryer reluctantly pulled up to the back door of Book & Candle to bless any new inventory that might benefit from such a blessing, as well as to replenish her stock of holy water. She couldn't trust her wholesale vendors, who'd tried sending her false holy water because they'd assumed she wouldn't be able to tell the difference.

The only reason she thought Father Bryer did her the courtesy was because the good stuff didn't melt her like rain to sugar and she was the one who knotted the prayer beads and crucifixes for the necklace rack, with nary a cross-shaped scar on her palm.

She and Clive also hand-carved vampire stakes from ash. Plenty of vampire hunters did their own rough carving, because a working stake didn't have to be fancy, but sometimes a demon hunter had to dispatch a surprise bloodsucker from his territory or a civilian learned that there were real monsters in the shadows. They'd creep furtively into her magic shop, hoping she had more than New Age crystals. And she did — a whole wall of weapons, in fact, with stakes and knives of varying degrees of artistry. Most hunters and civilians were strictly practical, but even veterans appreciated a little embellishment now and then. Or she'd get the odd tourist who liked the idea of displaying a pretty stake next to their collection of Monster High dolls.

She turned over the 'Open' sign before Clive made it down, because it was eight-fifteen, and she didn't like the idea of staying closed much longer after her posted hours. Granted, her more serious clientele usually called this hour bedtime, but walk-ins could happen at any moment, and tourists were sometimes early birds.

Clive finally turned the corner from the stairs as she took her place behind the counter. He handed her the latte he'd made for her, with extra foam as an apology.

"Late night?" she asked.

"Me and my insomnia." Clive settled next to the weapons display and the raw materials to make more. Customers loved watching a handsome man working with his hands.

"Did you try my tea?" Violet tried to keep her tone even, because this was far from the first time Clive had come downstairs with dark circles under his eyes.

"You know I don't like tea."

"Better than the five mugs of coffee you use to try to caffeinate your sleep deprivation into submission."

"I'm working on it."

Violet sipped her coffee. Milk foam didn't quite make up for the last four weeks of complaining about sleepless nights without doing anything about them, even though he knew anything she gave him would be more effective than over-the-counter pills, folk remedies, or sleep hygiene rituals. She'd heard the creak of his bedsprings deep into the night as he would toss and turn. She would then light an unscented candle to chase off the darkness and pray until the spring-creaking stopped and her chest ached like a heart attack.

The bells over the front door jingled. Two girls who Violet assumed were morning birds between their coffee and a yoga session entered the shop, followed by a meticulously styled woman who Violet knew wasn't as frivolous as her costume would suggest.

Someone might look at Cam Brumley and see only a pin-up girl at the end of a themed-diner shift—or perhaps from a classier strip joint—but Violet's shoulders immediately tensed. As Clive carved, he kept an eye on Brumley while she browsed with the civilians. She was silent, deceptively casual, as the other two girls chattered and picked up things to smell them, inspect the craftsmanship, or try them on.

Brumley moseyed to Clive's station to watch him sharpen the point at the end of the branch. Her lips were set in a smile, but she smiled like a predator, showing her teeth in an aggression display.

Brumley finally gathered a dozen practical stakes from the bins in front of his station and carried them with a small basket of holy water and two new crucifixes—one made with black onyx beads and the other in ruby—to the counter for Violet to ring up in a series of practiced codes. She had a spreadsheet somewhere for when Clive had to take the counter or she brought in her cousin's friend Claudia to cover for her during convention weekends, bead shows, and ingredient-purchasing trips, but she knew the codes by memory—not by heart, because her heart wasn't necessarily in the business, even though she was still damn good at it.

The vampire hunter handed Violet a hundred-dollar bill. Violet handed over her change. There were no words exchanged, because Brumley didn't like Violet and Violet didn't like Brumley. They tolerated each other strictly for business, because business didn't care about vendetta, blood or otherwise.

Taking her paper bag, Brumley smiled again, showing five hundred teeth between carefully applied red lipstick. Petticoats swishing, she sashayed back out of Book & Candle. The bells sang merrily behind her.

Both Violet and Clive sighed in relief, almost in cadence.

The other customers didn't notice. With suggestive grins and barely restrained giggles, they gathered in front of Clive's station to watch him lean between his spread legs while he sharpened a stake. Clive flexed his muscles, built from years of physical labor, and grinned winningly right back at them. Violet didn't recommend using the stakes as dildos—from either end, because even the less pointy end could splinter—but Clive sometimes inspired the odd adventurous woman to purchase one of the more decorative pieces.

These girls weren't that kind of adventurous. They meandered instead over to the crystal section and selected small amethyst crystal balls, larger clear quartz shards, and a grab-bag of smaller, tumbled stones— popular among young and old alike.

Violet didn't generally work with stones, other than clear quartz and the occasional carnelian or chalcedony, but there was no denying that they were pretty. She had a bowl in her apartment bedroom for her own collection of smooth stones through which she sometimes ran her fingers to ground her as effectively as touching grass. In the city, she sometimes felt so disconnected from nature. It didn't hurt to have an abundance of it within her place of business and her home above.

Violet slipped the girls a beginner's guide to crystal use—most of it useless to them, but in Violet's experience, crystals tended to end up on a shelf and made people feel better just to look at them, so no harm, no foul.

She'd always trod the line between fraud and folktale, because when civilians entered a place like this, it was usually for fun, only occasionally desperation. In the same way they consulted a priest or read their horoscope, they visited Book & Candle for one of her protection pamphlets and a blessed silver knife, or they sneaked in on Thursdays for Frida's fortune-telling gig next to the crystal corner. Frida was as much a psychic as Clive was a witch, but Book & Candle collected the table rental fee and people rarely stormed into the store to demand their money back, because Violet promised nothing to anyone who didn't have knives strapped in unexpected places. As far as civilians were concerned, Violet was just another novelty New Age occult granola tattooed hippie Wiccan who played with plants and rocks and called religion by another name.

But she wasn't. And the people who mattered knew it.

The real Wiccans and other Neopagans tended to look down their nose at her, but they still bought their accoutrements from Book & Candle because she was local, almost as cheap as online, offered the occasional hand-crafted piece people couldn't find anywhere else, and nurtured the coolest carnivorous plants. Also, she sometimes sold herbs that weren't strictly legal – for a price.

The hunters tolerated her, too, because she provided an endless reserve of spells and sharp objects they could use against the demons in their fair city, and she could guarantee valid blessings and spells upon them. Some of their patrons got them the good stuff, the really rare stuff, or made their own, dabbling in magic and alchemy as only the rich could afford to do. But some of those same patrons surreptitiously purchased those things from Book & Candle anyway.

The demons wanted to eat her heart, in the most flattering way, but they left her alone, too, because she sold them the same extralegal herbs, spells, and weapons of their own.

Book & Candle was neutral ground. By Meridian standards, Violet and Clive were diplomats—untouchable. Everyone needed them as much as they resented them. At best, she balanced precariously on the fences between the factions, but as long as no one pushed her, she stayed out of everyone's way and let them have their war—somewhere else.

Perhaps she was simply an inevitability in a place like Meridian—a capitalist with a solid market grip on the guns and gauze, metaphysically speaking. If that were really the case, though, she'd probably be richer. As it was, Violet just felt fortunate that she could keep up with rent on the store and apartment and employ Clive full-time. She even had a nice little nest egg growing under the care of her financial planner, who'd been recommended to her by one of the demons who frequented the store. It was in that demon's best interest to keep her happy so she could keep him in secretly donated virgin blood, so Violet had taken the referral and hadn't yet been disappointed.

Her stretch of work hours saw another steady trickle of unpredictable customers, civilians rubbing shoulders with demons in disguise, angels sharing uncertain glances with hunters of every shape, size, and variety—and all of them wary of the witch with whom they did business. But in the end, money was exchanged and everyone left in better condition than they came, which was why Book & Candle had been able to operate smoothly for the last eight years.

Her parents had thought she was crazy to leave the mountains, the forest, the security and safety away from prying eyes. Crazy to leave family and venture out on her own with nothing but a spell, a prayer and a booth at several of the farmers' markets before putting six months' rent down on what had once been old tea shop in the downtown square—a relic of when downtown had still been a quiet little side town too far from I35 to garner much notice.

The historical downtown district had been the first place touched by Angela Cabrera's Gothic hand, the façades renovated to a haunted-house grime thoroughly taken advantage of for Halloween festivals and perfect for Violet's aesthetic. Sure, the store was, by generous description, cozy—and, by less generous description, cluttered—but it and the cramped two-bedroom upstairs did their duty.

She'd been alone at first, and that had been lonely and sometimes frightening, considering the element she and her store attracted. But after three years making it on her own, Clive had moved into the second bedroom. Both bedrooms could pretty much only hold a bed and a dresser each, but they liked having separate sleep space, even if they sometimes shared a bed.

She might have been the more powerful of the two, but hunters and priests could be a misogynistic lot, and having visible muscle nearby also dissuaded demons. So she'd effectively gained a bouncer, a good friend, and a portion of the rent covered in the bargain.

The city rang with cold stone and concrete and steel, but she heard birdsong here as well as home, she kept grass and earth in her shop and within walking distance, and she had easy access to the dead. She wasn't completely cut off, and the dark and light magic that threaded like lightning through each lodestone, cornerstone and headstone charged her almost as well as climbing trees, digging for earthworms by the pond bank, and cultivating her garden and greenhouse rows.

Because of Meridian's later nights and her most popular clientele's sleep schedule, she kept the shop open until nine in the evening — sometimes later, if she was working with a historically good customer on something custom.

Tonight, however, was relatively quiet. Clive had left his station to package dried herbs while she tended her indoor gardens ensconced under sun lamps on the other side of the room from the weapons. After she turned the sign to 'Closed', Clive held up an Indian food menu, which meant they'd have dinner together tonight instead of alone. She smiled, pointed to her favorites that he already knew then vacuumed the shop while he left out back to pick up the food.

It wasn't the most glamorous job in the world, and she and Clive didn't speak as much as they used to, especially back when they'd met each other through his stepbrother, a hunter.

More adjacent to her world than part of it back then, Clive had taken to her immediately, intrigued as soon as he saw her under the stained-glass lamps hanging above the counter. He'd said she looked like an angel, the golden and colored lights caught like fireflies in the halo of her curly hair and glittering in her dark brown eyes. His stepbrother had replied that she was no angel, and she'd concurred. Despite the warning in the hunter's voice, Clive had slipped her his number and hadn't had much contact with his stepbrother since. As far as that hunter was concerned, Clive had stepped over to the other side. Clive, however, could better tell the difference between what demons did and what she was. Magic flowed through her veins and seeped out of her skin, as incense seeped in, but it wasn't the same kind of magic as demons, any more than that of angels.

Violet checked the locks and wards, then headed upstairs to their shared living area, arranging the small coffee table with utensils and glasses. She started that evening's wine without him as she listened to her uncle's record collection and let the coil of her magic unwind, draping over her shoulders and curling through her hair like little serpents. Her magic never completely left her, but it needed to relax as much as she did. She wondered if she could convince Clive to use those well-worked muscles on her shoulders and back tonight—and maybe more, although she'd been sleeping solo for more months than she was used to since leaving home.

Clive re-entered through the back, set the security alarm—although her wards were more effective than any security system—and trod up the stairs with new smells much less familiar to her nose-blind senses and therefore welcome.

He kissed her hair as he set the bags on the coffee table. "So, how was your day?"

"Oh, you know, same shit. Wine?"

"I'll get it."

She unpacked everything and set out plates. Then she put another Billie Holliday in the player. She'd made no secret about the fact that she didn't like most technology. The security system was a requirement from their leasing company, but she'd never had a television, depended on an older code-based cashier machine, and merely tolerated telephones. She'd been pulled into the smartphone era kicking and screaming and ordered from her vendors online by necessity but refused to put her own store online, although Clive had offered to be in charge of it. One of these days, she might be desperate enough, but today was not that day.

She and Clive settled on the loveseat and said little, because they'd already shared their whole day. Violet didn't mind the quiet, and Clive seemed preoccupied as he ate. They finished with mango lassis, Violet reading a novel and Clive staring into nothing with whatever distracted him these nights. When he was done, he rested back on the cushion and rubbed at his face and eyes, stretching his back in the opposite direction he hunched during his work.

As much as she wanted him to give her the massage, she set down her book to crawl over and ease his fingers from where they dug at his eye sockets. She rubbed his temples, over his forehead, until his hands fell away from his face entirely and rested slack in his lap. She inhaled the mixed bouquet of garam masala with the spiciness of infused incense through the apartment and used the power of both to warm her fingers. If he wouldn't take the tea, maybe she could help him sleep in other ways.

Violet moved the massage to his scalp, lightly scratching through his feathery hair with her nails, then over the base of his skull, then down to the knotted muscles of his neck and shoulders. He groaned in a way that curled like candle smoke in her lower abdomen. When she pressed a kiss to his temple—feverish from her fingers—he leaned against it, then lifted his head to meet her lips, though he kept his eyes closed.

They weren't exactly a couple and never had been, unless Violet just hadn't known otherwise. They might have dated or might have just gone out. They'd had sex plenty of times, but neither of them discussed it, as though that would solidify the ghost of what was between them into something less mysterious and ethereal. Sometimes they fucked and sometimes they didn't, sometimes they went weeks without being seen together outside the apartment.

And now it had been over two months since they'd even kissed, and Violet hadn't known how thirsty she was until she drank from him. The whole point of whatever they were was that they'd never be alone when they didn't want to be, that they'd always have a friend or a lover or a partner on the other side of a wall or right next to them if they needed. But although their daily routine hadn't changed, she'd felt so alone at night. She didn't think she was supposed to, not in Meridian, which fairly seethed with ghosts and monsters and everything in between, and where someone or something was always watching. So why did she feel so unseen?

She'd just eaten, yet below her stomach, how she hungered. She framed his face between her hands, sending whispers of wish and suggestion, not to manipulate but because it was easier to make him feel what she wanted than to say it. And she was, in the end, a witch. If he'd wanted just a woman, he wouldn't have moved in with her.

He gathered her in his arms as she climbed over his legs, but although he was hard against her when she straddled him, he drank less and less from her, his kisses more passive, and his hands too gentle on her, as though running over the same paths again and again to only mimic desire. He wasn't there with her.

Violet sighed and sat back on his thighs.

"I'm sorry." Clive rested his head back on the cushions. "I want to. I'm just tired. The magic can help with a headache, but..."

"I'll put the tea on your nightstand this time," Violet said. "If you drink it with a straw, you barely have to taste it."

He managed a weary smile, kissed her back when she kissed him, but it wasn't the kiss of a lover.

As she climbed off him, they might as well have been on different sides of the same mountain on the loveseat. She didn't like it. Even during previous dry spells, they'd had companionship. Without the benefits, they'd still been friends. But every night he felt farther and farther away, and she didn't know what she was doing wrong.

Other men—good and evil—wanted her, for all kinds of reasons. She didn't know why the one she needed didn't want her anymore. But she couldn't say anything now, because they hadn't said anything from the start, and she knew better than to hold too hard, or else what was already slipping through her fingers wouldn't be there anymore at all. Whatever distracted him, he'd tell her about it in his own time, or he'd resolve it on his own.

They'd promised each other nothing. She couldn't expect more than his portion of the rent and what she employed him for, and he could leave at any time, although she dared him to find a better deal so close to the historic downtown, a stone's throw from the best of Meridian.

She made the chamomile and catnip tea and stirred turmeric, honey, cardamom and cream in with the straw. Then she laced it with an under-breath chant, *"May slumber strike soon and swiftly and as gentle as the stroke of a feather."*

Violet brought the drink to his nightstand, as promised, then made one of her own, without the catnip or chant. She stopped the record player, which left the apartment too quiet while the two inhabitants knocked about with their evening rituals.

She considered leaving the loneliness of her own home and going to one of the clubs. She was as untouchable there as in her store, but any antagonism toward her could be its own deterrent. It had an energy effect on the people around her, whether they knew why or not. She thought about visiting Cemetery Grove to commune with the graveyards, although the stone angels there refused to speak to her. Or maybe she could bring herself into the twentieth century only a few years too late and go see a movie.

Anything she thought of made her more exhausted than she already was, despite the nervous, horny energy she'd yet to exorcise.

After Clive finished in the bathroom, she took a long, hot shower, then lotioned herself slowly to rub against the muscles that he hadn't. She wasn't sure when she'd started to ache like this, joint and bone deep, untouchable by herb or incantation. Maybe there was a storm coming. Maybe she was more upset than she'd thought.

Or maybe it was just that she was older now — although far from old — and with wisdom came pain. She'd consult her grandmother's grimoire in the morning. If nothing else, Ethel Panabaker was no slouch when it came to her remedies, for anything from the sudden onset of a cold to the most violent heartbreak, sour stomach to lingering grief. Violet modeled her own grimoire on her grandmother's, wished she'd known her longer in life so she could seek advice more directly than through fading scribbles.

Violet uncapped her hair, then wrapped it up before taking the rest of her tea into her room, where she read until she couldn't keep her eyes open. Clive had already closed his bedroom door. He might as well have locked, bolted, and sealed himself away.

She needed to go to his door. She needed to knock. They needed to talk. It needed to happen, and soon. She needed to ask if their arrangement was no longer adequate, if there was anything she could do, or if what had brought them together had since frayed away, like a boat untethered. She needed to know if he still loved her as a friend, as something more. She needed to know if he wanted out, if he wanted to leave as her lover, as her friend, as her coworker. It would hurt to cut ties, but she hurt more not knowing whether she should reel him in or set him loose. It was time for a change, instead of this constant holding pattern, like a haunting — ghost ships passing in circles. Boundaries encouraged healthy growth, but once a plant outgrew its container, those borders could suffocate.

Violet reached up to stroke the shoots of the spider plant hanging above her bed as though to ask it what she should do, but plants didn't concern themselves with the doings of people, as long as the plants were fed, watered, and put in a place to soak up sun.

She tucked her book back in its nightstand drawer and switched off the lamp, sighing.

Just as she started drifting to sleep, she jolted awake as though falling.

At first, she didn't know what had brought her back, but then the creaking of mattress springs through the layers of dry wall between her and Clive's bed grounded her. Not the quick series of squeaks that meant he was restless in his inability to fall asleep, but the kind that meant he was either with someone or engaging in particularly enthusiastic masturbation.

Either one hurt her from chest to fingertips, because she'd been *right there*, and he'd told her he was tired. She hadn't heard any of the door alarms go off, any floorboard creaks on the way up the stairs. So he would rather jerk himself off than fuck her.

She was a goddamn folk witch of the Panabaker and Corinth lines, and even those who hated her watched the way her breasts moved under her dress when she chose not to wear a bra during summer, which in Texas lasted well more than half the year. Her body was wanted, whether whole or in parts, yet she was sexually frustrated in her bed while the man she'd thought still wanted her was roughly rubbing one off instead of knocking on her door.

Over and under the skin, her flesh tingled. She slipped her fingers beneath her sleep shirt to stroke over her abdomen but still resisted sliding her hand down. Her magic roiled inside her so deliciously that she would rather have someone to share it with.

Violet sighed, considering whether she should turn over and cover her head with the pillow to muffle the slow rise of his moans. It wasn't like he was going to take much longer, not at that pace and with that kind of insistence.

Instead, she released the pillow and raised herself up on her knees. She pulled her T-shirt over her head, leaving herself only in her underwear in the cool, air-conditioned room.

Then she lowered herself back down to sit between her heels, and she listened. Felt the vibration of the bed springs through her fingers. Found his rhythm. Imagined herself over him, imagined him inside her, imagined she was the one making him moan like that, imagined he was stroking over her instead of himself, imagined that when she shifted her hips up and down over nothing that she was taking him in. She rocked in her bed to the beat of his, biting her lip as her bed springs started to creak in time.

He wouldn't notice the sound, but maybe, just maybe, he would feel the tendrils of her magic within him. Arousal sang inside her, opened her like ferns unfurling toward the sun. The things she would do to have him beneath her. She'd knock his hands away from his cock and swallow him bare and straining down her throat, let him hold her head down. She'd moan and gulp and swallow and swallow until he knocked his head against the headboard and pushed up into her tightening mouth and let loose *that* sound, that one right there he made because he thought she was already asleep and couldn't hear him come without her.

Violet slumped, chin against her chest, turned on but a little nauseated.

Because his moan wasn't the only one she'd heard.

Chapter Two

Long after Clive's room finally went quiet—
following muttered conversation that Violet obscured
by largely ineffectual attempts to keep herself from
crying—she managed to fall asleep before the sun rose
to pour through her open blinds.

She extricated herself from the blankets and rubbed
crust from her eyes, made worse from all her tears—
like sand in oyster shells, although she'd yet to make
pearls from her pain. She felt like she'd downed the
whole wine bottle instead of just two glasses.

She didn't even know why she was this upset. She
certainly didn't have any right to be, not with the way
they'd arranged their lives. After all, when everything
was good, it didn't matter if they dated outside their
relationship. Why wouldn't he make plans with
someone else if he'd done it before?

He didn't even need to have sneaked them into his
room through the fire escape. He might have switched
on his computer or his phone and had cybersex, which

was one of the few things Violet was categorically unwilling to do.

The more she thought about it through her morning ablutions, the surer she was that his dalliance had been digital. She wasn't that far from him. She would have heard someone arrive and leave through his window.

Violet unwrapped her hair and splashed her face as she washed the morning oil away and moisturized. Scrubbed and new, she tried to see herself as beautiful, worthy, valuable, powerful, but she could already tell today was going to be a fragile day. She finished in the bathroom, then left it open for Clive to take his later morning as usual.

She climbed up to the roof to meet the dawn.

No temporary greenhouse this time of year, so she had a perfect view of her little patch of nature in the middle of Meridian. She didn't even use all her plants for the store. Sometimes she just wanted to wake up to a beautiful bougainvillea or hibiscus or to sit under the shade cloth that shielded her Japanese maple. But she did have the Meyer lemon tree, from which she made lemonade infused with herbs or flowers as the days grew warmer and warmer, and she had her herb garden, everything from balm to poison—although poison was sometimes just a matter of scale.

She gathered herbs and flowers to dry in bunches in the kitchen and living room—just another series of notes in the symphony of scents she barely smelled anymore, oils that rubbed into her fingers—mint, basil, rosemary that was just as good for smudge sticks as sage, parsley, catnip, chives, things she used as much in cooking as for the store, because cooking was magic and spices were spells. Then she collected the things she never used in cooking and dealt with as far away from the rolling island as she could—tansy, foxglove, nightshade, lily of the valley, oleander, as well as mushrooms of the psychedelic, poisonous, and edible varieties, carefully separated before being stored or dried.

When the health inspector visited, all it took was a stroke to a few careful words inked on her skin, and they never saw the poisons, lest she end up on a list somewhere that the wrong people might use to assign blame in the event of odd deaths—of which there were many in Meridian, and she'd surely contributed to a few of them. But some poisons were also absolutely essential for beneficial potions and spells, neutralized by magic or counteragent. It wasn't her responsibility to decide what kind of magic her ingredients could be used for. *Everything* in her store, from the harmless to the violent, could be used for good or evil. She gave warnings, and the poisons were labeled and out of reach without request. Everything else was in the hands of her customers, as much as it was at any grocery store or plant nursery.

Her mother wouldn't agree. *"You're putting weapons on the street, Indi. You're responsible for what you send out into the world. That you sell evil for coin doesn't make it less evil. It stains your hands like squid ink, baby girl."*

But Violet was neither a good witch nor a bad witch, and nothing in her greenhouse or storeroom was evil in and of itself. She found cursed objects in antique shops, estate sales, garage sales, flea markets. She honed in on the pain collected in the pieces and rescued them—sometimes by binding them, sometimes by releasing them—but just because an object was cursed didn't mean it was evil.

There were only a few things in the world she'd held in her hands that felt truly evil, cold as blue ice broken from a glacier. Not even the handshakes she shared with demons gave her the same chill—because free will was a funny thing, and if a demon could sublimate its impulses long enough to treat a witch with respect, it was not, at that moment, evil.

She gathered her morning herbal haul to hang in the apartment. On the way back down, she crossed paths with Clive heading into the bathroom to shave. His bedroom door was open, as was his window. If the wards, garlic flowers, and anointed salt remained on the windowsill, it didn't matter that he liked to sleep with outside air circulating through.

His sheets were rumpled, because he never 'made' a bed so much as slipped into its comforting nest night after night. Clothes from the last week were strewn over the limited floor space. He was as messy as Violet was cluttered—these things weren't the same—but as long as it stayed in his space and not hers, that was his prerogative.

Violet stared a little too long at the chaotic folds of the blankets, wondering if those dents were from someone else's knees, if there was a damp spot covered by the top sheet, if someone else's limbs had tangled around his while she'd slept in an unlocked room just one long stride away. She wanted to be angry at the other woman, but she wasn't. Clive wasn't even cheating, just…drifting away from her, from her magic, even though they spent so much time together, physically inescapable. And maybe that was the problem. But unless one of them actually *spoke*, she wouldn't know what was wrong, so she wouldn't know how to fix it.

Violet squeezed her eyes shut against the cyclone of circular thoughts, of feelings more painful than she'd like to admit. She had a store to run, which ran much better when Clive was there. She couldn't afford to rock this seasick boat.

When she opened them, she paused, her gaze not upon the bed but the open window.

She sold protection spells against nocturnal predators of the spiritual persuasion, and she'd warded both her window and Clive's from all wandering demons, hybrids, and mares. The salt rubbed into the sill and the carved spells were designed to shut out demons. The garlic flowers pinned on either side were for vampires. Not all night spirits required invitation. Mares, for instance, could climb in whenever they pleased without something to ward them out, but they were largely harmless except for the terrors they inspired. For the creatures that did require willing trespass, however, it didn't hurt to have extra protection.

The garlic flowers were still up, but the sills had been scratched, her first impression that of claws. Violet's inner hackles immediately went up, as though her magic stiffened into porcupine quills. But the lines crossing her wards weren't as ordered as claw marks. Cutting through a carved ward wasn't as complete of a cancellation as opening a salt circle, but it definitely lessened the efficacy of the spell. That, plus the worn-down sigils at his bedroom door from good-luck rubs meant that he wouldn't be as well protected.

Violet tilted her head, searching the shadowed corners, as though she'd see the sylph-like dark form of a demon trying to hide from her, despite the fact that no amount of magic could conceal a demon from her sight. Nothing there but the odd cobweb, which was supposed to be good luck.

She'd have to refresh the wards soon. If she carved them deeper than the scratches, they'd have more power than the interruption. The only question left was what had caused the marks, because the angle suggested that they were scratched inward, not from outside.

If she didn't know that Clive knew better, she'd think they were from a knife.

* * * *

Clive was working on more elaborate stakes today, which meant he could bring out the lathing machine and copper and silver wire and go nuts, and he was far more entertaining for people to watch while browsing. Sometimes, people came into the store just to see what new thing he was doing, and apparently, he had a decent online following on some video blog thing. Violet didn't mind him having his own life and revenue stream, because it brought more people in on their little digital pilgrimages to the highly viral city.

Three pagan keychains, five computer protection stickers, five bags of assorted tumbled rocks, a dozen quartz wands, two dozen practical stakes, three decorative stakes, and two etched knives later, Violet refilled the bins that were low on dried flowers, leaves, and spices, then checked all the living plants for sale, some more high maintenance than others — particularly the carnivorous ones, which had to be kept in a much different environment than the cool dryness of her store.

Some people found plants fiddly things, but Violet liked that they were quiet and their needs were specific but measurable. She liked that when she walked by them, they sent warnings and wishes to her in the same whiff as scent, and she liked that the ones who recognized her trusted her. They were much less concerned about any moral code than they were what was dangerous to them and what wasn't, which Violet found a much more useful metric.

The bells above the door jingled. Violet had chosen a set that were gentle to the ears, like the song of coins at the hips of a belly-dancer. It kept the ringing from becoming grating, tiresome, or dread-inducing.

The customers who entered her shop were dread-inducing enough.

Clive stopped working the lathe to hand-carve instead, which allowed him to better keep an eye on the three men wandering the aisles. Hunters, with their sometimes rigid ideas about good and evil, were who she most feared would breach the demilitarized zone and burn her in the town square under one of Cabrera's more militant watchful angels.

It was a topsy-turvy world where she was more afraid of the demon hunters than the demons themselves, but hunters generally didn't self-reflect in shades of gray.

Violet waited in the plant-ridden wings until one of the hunters met her eye and nodded in the direction of her back room. Risk or not, that was her cue. She shared a glance with Clive, who nodded and left his work station for the counter. Violet went first, leading the three hunters from the aisles into the equally crowded and seemingly chaotic back room. The storeroom was as large as the primary store, which was important, because more than half of it was additional inventory of the sort she couldn't put on the shelves and conveniently disappeared from view when police or inspectors investigated her product.

She stood on one side of the bargaining table — a literal dining room table, a once-cursed object rescued from an estate sale. It had really only wanted to be used more often, and now got its wish in return for not making everything set out on it rot at an accelerated rate.

The three hunters, ragged after their long night, stayed on the other side.

"Understand, you were just the *closest* broker," the hunter immediately across from her said.

Violet nodded without comment and spread her hands to offer the table top to them.

There were all kinds of black-market brokers for demon and human parts in Meridian. She was merely one of them, and the only human parts she ever dealt in had been irreparably cursed into some kind of hybrid and put down for their own good. Also beatified relics on occasion, although she sold those more by reputation and questionable provenance than magical verification, since half of them seemed to have no spiritual power at all from her assessment. There were probably at least four dozen fingers of Saint Peter in the world. As long as they were older than two centuries, she figured the dealers and collectors of such things weren't hurting anyone.

She wasn't even the best body broker, but she was the most neutral, and her back room promised a certain level of confidentially, protected by spells that repelled and sometimes aggressively destroyed active recording devices.

The hunter who had taken point with her was smaller and younger than his counterparts, with sweaty, messy blond hair and a week's worth of scraggly stubble. He unslung his backpack — undergoing its second life after military use — and pulled out a butcher-paper-wrapped heart and clawed hands. "Pestilence demon ravaging an apartment building."

He checked his hastily bandaged arm as she inspected the parts. Blood and something yellow seeped through. To the untrained eye, it looked like pus. It was more likely a specialized antibiotic ointment in common use among hunters and cultists who engaged in frequent ritual blood-letting—of their own or others'. She sold that kind of ointment in glass jars and sometimes in bulk to the odd hunter collective or cult group when they anticipated a greater spate of wounds.

The heart and hands had been expertly cut, at great risk to the hunter's limbs and perhaps his life. Most pestilence demons were relatively amoral, but it wasn't her place to question the conditions of the acquisition, only to determine value.

"I can offer seven hundred for the set." Whole pestilence demon parts were valuable among healers, but contact and proximity put her at risk, too, which was why she didn't offer eight hundred.

The hooded hunter, who had backed into one of the darker corners to pick dirt and other things out of his fingernails with one of his knives, snorted. The hunter with whom she was negotiating, however, didn't disparage her offer.

"Six hundred fifty if you throw in a box of healing potion and a bottle of gastro-salve. Damn dirty demon. I'm going to be puking purple for a month."

Violet slid out a box of twenty-four-count healing potion tubes—more expensive but also more effective than the antibiotic ointment—then climbed up from the bottom shelf to reach the collection of gastro-salve potions. Her shelves were sturdy, and she was always misplacing her stepstool. She wasn't short, but she used every bit of available space, and that meant storing high.

From a cashbox that had also once been a cursed object that ate cash and opened to lint—and still did when anyone but her used it—she pulled out the money she'd promised. She slid the amount across to the hunter as he passed the cuttings to her.

She pulled on a pair of gloves to handle the meat. Mess with the wrong pestilence demon's flesh, a person could end up in a hospital with necrotizing fasciitis and lose whole pieces of themself, which was a big reason why most hunters avoided them or left their bodies to the predations of other pestilence demons. But plants had the same protective and sometimes vengeful defense mechanisms, and she was careful as she slipped the heart into a glass jar, the hands into another. She didn't bother with formaldehyde or other preservative fluid. Symbols drawn and etched into the jar lids would keep them fresh until she could find another buyer, probably for nine hundred or an even thousand.

There were nefarious uses for demon parts, of course, just as there were for human parts, but most of Violet's contacts were healers or healer-adjacent, researching and experimenting with more targeted or effective healing potions and pills. On occasion, she sold back to demons, but once she owned the pieces, they were hers to disburse at will, not at any hunter's discretion.

The smaller, younger hunter beckoned to the man on his left to hand over his pack. The hunter, a large black man with salt-and-pepper hair and a completely white beard, shrugged off his satchel, from which the younger hunter retrieved a packet of vampire teeth and a vial of its blood.

Teeth were standard if hunters could gather them before the bodies deteriorated. Vampires didn't quite burst into ash, but they were nearly dust after a day — faster the older the vampire was. Blood wasn't so standard in the body market, because the primary use of vampire blood was to turn someone into a familiar. Add the teeth in, and you had a vampire maker. Selling both seemed counterproductive for an intrepid vampire hunter. But vampire blood was also used by the researchers Violet sold to, so she was one of the few brokers who bought it, and she'd rather have it in her fridge than on the streets, because there it sometimes surfaced as a new drug that went well for absolutely no one.

The teeth were broken rather than whole. They could still be used ground down, but for rituals and reliquaries, they were better with the root.

"The best I can do is a hundred, and that's because of the blood, not the fangs."

The hunter whose wares she dickered over sucked his teeth and looked like he wanted to spit something more than saliva on her offer. "I'll do a hundred if you throw in a touch-up of my all-seeing eye."

"Ninety with the touch-up," she countered.

"Highway robbery."

"Feel free to take your business elsewhere, but that blood might keep coagulating."

The hunter held his hand out with a snap that did nothing to make her snap to.

She opened the cashbox again and removed ninety dollars to give to him. "I'll touch you up when we're finished, if you can spare the time."

The hunter took the money, then backed against the wall, crossing his arms.

The hooded hunter had wings hanging from his pack. She already knew what kind of demon parts he was selling, but she salivated anyway, and not just because of the magic intrinsic in every barbule.

Most incubus and succubus bodies were sold to specialists, but so many people came to her looking for love potions. Of course, she didn't make full-on love potions, because they were creepy as hell. But in small doses—a feather, for instance—a person could make themselves more attractive, to the degree of potent social lubricant. Or people sought to boost or sustain their libido or spice up their established love lives. There was a risk of addiction or dependence, but with judicious use, it could be a hell of a relationship enhancement. She'd enjoyed a succubus feather powder pill more than once. So had Clive, especially when she had an incubus feather to give him, too. They'd received several noise complaints that weekend.

Violet swallowed and tried not to show how much she wanted what the hooded hunter had brought, despite the death that had been required to get it. Hunters were going to hunt. Might as well use what was left behind.

The hooded hunter handed his loot to the one they'd all decided was a mediator. With the more pronounced muscles pressing against his shirt, one wouldn't expect him to grunt when the hooded hunter passed the pack to him, but he nearly dropped it.

Violet couldn't read much from the hooded hunter, given he was clearly dressed for hunting sex demons. His gloves hung out from his coat pocket, so his hands were the only visible part of him, but the prominence of his veins, the lessened elasticity of the skin, and his mottled paleness—not from age spots so much as uneven sun exposure—suggested he was an older white man, and strong, since he'd entered the store with such a heavy pack and hadn't hunched like a schoolgirl with too many books. Older than the go-between, yes, but older than the bearded man? Hard to say.

The negotiator unhooked the wings with his bare hands, which left him licking his lips and unable to look away from the front of Violet's sleeveless shift shirt.

She put on a new set of gloves to inspect the wings as the negotiator continued unpacking the bag. The man had already packaged his parts in enspelled glass. They looked like hers, with her style of etching into the lid, so she must have seen the hooded hunter before. He wasn't the only one who preferred anonymity in Book & Candle, so he could have been any of a number of hunters who'd purchased preservative glass from her.

She hesitated before the full scalped head of hair that he'd wound into a loose hangman's knot—a dark joke to the succubus, or possibly to her. Succubus hair could be added to weaves and extensions or even just braided in with one's own hair for a similar effect to their feathers, if not quite as strong. Practitioners of regular sex rituals paid through the nose for sex demon hair. Violet might have woven a lock or two through her own before, if she braided before sex magic.

"I know what it's worth," the hooded hunter said. He had a touch of an accent, perhaps from his youth. She wanted to call it British, but it was so mild that it could have been Scottish or even leftover from a broader New England accent.

"It's not about what it's worth. It's about whether I can make a profit. Don't insult me with false ignorance, and I won't insult you by undervaluing this." Violet did some quick mental calculations for the use she could get from the wings and hair and what she could sell the heart, claws, and teeth for. "Do you want to keep your containers?"

"The containers are mine." In addition to the slight accent, his voice sounded like it had been smoked, marinated in bourbon and lighter fluid, then taken out back and run over new black asphalt a few times with a muddy all-terrain vehicle.

"I'm not interested in a back-and-forth. I can do seven thousand five."

The hunter stared at her through the shadow of his hood. All she could see was the gleam of his eyes, not shape or color. Finally, he nodded.

Violet transferred the pieces to her own jars, then nudged the empty glass back across the table. She squinted when light bounced off the hunter's knife as he continued to play with it against his palm. There was still blood near the bottom of the blade—harder to clean there right after a kill.

She pulled out the price they'd agreed upon—steep, but entirely fair. She could make over ten thousand eventually.

Violet pushed the empty pack across the table and held the money out for him, but he pointed the knife down to the table.

So he was one of *those* hunters. The kind who would rather not be dealing with her at all but considered her a necessary evil in a city full of unnecessary evil. Didn't want to talk to her. Didn't want to touch her. Could take down a succubus and steal all of its parts. Happily got his hands and his boots dirty. Survived to an older age, stronger than his younger companion. There was no point trying to reach across a table to someone so good at killing, someone who would slaughter her the moment she stepped out of neutral territory.

Business could be its own necessary evil.

She put the money on the table in front of him, then gathered the wings with a rustle of arousing feathers to hang them in the back by the air conditioner. The regular dry air would help keep the fleshy parts from decaying too much until she could pluck the feathers. The feathers caressed her arms, her cheeks, her belly through her clothes, felt as though they surrounded her. She trailed her fingertips through the lower part of the wings like hair. Her whole body had broken out in gooseflesh for reasons other than the A/C. The sensations would be even more intense were they incubus wings.

Her nipples were unsettlingly prominent against her shirt, but she didn't hide herself as she returned to the table for her jars—the hunter's money had disappeared, probably secreted into his pocket or his pack—which she shelved with the rest of the hunters' loot.

"Pleasure doing business with you," she said, after returning to the table and closing her cashbox to signal the end of the transaction.

The negotiator's Adam's apple bobbed over his shirt collar. "We can see that."

"Get out of my store."

The negotiator put down a hundred dollars cash. "You sure?"

The white-bearded hunter slapped the back of the negotiator's head. The hooded hunter grabbed him by his arm to drag him out of the back room. The bearded hunter remained.

Because the procedure would be quick and she didn't need to pull out the dentist chair, Violet moved two folding chairs over to the shelf she devoted to her inks and tattoo gun. It wasn't as shiny as some of the tattoo parlors, and it probably wouldn't survive a real health inspection, given the ingredients in some of her inks, but she only had to use standard black ink for this touch-up. The magic of the all-seeing eye was in the symbol itself and needed no additional bolstering.

The bearded hunter looked away while she prepared the ink in the tattoo gun, but he lifted his shirt as she drew her chair closer to his. After disinfecting, she brought the needle to the blurring edges of the tattoo—harder to discern on his darker skin, but she knew the design by heart, even though it wasn't one of hers. They varied in style, but the symbol remained the same, and hunters weren't too interested in making their spells works of art. They just wanted the spell to work. And almost all hunters had an all-seeing eye to more easily discern their camouflaged prey. It was practically a rite of passage.

She wiped away the excess ink and blood, then covered the tattoo with a bandage.

He abruptly stood to leave, removing his vulnerable belly from her reach. He didn't say thank you, but that was the hunter way. Their relationship with her was strictly transactional. He didn't have to show gratitude when he'd paid for the service.

The other two hunters were still in her store when she emerged from the back room. Clive wordlessly returned to his work station, where the hooded hunter inspected the stakes and other weapons available.

He lingered over a katana she'd rescued from a garage sale, but he finally stepped in front of a bowie knife. Most hunters preferred smaller knives for the same reason they preferred small or slender guns—balance and control. A bowie knife required steadiness as well as strength to manage the additional weight. But if a hunter could handle it, the silver-inlaid bowie knife could give them extra distance in hand-to-hand combat, which was helpful with both pestilence and conquest demons, who could infect with a touch.

If he was anything like other hunters she'd encountered, he probably had a whole wall of weapons of his own, but knives were shiny little things. She'd never had trouble selling them in Meridian.

Which meant she wasn't surprised when the hooded hunter beckoned for Clive to remove the bowie knife and its sheath from the lighted display. Clive gave the knife to Violet, who rang it up with the dozen practical stakes that the hunter had dumped on the counter. The hunter gave back eight hundred of the dollars from their less official transaction.

"Knife is new," the hunter said, no emotion in his tone as he gathered his stakes into his pack.

"The commission was completed two weeks ago," she replied just as evenly.

He folded back his duster to attach the bowie knife to his belt like a modern-day Quincey P. Morris. That was how a lot of hunters seemed to her—cosplayers, the sort of people who dressed themselves up in military fatigues to play laser tag. But although some hunters donned the costume of an urban cowboy, she knew for a fact that the good ones used every bit of it for its intended purpose, which was primarily protective but also provided concealment and storage. This hunter fell into the latter category, a real gunslinger instead of someone playacting tough. He even had at least one gun on his other hip, and he probably had other weapons on his person that she couldn't see.

He slipped a five across the counter. "You got any of those cinnamon sticks?"

Violet nodded toward the herb and spice sections. One of her most popular ingredients, especially in fall and winter.

"I'll take three of those and a jar of honey."

Violet didn't keep a beehive on the roof with her plants. Her business neighbors would have a thing or two to say about that, and Clive was allergic. But she sourced her honey from local hives for pollen allergies. She gave him a quarter in change, which he flipped into Clive's tip jar on his way to the aisle.

Clive flipped him the bird behind his back in response, which the hunter probably saw in one of the corner convex mirrors, but he didn't react as he gathered his cinnamon and honey. Violet pegged the ingredients as additives to tea to treat what sounded like a seriously sore throat, but it was impossible to know for sure if he didn't ask for her advice.

The hunter didn't try to steal more than what he'd paid for, and he strode out without looking back. The other hunters stopped loitering and followed. If he wasn't a leader, he was certainly respected or feared, which in their circles sometimes meant the same thing.

As soon as the hunters were out of the store, both Clive and Violet exhaled in relief.

"Is it too early for wine?" Clive muttered as he left his station and came up behind her, resting his head on her shoulder as she rested hers on her arms crossed on the counter.

"I've got vodka in the back. Shots?"

"Do you know who that was?" He pulled her by her waist to the back room with him.

"I know he's been here before, but he's not the only one who doesn't show his face."

"I think that was Abel Simmons. He's a scary dude."

She shivered, but she let herself be led, then took her own lead in the back room, grabbing one of the bottles and two shot glasses she kept in a fake file cabinet. It *was* early to be drinking, but she wanted something to loosen the steel rod her spine had become, and this was quicker than almost anything.

Clive hadn't let go of her waist. He pressed the front of his jeans against her ass while she bent over for the vodka. When she straightened, his breath was warm and gentle over the little hairs on her neck.

"When they're dead sure he's nowhere near the room, they call him Willing and Abel. I heard he stabbed someone or something in the financial district in broad daylight and never got arrested. Sure, maybe they couldn't prove it was him because he covers up, but rumor is that he just found demonic dirt on everyone who tried. Every time they think he has a line, he crosses it."

"Glad he's such a regular customer then. Good product is good incentive to keep us alive." She turned in his arms, and he didn't back away.

He breathed her in where her pulse quickened, then up to her hairline behind her ear. When he withdrew slightly, he gazed where she was still perky under her shirt and licked his lips. He crowded her against the cabinet, sliding his hands up to brush his fingertips across the undersides of her breasts.

Then he lowered his head, letting his hands drift back down until he wasn't touching her anymore. "It's the wings, isn't it? He brought parts."

She nearly sobbed to have been so close to having what she wanted, what she *needed*, what the succubus feathers had inspired in her. "Some dander must have brushed off on me. It wasn't on purpose. Clive…"

He took the vodka bottle and poured them both a shot. After he handed hers to her, he took a step back with a slight frown, but not so far back that it seemed he blamed her for the erection pushing against the front of his jeans.

He held his shot glass up to clink with hers, then joined her in gulping it down, and in the weird face they both made after. "Violet..."

She touched her fingers to his lips to make him stop, but he shook his head.

"We do need to talk," he said. "If not today, can we sit down tomorrow?"

Clive didn't look like he was holding a grenade, but she could take a hint from the way he kept their bodies at friendly distance. And she certainly couldn't ignore what she'd heard last night. There was only so much avoidance they could manage when they couldn't really escape each other.

"Yeah." She sounded deflated, even to herself. "Tomorrow. Dinner?"

Friday night. Not a date night, clearly. But Saturdays and Sundays, the shop had later opening times, so tomorrow they could spend more time and perhaps more bottles of wine to say what needed to be said.

"Dinner tomorrow night," Clive agreed. He set his glass on the cabinet and took hers. As they left the storeroom, he glanced behind her at the pair of wings hanging from the ceiling.

Chapter Three

Clive went out alone to dinner that night, then sneaked into the apartment far too late, presumably to avoid talking with her until they'd agreed to it. And Violet drank more than her share of a wine bottle, past the point of enjoying it anymore, but at least she barely awoke when he clattered around in the bathroom and did whatever he was doing—with whomever he was doing it—in his bedroom. She wasn't even positive what she heard. It could have just been her dreams playing a cruel joke on her.

By morning, being upright seemed like a terrible idea, but business waited for no headache, and if she could make it to the kitchen, she kept hangover remedy in the fridge.

Violet practically melted from her bed and crawled to her door, then used the knob to pull herself to her feet. She held her head against the throbbing with no success, but it seemed better to try something rather than just let the beat take over her skull willy-nilly.

She drank down the remedy as quickly as she could so she wouldn't have to think about what was in it. Multiple sides of her family had their own recipes. Plenty of other families did, too, but the added element of magic meant that each faction could get catty as cooking divas over theirs. Violet could only work with the most effective, though, regardless of who might be offended in the process, and the one that worked required a raw egg in the mix, which made an already slimy concoction even worse.

She sat at the small dining table that mostly functioned as a spice and tea sorting station and stayed as still as possible while her stomach decided whether it wanted to regurgitate everything she'd eaten in the last twelve hours, and possibly things she'd eaten last month. But after about fifteen minutes, the waves of nausea passed and the headache receded to something more manageable in the brightening morning sun.

After going through her usual rituals, she headed down to the store. She hadn't heard Clive yet, but given that both of their worlds as they knew them for the last eight years were about to blow up, she wasn't in any hurry to get the day started.

Upon reaching the bottom of the stairs, the open storeroom door told her something was very, very wrong.

Every night, in addition to the front and back doors, she locked the back room and the door to the stairs leading up to their apartment. That was just part of the routine. The single biggest deterrent to burglary was doors. The second was locks. Even if someone broke into the store, they might stop at another locked door and stick with looting what was right in front of them. Well, no one had been in the apartment—as far as she'd been able to tell from her room to the kitchen—but someone had unlocked the storeroom and left it open.

There was no splintering in the door or the frame, so they'd either had access to a key or they'd picked the lock. There were some powder potions that could effectively undo a lock, but they would have left residue, like talcum.

Violet tiptoed to the side and opened the storeroom door completely, peering in but ready to jump back if someone was there.

She was alone. But someone *had* broken in, because they'd left a mess.

The first thing she noticed was that the wings were gone, and when she peered in further, she confirmed that the hair was gone, too, and so were the locks from other dead succubi and incubi. In addition, bottles and bottles of pills she'd made from previous sex demons' feathers had been raided, although the slimy bits—hearts and other organs—had been left behind.

Other shelves had been ransacked as well—poisons, spices, dried flowers, shrunken heads, vampire teeth, pestilence blood vials, even things that were common elsewhere, like needles and leather string. Her chaotic system had been left in disarray.

Violet backed into the hallway and slowly approached the store counter.

Book & Candle was in ruins. The books, which lined every wall and aisle in one way or another, had been raided, half of them removed. The crucifixes and prayer beads had been broken, slashed, or unstrung. Several knives were missing. Stakes had been snapped. So much of her spice and dried plant inventory had been taken, while the candles and incense sections were conspicuously neat, although she suspected some of both had been removed.

Her living plants had been left alone, which was probably the only thing saving her from a cardiac event brought on by grief.

Neither the back nor front doors looked broken into, and the windows were unshattered. There was no graffiti to indicate rancor toward what she was or what she sold in her store. If anything, what had been stolen indicated an appreciation of its value.

Except the only ones who knew its value also knew who she was, and that she and her place of business were not to be touched.

Someone had broken the motherfucking rules. And Violet didn't know what the hell to do with that.

She also didn't know where to start with the mess, with cataloguing the inventory taken or damaged, determining how much someone had carved from her chest—both financially and personally.

She ran back toward the stairs. A check of the security system indicated that it was still on. All her protective wards on the front and back door frames were still intact.

Which meant no one had actually broken in.

They'd been let in.

Her booze-dizzy memories replayed from when Clive had returned late last night. She'd thought she'd heard him stumbling in. She'd thought the sounds she'd heard from his bedroom had been those of pleasure. But by that point, the apartment had been a ship in a storm-ridden sea, and she couldn't trust her interpretation of muffled sounds when she couldn't have said which way was up.

She darted up the stairs, then braced herself at the hallway to the bedrooms—his to the left, hers to the right, the bathroom between them. She thought of carvings rubbed for luck, of all-seeing eye tattoos blurry with age and blurring a hunter's sight. She thought of broken symbols and broken wards, smeared salt, chain-link fences breached with bolt cutters.

She twisted her neck to look back at her kitchen counter, where her grandmother's and her own grimoires were supposed to be close by for whenever she needed them.

They'd both been removed, with only the bookstand left where her grandmother's grimoire had taken its place of honor. Her heart ached like when she'd stood over her grandmother's freshly turned grave, with daises instead of lilies because Gran wouldn't have wanted a stray cat to breathe lily pollen and the daisies were from the field outside Gran's house, higher on the hill than the one Violet had grown up in.

Although she'd been startled sober, she almost couldn't get her legs to work on the way to Clive's bedroom.

Inside, his window was open, and Clive was gone.

There were claw marks on the wall above his headboard.

Violet went to the window, then climbed out onto the fire escape to look down. The ladder was still up. She supposed someone could have climbed out of the window and down the ladder, then pushed it back up with something, but she didn't know how someone would enter before the ladder had been released.

Unless Clive had let them in that way.

But if Clive had been in on it, if he'd facilitated the burglary, there would have been no reason to ransack or leave through the window. He could have just let them in through the back door when he came home, they could have removed her products and possessions in an orderly fashion, and left the same way they came, and all he would have had to do was set the alarm after them.

Why the window?

Violet crouched in front of the window and ran her nails over the marks in the sill. No, not claws. They definitely looked more like the crude cuts of a knife. Clive had knives for both protection and ritual, and access to plenty more. But why mar wards that kept his sleep safe?

She climbed back into the room. Then, after a moment of hesitation, she crawled onto Clive's bed, all the way to the headboard. She put her fingernails where the grooves were, confirming that these were, indeed, claw marks, too deep to be Clive trying to grab at the wall while something dragged him off.

But claws over plaster could also be a threat. That there was no immediate sign of struggle didn't mean that Clive was safe and complicit. A knife to the throat didn't have to draw blood to intimidate.

Violet didn't want to do it, just like she hadn't wanted to sit down and talk with Clive tonight, but she pressed her hands against the wall over the claw marks and closed her eyes. This sort of thing wasn't something she was good at, but maybe the recent trauma to the wall and the recognizable radiance of Clive's energy through either pleasure or pain would show her what happened.

Nails narrowed to a fine, sharp point. It is not pain or threat that drives them into the wall. The two of them are crying out in pleasure. His entire body is taut, an exquisite twist of agony, if one trusts his expression, but he is so hard inside her, as hard inside as he seems outside with every muscle tense to bring himself to climax. But she withholds, because it pleases her to string out his pleasure until he shouts when he comes, until he pleads and promises and tells her truths she never asked for, because she is the best kind of interrogator — the kind that gives her victims what they want most, whether dreaming or awake. Her lover is awake, while she is a dream.

Violet jerked away from the wall, but her knees were still on the mattress, on the sheets in which Clive had writhed. And now that she knew it was there, she found sex demon signs everywhere she stretched her magic—soaked through the sheets, splattered on the walls, hovering in the air, rubbed into the floor, on the windowsill. A succubus wouldn't have been able to smear away the anointed salt on the sill, but once the ward had been broken, she could have perched on that sill while Clive fucked her. If the protection spells had been unmarred, she wouldn't have been able to be in there at all.

He had let her in. He had let a succubus into his room. He'd invited her, and not just with words or wishes. He'd removed the spells that would have forbidden her from crossing the threshold.

"Goddamn it, Clive!" Violet slammed her fists against the bed. It sounded weak, like punching a bag of loose sifted sand.

Didn't he know better? Didn't he know that if he let one in, the protection wards didn't protect him anymore, and they didn't make sex demons safer? Didn't he know he could have died? Didn't he know that he still could?

But she didn't feel death here, at least not of the permanent variety. And if this whole heist was a succubus attack, why *wasn't* Clive here, dead on his rumpled bed with a smile on his face, now that she'd gotten everything she needed? And what did a succubus need with magic shop ingredients anyway? Like vampires, sex demons' needs were few.

She had pieces of the mystery, but she couldn't make them fit together. If it had just been Clive missing, a succubus could explain the absence, but the store... No matter how she put the stolen ingredients together, they didn't add up to any one or even three potions or rituals. They might have gathered big-ticket and useful items to hide what they were really there for, but it also could have just been a smash-and-grab. She couldn't find the sense in anything, not even in a succubus taking the man with her when she'd had him for the taking in his own bedroom. Vampires occasionally collected humans as familiars or donors, but sex demons didn't generally bring their food sources home with them, not even to hide the bodies. For the average coroner, death by sex demon read as an unexplained heart attack, nothing more.

Violet clasped her hands against her breastbone. She was afraid and angry and confused and angry and violated and *angry*, fighting to hold all those feelings in her delicate chest. She didn't know if her ribs would be an adequate cage to contain it all.

She sat there, kneeling on her best friend's bed, until she was sure she could unclasp her hands from their interlocked fists and not shudder apart.

She left Clive's room and entered her own, where she pulled off her dress. Her store uniform was usually flowy, flowery, bohemian, the kind of thing people expected from the proprietor of a magic store, and she loved the uniform so much that she wore it off-hours as well. But a flowing skirt wouldn't serve her now.

She pulled on a pair of jeans. They didn't even fit right, a little big so that she could move comfortably through the forest. She'd bought them from the men's section because the stretch added to women's jeans made them prone to fray at the thighs, and she needed the extra layer when at risk of copperheads.

Eschewing the hiking boots she usually wore with the work pants, she chose steel-toed boots she'd worn back on her parents' property and that she still used when doing her own repairs. Then, after strapping herself into a practical bra that did its job holding her in place and not much else, she pulled on a long-sleeved plaid shirt she hadn't worn since she'd painted the apartment. She almost didn't recognize herself in the mirror, but at least half of that was the wide-eyed terror, no trace of smile or cock-eyed optimism. And as someone who had deliberately leveraged her femininity for the last eight years, it was strange to see all of that stripped away, to see the girl she'd been when she first arrived in Meridian. The kind of girl who knew harder work and harsher winters, with calluses on her hands and knots of scars on her skin from both ritual and accident. The girl who hadn't needed to wear a skirt on Sunday because she'd celebrated the last pagan holiday nude.

She grasped the quartz pendant of her necklace. Then she grabbed her phone and selected one of the contacts she'd never had to use before but that she'd entered for emergencies she couldn't take care of herself.

"Hello, this is Detective Andrea Black."

"Good morning, Detective. This is Violet Panabaker. I know this is your personal line, but I received your number from a friend a long time ago."

"Violet Panabaker. Yes, I know who you are. Of Book & Candle." The better half of the unofficial Q division of the Meridian Police Department kept her voice conversational and friendly, but she was unable to hide the wariness underneath.

"I've been robbed, and my coworker, Clive McCormick, is missing."

There was a moment when Detective Black covered her receiver, muffling when she spoke to someone else. Probably her other half. Then she lifted her hand from the receiver again. "What do you need us to do, Ms. Panabaker? We can head that way now."

"No need for a police report. I'm calling as a courtesy. Someone's crossed the line, and I'm entitled to make myself whole. I just wanted to let you know why I'm doing what I'm doing."

"Ms. Panabaker, please, let us do our own investigation. We have more resources —"

"You don't have anywhere near my resources."

"No one needs to get hurt."

"You're right about that. I'm not a violent person, Detective. I will not spill unnecessary blood. But I can assure you, I will find my friend, and I will get back what's mine. Consider this your heads-up. Someone else stepped out first. Remember that."

Violet ended the call, then slung a satchel over her shoulder and went downstairs to fill it.

Chapter Four

When Violet entered Chasing the Dragon, not everyone turned to look at her like in some western saloon scene. Women might have been the minority, but they weren't as unusual in hunter circles these days.

Nor was it surprising for just anyone to come in and order a drink. This was a twenty-four-hour bar. There were no ugly lights, and at least one of the clocks on the wall read five o'clock. Evil slept, but when it slept depended on the evil, so Meridian had a solid incentive to provide twenty-four-hour venues for its nocturnal element—both hunters and hunted.

She accepted an Irish coffee and a bowl of scrambled hash, then found a table where she could keep an eye on the clientele while she ate. She wasn't the only person there looking to eat breakfast in peace, nor was she the only one scanning the bar. Pack a bunch of Type A, loner demon hunters into the same place, especially among those who weren't hunters and didn't realize where they'd decided to have their hair of the dog, it led to understandable suspicion.

The double takes she kept receiving suggested that at least a few of them found her familiar, although they would never have seen her quite like this before. They were probably trying to figure out how they knew her, whether she was a demon they'd tried to kill or a victim they'd saved—neither of whom would have been particularly welcome in Chasing the Dragon.

Violet stayed in her seat long after finishing breakfast. She switched from Irish coffee to regular coffee after the first cup, because although she'd needed something to help her calm down, now she wanted to take advantage of the caffeine to hone her focus and keep her alert.

By afternoon, she thought it might be time to find another place to perch to find whom she was looking for, but then one of the hunters who'd been in her store the previous day pushed his way through the heavy doors with his boot, hauling his pack behind him.

The hunter—the younger one who'd acted as the primary negotiator—strode in. She wanted to say that he swaggered, but he didn't. Although he was somewhere in his twenties, demon hunting had a way of stealing a youngblood's swagger. It was lean, mean work, and they weren't exactly superheroes. They couldn't proclaim their good deeds to the world, couldn't be celebrated with free drinks and other perks. A hunter worked in anonymity whenever possible, because what they did was more akin to vigilante justice than the kind of thing cities handed out medals for. Any strut in this hunter's step probably had more to do with premature aches and pains than pride.

She waited until he'd settled at the bar and ordered a drink before she headed straight for him. The hunters keyed for a predator's attack angled themselves toward her. Some slid from their seats, reaching for weapons.

But she got to her hunter first, grabbing him by the back of his jacket and jerking him out of his seat to land like an anchor on the floor. She hauled him away from his pack and the bar, then pulled him up to his feet and whirled him around to grab him by his neck. That left him with two arms and two legs with which to attack.

If she were just an ordinary woman.

She hadn't used magic like this in years, but that didn't mean she couldn't, and Meridian had endless reserves from which to pull when her own magic considered faltering. Even this bar had been built as one of a million metaphysical conduits. It was like being plugged into the sun. The hunter wasn't even a spot in her eye.

"Whoa! Jesus, what did I do? Fuck, someone had their spinach this morning." The hunter dangled from her hold the higher she lifted him. He tried to punch and he tried to kick, but she sapped strength from him as long as her hands touched his skin, so all he managed was a half-hearted twist dance.

Other hunters coming to protect him hit invisible walls on every side of her. When she reached into her satchel and pulled out a glass vial, the circle around her immediately stepped back. She opened it with her teeth. All the glass in her bag was shatterproof, so she couldn't smash it like a glitter bomb, but the powder inside was incredibly obedient and would go where she told it to.

"It's too early for this shit. Did I insult your mother or something? God!"

Violet throttled him to let him know she could kill him one-handed if she chose. "Now that I have everyone's attention..." She slowly lowered him so that he could reach the ground with his toes, but she could always lift him higher again. "I'm Violet Panabaker. Most of you here know me."

"Geez, I didn't even recognize you without—"

"Stop talking." She didn't speak to him, per se, because he apparently didn't know how to shut up when it was good for him. Instead, she spoke to his tongue, which listened to a folk witch much better.

The hunter made all kinds of amusing faces as he tried to convince his tongue to work. Instead, it lolled like a slug in his mouth until the hunter finally understood no amount of strength or will would change that he was powerless.

"I know what you're all thinking. Yes, all of you. Even you. Among those thoughts, the most relevant is, *She can't possibly be doing this. She's breaking the rules.* Most of you know I run the Book & Candle magic shop in the historical district. It's never been codified into any law, but for those of you new in town, it's pretty much understood that Book & Candle is one of the several places in Meridian where everyone is expected to play nice and share—like Chasing the Dragon. It's important for Meridian to have spaces like these, because not even your bed is safe, but at least your beer is."

Violet looked over her shoulder at the bartender, K.D., who nodded back in acknowledgment, although she maintained a certain coiled tension. However, from one true neutral to the other, K.D. was clearly willing to give Violet the opportunity to state her case.

"I'm here because someone entered Book & Candle and stole from me, and they also abducted my partner for reasons yet unknown. Whether for ransom or spare parts, they took what wasn't theirs. They crossed the line."

The hunter in her hand shook his head emphatically as he made unintelligible noises, his tongue sloshing from side to side behind his teeth.

"I didn't say you did it. I'm here because I now have leave to cross into both sides of this never-ending war and do whatever is necessary to get back what has been taken, by any and all means available to me. Now, most of you know that I would rather pick up a cockroach and let it out back in our alleyway than crush it to feed my carnivorous plants. Book & Candle is and always has been neutral because I am, by nature, slow to anger. But see, someone done fucked up, and now I'm angry."

The hunters around her took another step back. When magic burned hot right under her skin like this — as though she would shed her girl-flesh for something monstrous beneath if she concentrated hard enough — she knew her eyes glowed like St. Elmo's fire. Not red like some demons, but she couldn't say whether her energy right now was amber or as violet as her name. Neither boded well for anyone who got in her way.

"Anyone who tries to stop me while I figure out upon whom to rain a beating of biblical proportions gets a share of those profits. It's in your best interest to comply with me, because being a peaceful person doesn't mean I'm weak. Now, as for you, I don't think you did it. At least, you better hope to hell you didn't."

Violet released the hunter's throat and his tongue. The circle of hunters around them kept him enclosed — not least because of their sheer curiosity. To her frustration, her violence seemed to grant her greater respect, but for what she needed to do, it would work in her favor.

"I'm here because you visited the store with two other hunters who I assume are part of your collective, yes? You can talk now."

"Fuck, sister. If I'd known you could do all that—"

"Don't make me regret giving your tongue back."

"Yes. Okay?" The hunter adjusted his shirt and jacket, attempting and failing to save face. "We're part of the same collective. If someone's feeling suspicious another hunter is keeping too much of their cut, sometimes we sell at the same time. What of it?"

"Are you skimming?" she asked.

"What? No. What's it to you? But no."

"Maybe you decided to steal from me when you couldn't steal from someone else. Maybe you thought I was an easier mark than a fellow hunter, and less dishonorable to steal from."

"*No.* I don't steal, okay? Hunting isn't a greedy person's game. But the old guys, they get paranoid sometimes. They already see demons everywhere they look. Why not sinners, too?" He didn't bother adding 'no offense' to the older hunters around him, and they didn't bother taking offense. He wasn't wrong. "And I'm the new guy, because to old-timers, everyone under forty is the new guy, so I'm the one he suspected. I was the front man so they could watch me work and know I was honest."

"Here's the big question, then," she said. "Where does Abel Simmons live?"

When the hunter looked at her like she was crazy, Violet glanced around the circle at the others.

"Feel free to chime in. There's no cash prize here. There's scorched earth or no scorched earth."

"Are you nuts, lady?" the young hunter said. "Do you think we have neat little address books with the home base of every hunter in the city? You think just because we're in a collective, we all live dormitory-style with the little old lady in the shoe? If my own mother was a hunter, I wouldn't know where she crashed."

"So if there's an emergency, you just collapse in your home and hope the landlord finds you before the flies do?" In such a deadly profession, it didn't seem very practical not to have an informal buddy system of some kind—like girls texting each other before, during, and after meeting a new date—but rugged individualism apparently didn't care about practicality.

"Pretty much."

"Fine. But as a collective, you must share some resources—the same laundromat or dry cleaner, favorite pizza place, discount at the doughnut shop. And you have to at least have a way to bring everyone together to pay and get paid."

"We don't do team meetings, if that's what you mean. We don't do potlucks or family dinners. This is the closest we get to a group hug." The hunter spread his arms to indicate the bar and its patrons.

"That's the saddest thing I've ever heard. If you never meet, how do you split your profits? The honor system on a cash-sharing app?"

Now the hunter looked from the hunters around him to his shoes. "We're really not supposed to talk about—"

"Do you know what this powder does?" Violet held up the vial. "It's the mother of all itching powders. That may not sound like the worst thing in the world, until you remember what the worst itch in your life was. Now compound that by seventy-five and imagine no numbing cream or steroid will make a dent. I'll start with you, but then I'll start spreading the misery around. I don't need to fight violent to fight dirty. Now, answer my question."

"Fine! Fine. The treasurer of the collective takes most of a hunter's profit, and he distributes the money twice monthly."

"This treasurer probably needs contact information on everyone in the collective. Seems unlikely that he'd have banking numbers but not know where to go knocking if someone needs cash or they're suspected of withholding. And you would need to have his information, or else how would he know you were coming to him after a job?"

The hunter hung his head as though she'd slapped him twelve times in front of everyone, but he nodded.

"So I'm betting you know my next question." Violet stepped closer to him and insinuated her hand under his jacket to slip into his back pants pocket.

He swallowed hard and did his best not to touch her beyond how she touched him.

Good boy. Smart boy.

She pulled out his phone and held it out for him to take. "I need the contact information and address for the treasurer of your collective, please. Unless someone else knows where I can find Abel Simmons. No? Looks like you're on the hook, Junior."

"Fuck. I'm going to get kicked out of this fucking collective. *Fuck.*"

"Cheer up, Junior. With any luck, once word gets around, everyone will realize you did the only thing you could."

* * * *

The treasurer of the chatty hunter's collective lived in one of Meridian's small suburbs, in an older neighborhood sometimes called the Mini Mile for its detached-townhouse starter homes, most in some degree of disrepair, from before certain regulations for single-family homes went into effect. The paint was chipping, the lawn in disarray and disrepair. Violet didn't have time to tend to or mourn the slow deaths of his hedges. The fact he didn't have an old armchair on his porch put him miles ahead of some of the other houses on his street.

Violet could have opened the lock in any number of ways, but it didn't seem a good idea to break into a hunter's house, especially if she didn't know where he could be waiting for her. He could already know she was there. He could even already know why.

She knocked. There was movement inside, but no one came to the door, as far as she could tell through the window.

She rang the doorbell, then knocked again.

"I hope you realize I'm not going anywhere," she said through the door—not quite yelling, out of deference to his neighbors. "And I have skunk musk in a powder bomb. I don't even have to let it off in your house. I can just throw it at your porch, and you'll never get the stink out in a million years. That tomato sauce trick is an old wives' tale."

The shuffling inside the house increased. Finally, the man inside shouted out at her, "It's open."

A shotgun cocked as she entered, but she'd anticipated that. Firearms didn't worry her unless they caught her by surprise. She put a block on the gun so that if the hunter decided to shoot, it would only blow up in his face.

Other men's fear wasn't something she often sought, but she was oddly gratified by the sight of it now, that not just a young buck but a veteran hunter could shake in his boots because the mean little witch had come knocking on his door.

He was the white-bearded man who'd joined the younger hunter at the store. In his own home, the man was dressed down in sweatpants and an old Cowboys T-shirt. He looked like anyone's father, even a young grandfather, except Violet could tell how powerful he was under the loose clothing. If he'd been wearing something more tailored instead of dressing like a slob in the comfort of his own home, she could only imagine how many people would call him a 'silver fox' behind his back.

"What do you want, witch?" the hunter snapped.

"Were you displeased with our deal yesterday? Did you come back in the night and take what you thought you earned?"

"What the fuck are you talking about? I didn't make the money I wanted to last night, but I still killed some vamps, which is my job, and I did it well. You dealt fairly with us, no different from any other broker, except your bills are crisper." The hunter lowered his gun but didn't take his finger off the trigger, nor did she release the block. "I don't like you, witch, but you're no skinflint, and I'm no thief."

"Then you have nothing to fear from me. All I want is to find Abel Simmons."

"He didn't do it, either. And he hates you more than me."

"I don't think he did it, but I want to find Abel Simmons, and you're going to tell me where to find him."

The hunter finally took his finger off the trigger and set the gun on his coffee table. "If I give you that information, he'll kill me."

"Sir, I will find him with or without your help. Given that you and your collective might be in the running to make quite a bit of money in the bargain, it's in everyone's best interest to help me find him sooner rather than later. If I find him later, I might be in a less civilized mood. And you're assuming that, should you refuse, I won't kill you myself. Oh, maybe not today, but if your delay means my friend dies, who knows what'll turn up in your next autumn squash soup?"

The hunter sighed and lowered himself into his rocking armchair. "Do tell."

"I have three dozen poisons that I grow myself and three dozen more that ship straight to my door." Violet didn't show him her wares. The vials in her satchel didn't contain anything fatal. "These poisons might not kill you immediately, but they should make you miserable until you die of the toxin or by your own hand, because without knowing what poisoned you, doctors won't be able to help you—especially if I bind the poison with magic rather than letting nature take its own terrible course. Make no mistake, I don't *want* to do any of this. But I will do what is necessary, and you have a better chance of living through it if you don't get in my way."

The hunter closed his eyes, rocking, rocking. "Do you know what he'll do to you?"

"I've seen his handiwork. I'm more useful to him alive than dead."

"Unless he decides that your usefulness doesn't exceed your evil."

"I'm not evil, or at least no more evil than him. How is it that you can purchase my weapons, my spices, my magic, my spells, all for your crusade, but you call me evil for providing what gives you the means to defeat your enemy?"

"We use money, too. We pay taxes. We facilitate evil systems that tear the unfortunate and disadvantaged apart. We support evil people. We pay evil people's bills. It's not what you do, witch, but who you are and from where your magic comes that condemns you."

"Jesus Bloody H. Christ on a cross," she muttered. They really were those kinds of hunters who would have worked in tandem with witchfinders, inquisitors, and actual crusaders in the name of their God. There was no reasoning with people who believed in magic men and miracles but suffered not a witch to live.

The hunter was standing in less than a second, and instead of his gun, he pulled a knife from under his shirt to direct at her. It wasn't one of hers. The carvings in the blade and hilt were far more Christian in nature than she preferred in her inventory, especially on a weapon of battle. "Take His name out of your filthy mouth."

"If I can say it without bursting into flames, I *should* be able to say it. You know, the Panabakers are a long line of pagans, but the Corinths have woven in and out of the Christianity of whatever earth they called their native soil for over three hundred years. If you stab me, I bleed, and I don't burn where silver touches me nor scream when holy relics pass over my skin. If you want me to stop saying the name of your savior, then give me the location of Abel Simmons."

The hunter's knife danced in his hand from his restlessness. Anger of his own seethed behind his tended facial hair, but he swallowed thickly and nodded. He indicated an old roll-top desk in the next room, with papers, bills, junk mail, and all sorts of crap piled on top. "The address book is in the right drawer."

Violet backed into the office, sniffing for a trap, then opened the right drawer without looking. A small address book was inside it. Violet threw it at him. "Tell me."

"Fuck you."

"Don't make me open the skunk bomb in your house. You'll never be able to sneak up on another vampire ever again."

The hunter spun his knife again. "I think you're bluffing."

Violet conjured the address book to her again, opened the front door, backed onto the porch, uncorked the vial, threw the powder bomb into the house, then closed the front door before it went off.

At the very least, after the fifth straight month of the hunter trapped in exile because he couldn't shake the scent, he and others would believe that she was capable of far more effective retribution than any hunter, who only knew how to kill things. As far as Violet was concerned, if they weren't alive to suffer, then there could be no real retribution. People were stuck on the idea of blood feuds and making deaths look natural, but pettier problems could add up to special levels of hell. An enterprising witch just had to know what people took for granted and take it away indefinitely.

As she strode away from the hunter's house and his disgusted howls, she wished she could enjoy herself.

Chapter Five

Before Violet could knock on the motel door, it opened first.

"I hear you've been looking for me."

He wasn't quite what she'd pictured, nor completely dissimilar. The treasurer of the collective had boasted a mix of white and black on his scalp, but Abel Simmons had gone entirely gray, and based on the wear and tear on his face, it wasn't premature. One whole side of that face had been clawed by something, and his left eye had been caught in the attack. It was milky and distorted — almost a cliché — but the hunter made no effort to hide the fact that he'd lost sight on one side, even if that made him more vulnerable.

The scars were old. It clearly hadn't made him vulnerable enough.

"Aren't you going to invite a lady in?" Violet asked.

"People who have to ask for invitation aren't the kind I invite. Oh, save it, I know you're not a conquest demon or a hybrid and you can come and go as you please. But you ain't no lady." He pushed away from the frame and turned his back to her, leaving the motel door open.

It was either a test, a trap, or both. But he hadn't invited her. So although she technically could, she didn't enter.

"I've had a very long day," she said. "Now that I'm here, I don't want any trouble. I'm not going to pull your fingernails out to figure out what you did with Clive and why, because I already know you didn't do it."

"I don't need you to tell me what I did and didn't do." Abel faced her again, two full-size beds away. He crossed his arms over the white tank undershirt. He'd bathed since last they'd spoken, but there was still something disarmingly dirty about him, like the grit of old movies.

"I'm not here because I want to hurt you," she said.

Abel laughed, a loud, harsh sound that snapped from his throat like a rubber band breaking against skin. "You, hurt me?"

Violet breathed in, searching for whatever he'd set for her. She found it in a nearly invisible fishing-line booby trap that ran just above the floor from the beginning of the first full bed to the wall. She reached into her satchel and pulled out a rock the size of her fist. She'd packed it in case she'd wanted to get more personal with her revenge.

Abel brought his hand to the hilt of a knife at his hip. Not the bowie knife, which was too big for home use.

She threw the rock instead at the booby trap, which immediately fired four arrows from crossbows to the right of the wire. The tips lodged themselves into the wall opposite.

Violet raised an eyebrow.

"It's my motel. I can do as I like." He didn't bother retrieving the arrows or the crossbows, and he didn't move. Violet searched for more, but although she sensed weapons stored in every nook and cranny of the room, there were no more surprises.

"If you know I've been looking for you, I assume you know what happened."

"The way I hear it, your store was robbed, your employee kidnapped. I'd think the Wicked Witch of the West would have spells protecting against things like that."

"I do. Spells on spells. Those spells only work, though, if they're intact, and it's easy enough to break them from—"

"From the inside," Abel finished for her, still inscrutable at a distance—although she suspected he'd be just as inscrutable up close. "You think that boy you have carving stakes let the wolves in."

"I think he was bewitched first, but yes, I think he let them in. Or he let one in, and that one let the rest in."

"Bewitched." He scoffed slightly, raising his chin and staring down at her with his one good eye. It wasn't any extraordinary color—just an average blue, unremarkable. His regard was more intense. "Strange. I thought he already was."

"I didn't bewitch anybody. I don't do that. There's no fun in it, no meaning. He met me, thought I'd be interesting to get to know better, and we went out for a while. That was all. No potions. No spells. Just a spark of attraction and a suspicion we'd be pretty good in bed. But what's got her hooks in him now... She's using her kind of magic."

"You think a succubus has him? Succubi don't kidnap their prey."

"I *know* a succubus has been visiting him. More than three times."

He would know what that meant, about the hold a sex demon had on a victim after three feasts that didn't end in death—not that most sex demons bothered. He'd know the succubus would have Clive completely under her thrall by now. And while Violet wouldn't go so far as to say that Clive couldn't be held responsible for whatever he'd done, he'd almost certainly been manipulated by more than mere feminine wiles.

"If you knew, why didn't you stop her?"

"I knew he was seeing someone else, okay? And I was a little upset about that. But I didn't know the person he'd been having sex with was a sex demon. I don't go into his room that often, so I didn't know he'd scratched through the protective wards. And he's not dead, as far as I know. He's just not there."

"Sounds to me like you've been played, witch." The sentiment seemed to thoroughly please him. "My professional opinion is that someone took the money and ran."

"All he had to do was end our arrangement and leave the company. He knew better than to do something like this as a giant middle finger to me, because he didn't *have* to flip me off. We weren't exactly *together* to begin with."

"While this afterschool special is thoroughly entertaining, I don't see what your delusion has to do with me."

"I want you to find him. And if the person responsible for stealing is different than the one responsible for taking him, I want you to find them, too."

He looked at her as though she were the remains of a stomped grub on the bottom of his shoe. "I don't find missing people. I hunt demons, plain and simple."

"I can pay you fifty thousand dollars cash to find who took Clive and who robbed Book & Candle."

"You were just robbed. You don't have that kind of money."

"I've been brokering on the supernatural black market for years, and so have you. Despite the collective, you've managed to purchase a motel. I don't have a motel. I have savings. And if you own a motel, I *know* you need money."

Abel smiled. There was no humor there, no indulgence, but she'd at least amused him. "I don't want your money."

"Then do it for free. I just need you to do it."

"Why me? Why not Eli Fray? I heard he's shacking up with a hussy of his own, but he's still taking down sex demons like he wants her to be the only one left. I can't decide which part is sadder. I'm sure he'd take your case, and he'd be better at tracking a succubus than me. I'm an indiscriminate hunter. I'll kill just about anything. Anything, witch. That includes you. I don't care what you have in your bag of tricks."

"I'm not at Fray's doorstep. I'm at yours. Because you have a reputation, too. Do you know what they call you?"

"People don't talk as quietly as they think they do."

"They say you're willing and able to do anything to bring down demons. Are you willing and able to do anything to bring down mine?"

"Honey, you literally walked up to a hunter's door unprotected by the neutrality which you were shrouded in before. You think you're free to do whatever you like without being fair game?"

"I'm not fighting anyone's war but mine," Violet said. "And I'm not unprotected."

"Going to stink-bomb me?"

"I don't need potions to hurt you."

"But you do need to enter this room in order to do so."

"And I'm not going to enter it until you invite me in."

"So a witch needs permission?"

"My mama didn't raise a lady, but she sure as hell didn't raise a barbarian." Violet carefully slipped her hand into one of the pockets of her satchel, where she kept hex bags that were less alchemical in nature than what was inside her potion jars and vials. "Also, the defensive spells carved into your frames and the corners are activated if anyone enters without invitation. If you think I can't recognize spells *I* use, spells *I* sell… Your invitation would ensure this isn't a trespass, which would expand what I'm allowed to do if you treat me inhospitably."

"Do I look hospitable to you?" He indicated his surroundings — as anonymous as any motel room, spare, sterile, lacking personality.

"As part of the hospitality business, do you regularly attack your residents?" Violet asked.

"On occasion, if they're a certain kind of resident and don't know when they're being trapped."

"Demon traps don't work on me. And if you treat all your guests as potential victims, may your God smite you like Sodom."

Violet had never known anyone who smiled or laughed with such little warmth. He showed his teeth like a yawning tiger.

"If they're innocent, they can check out just fine," he said. "If they can't check out, they're mine."

"Invite me in. You'll know I'm innocent when you finally see the back of me."

"It's not the same for you, witch. I know that."

"Are you afraid of me?" she asked. He was a hunter of whom other hunters were afraid, yet he wasn't willing to risk her in his home, temporary though that home might have been.

"You're holding on to whatever's in that bag pretty tight."

"I'm putting my neck on your block to ask for your help — professional, charitable, courteous...whatever makes you agree."

"Then *you* are afraid of *me*. Which makes you smarter than you look."

She bristled, but she didn't say anything, because he'd clearly wanted her to bristle. He watched her the way a bald eagle fixed its fierce stare on a field mouse.

"Look, whatever you feel about witches, we're human — blessed by God, cursed by the devil, whatever you like. I don't think gods, angels, demons, or devils really have anything to do with it, any more than they give a damn about birthmarks or different-colored eyes. I'm just a human being with some magic who would prefer not to hurt a soul and who's coming to you with a paying job. You can broker parts collected on the way however you want. You don't even *need* to kill anything — just get Clive and as much of what was stolen back as possible. If I'm wasting my time, I'll give this offer to someone else."

She turned toward the parking lot, showing that she didn't have to fear him at her back, either.

"Get in here, witch."

Violet turned again to face him but still didn't cross the threshold of the door frame. "You know, I have a name."

"I don't want to know your name. Names make things messy. You name a cat, suddenly you're expected to feed it."

"I know yours."

"You looking to feed me?"

Violet remained on guard as she entered the motel room, but the fact he'd invited her had immediately disarmed the more magical protective spells. Though the man remained unwelcoming, the room welcomed her in—as much as a motel room could. "So you'll do it?"

"Show me the money."

"Come on. I'm not carrying that amount of cash around with me when the space in my bag could be better used for weapons. I can show you my account."

"Drop the bag. Over there." He pointed to the nightstand between the two full-size beds.

When she bent over to stuff it in the empty cubby hole there, she retrieved two hex bags, one for each front pocket of her jeans. She also kept a knife ready in her boot. As she straightened, she doubted she fooled the hunter for a second.

"Come here." He pointed now to the thin carpet right in front of him, then tucked his hands into the back pockets of his jeans as she slowly complied. "You must really want that boy back bad."

She took her place in front of him, close enough to feel the heat burning from his bare skin like it was a furnace. Apparently, he was just one of those people who ran hot, which had its disadvantages during the long Texas summers.

Rather than his mauled face, she found herself cataloguing every scar over his bare arms and the portions of his chest that the ribbed tank exposed — scars and tattoos, which either wound around the scars or had been done before the scars or into the scars themselves. Nothing sentimental here. He didn't have his all-seeing eye where it could be seen. Most hunters chose their side or back because it was easy to hide from civilians, and easier than hip or thigh if they needed to show a fellow hunter, like flashing a badge to prove they were on the same side.

The symbols on his arms were all spells. On his right forearm, he had Last Rites in Latin, tattooed in someone's handwriting — preemptive, but in someone's own words. That meant the hunter was probably Catholic, although sometimes hunters could be ecumenical yet prefer not to hedge their bets. The iconographical nature of the Catholic Church overlapped with hunter fervor, regardless of denominational preference.

Above the Last Rites, he'd had a cross tattooed and touched up over new scars as a ward against vampires and general discomfort for many demons. It would work more because he or the demons believed it would than any intrinsic power to the symbol itself. Conviction could be its own spell.

From what was visible on his left arm, a labyrinthine bracelet over the defined biceps and triceps showed the phrases *in the name of, heart of cold forged iron, against the Father of Lies, among the crawling saints, an innocent sinner for and against*. This one seemed like a cross between a prayer and a spell. There was plenty of overlap there, too.

"What are you looking at?" He didn't appear self-conscious, just annoyed that she'd become distracted.

"The story of your life. Part of it, at least."

"Whatever you sneaked from your bag, put it over there. If you're going to corner me in my own home, you're going to divest yourself of all your weapons. It's only fair. You understand fair, don't you, witch?"

"I don't see you removing your weapons."

"Even without your little hex bags, you have advantages over me if you're half the witch you purport to be. I'm evening the playing field. Thank whoever you pray to that I'm not demanding a strip search."

Violet removed the hex bags from her pockets, put them on the dresser, and knocked them out of her reach. Of course, she could conjure them closer if she needed to.

If the hunter knew what the hex bags could have done to him, he didn't mention how he felt about it one way or another. He just looked down his once-broken nose at her like she was something unpleasant and bloody blown into a tissue.

"I don't like you, witch. I never have. You can't put your feet on both sides of the fence and expect the other side not to have enough claim on you to outweigh what you do for mine. But you've caught me in a generous hour, because someone so happens to need that money. You need to decide, right here, right now, what *you're* willing and able to do for this son of a bitch you've decided to run after, even though it looks like he'd rather be anywhere but with you."

"You have no idea what things are like between me and Clive, or what happened to him," Violet said evenly, not letting him intimidate her so close. "I don't care if you insult me, but leave him out of your snide remarks."

"A man willingly joined himself to a witch, then fell under the thrall of a succubus. I think that tells me and you everything we need to know."

"Maybe people are the sum of their worst choices for you, but they're more to me. Just like you're more than scars."

"You think my scars are bad choices?"

"They're repaired damage, which suggests a certain amount of error. But you have more undamaged flesh than repaired, which tells me you're good at saving your own skin. I'm just here in hopes that you're good at saving others."

"Fine. I'll suspend my serious disbelief in the fidelity of your lover and brand him victim of lascivious circumstance instead. But you came to me. You know I'm going to step not only over your line but over lines other hunters might not cross. What lines are *you* willing to cross to get your things back? What are you willing to do in addition to what you're willing to pay?"

"Fifty thousand dollars not enough of a sacrifice?"

"Apparently not, sweetheart, if you give it away so easily."

"He's worth it."

"And what else is he worth?"

She flinched when he raised his hand, but only because she thought he was going to strike her. Instead, he drew some shorter locks from where she'd tucked them behind her ear and wrapped the curls around his finger, then traced the rough fingernail down the quickening pulse of her neck.

"What—" Violet jerked back, her hip striking the dresser. It jingled from the metal in the drawers.

Abel didn't move, but the glint in his good eye didn't change.

"You want me to— You just said you didn't like me."

"I don't. You disgust me. That don't make a damn bit of difference." Abel hooked his thumbs in the belt loops of his jeans. "I'm asking what you're willing to do to save your boy. The money isn't nearly as important to me as how far you'll go."

"You're sick," she hissed.

"Heard that and everything else before. But if I'm going to do this job for you, here's what you need to do for me, until such point you have your things once again in your possession—anything and everything I tell you. The only thing you need to know about me is that I don't have many lines myself, and I won't cross a single one with anything I'll make you do. Ask yourself now if you're still interested in acquiring my services. This could take quite a while. I may never solve the mystery of who stole your crystal balls. Now, never may not be a long time for a hunter. Hell, I may only have months left. But can you stand months of my whims? Years? Is your boy really worth that much?"

Violet strode to the nightstand, grabbed the satchel, and headed for the door. Where she stopped.

There were other things she could try. She could find a new hunter, one less suspicious of a witch's motives. She could let Detectives Black and Dunn into her store and hope they had some tricks up their sleeve. She could work on developing distance magic so she could try some kind of lost and found spell, although the only version of that spell she'd seen recorded had been in her Gran's grimoire.

She had other options. What she wasn't sure she had was time.

People under succubus thralls weren't like vampire donors. Succubi and incubi could keep a feed going for weeks, but the subject eventually buckled under the energy drain. She didn't know how a hunter like Fray could have a legitimate relationship with a succubus, but whatever was going on between them, it wasn't conventional. Most sex demons had no interest in long-term affairs with anything except other sex demons, who could keep up with their appetite.

Last Violet checked, the penalty for vague infidelity wasn't death. At least, it wasn't supposed to be. But death was on Clive's docket if she didn't tear him from the succubus's thrall.

And that wasn't even beginning to address the chaos someone could rain upon Meridian with the stolen inventory from Book & Candle.

Violet didn't turn around. She didn't want to see his smirk. She kept telling herself she'd done stranger things. She'd done stranger people. And her friend *was* worth it. "I'll give you a month. You don't find him by that point, he's probably dead and my product spent. And for this to work, you need to put in a good faith effort to find him. No kicking your heels up and playing master and servant for doing nothing at all. You don't get paid until I get mine. That means putting all your other hunts on hold. If you are my only job, I'm your only job, too. I won't kill for you. I can't even promise I'll kill to save you. You haven't earned that yet. But short of torturing myself for your wing-pulling pleasure…" She took a deep breath. "I'll do anything in return for you taking this job."

She felt the shackle, the stamp, the brand in the words. She knew more than most how powerful a promise — when spoken by the right tongue — could be.

"You've always been fair." Abel opened one of the dresser drawers and pulled out a knife from what looked like an entire drawer of large cutlery. "I'd like to amend. An expansion, really, because it's covered by the caveat that you do everything I say. I want one of your tattoos. Not the piddly things you give out like lollipops. I've seen what some of your larger protection spells look like on demons I've taken down — which just goes to show they're not foolproof, but stands to reason that having one will keep me alive longer than I can manage on my own. And I admired the artistry, like Arabian love poems. I might as well take advantage of it while I have you."

Violet finally turned around, although she didn't want to. "Arabian love poems?"

"I'm a multi-layered hunter. Are my terms acceptable?"

"Are mine?"

Abel held up his knife and brought it to his palm. "Shake on it."

Violet grabbed his wrist before he could cut through his hand. Abel spun the knife toward her so fast in reflex that it cut her palm instead.

"*Fuck.* I was trying to *stop* you from cutting your hand. They're a pain in the ass while they heal, and all that's required in oaths like this is mixed blood, not crossed lifelines. You sure you want a witch's blood in your veins?"

"Not in the slightest, but of the two of us, I'm getting the better deal. And you're getting hunter blood in yours. Think that'll be enough for the demons to finally reject you?"

Violet wriggled her fingers. "Are we going to do this, or do you just want me to bleed on your carpet?"

He cut his hand with ease that suggested he'd done this for a ritual more than once, slicing through the webbing between thumb and forefinger, close to where he'd cut her by accident. Then he grasped her hand in a firm hold that she wouldn't be able to break even if she'd wanted to.

"I'll find your boy for you, and the loot, if they're not in the same place. You do whatever I say short of murder, justified or not, and compensate me for my time and effort with fifty thousand dollars once the job is finished. That cover it?" he asked.

Promising in blood was stricter than signing a contract, but it allowed for obeying the spirit, not the letter. Where there was confusion, it bound the bloodletters through continued negotiations.

There was no confusion here.

Abel withdrew his hand and grabbed for a roll of paper towels, which he tossed to her after he'd bunched some in his fist.

"If you have first aid, I can wrap them," Violet said evenly.

Of course he had first aid somewhere, with all these knives, and she doubted he'd gone to the hospital for most — or any — of the scars showing on his body. There was a reason she had trouble keeping healing potions in stock.

Abel pulled a first aid pack out from under the bed and kicked it over to her. She tended her own hand first, because that would make it easier for her to work on his without getting any more of her blood on him.

He said nothing as she stuck his hand under the sink water approaching hot, not so much as a hiss of pain, just flexed his hand when she was done to check his range of motion. It wasn't enough of a cut to justify a healing potion, although if it still seeped tomorrow morning, she'd probably recommend some, just to be safe. And she didn't need to waste his healing potion on her when she still had plenty of her own back at the store.

"Follow me."

Seemed they were back to using the minimal number of words to convey meaning. But with dread cold and sick in her belly, she preferred fewer words.

He led her to the adjoining door, unlocked it, and stepped into the motel room next door. In such a cheap motel, she was pretty sure there weren't supposed to be adjoining doors in the first place, but this room had been renovated into a living room with a full working kitchen, which other motel rooms wouldn't have, either. As impersonal and jangly as the bedroom was, this room was practically homey.

Not that it was particularly well decorated, but at least it felt like someone lived there. An overflowing laundry hamper next to a washer and dryer. A mini-fridge with a transparent door and nothing inside but canned and bottled craft beer. A full-size fridge against one wall with magnets on the doors, including one that held a marker drawing that had to be from a child in his life. A *Casablanca* movie poster right next to one for the original *Wolf Man* with Lon Chaney, Jr. — surprising choice for a hunter. A pan soaking in the sink. A threadbare loveseat opposite a large plasma screen. A laptop on the coffee table next to *National Geographic* magazines—and since he didn't seem like someone who got a lot of visitors, he probably read them, too.

And here, as in the other room, the corners and frames were all warded against demonic entry without invitation and barred sex demons from making their more insidious requests entirely. He even had a spell against nightmares, which sometimes had the side effect of more broken sleep, but it ensured demons couldn't find a way into his melon when he was unconscious, inflicting psychological warfare while the wards physically kept them out.

There were ways to make good dreams torturous as well, but if he had those, he didn't seem to mind, because he hadn't applied the spell for entirely dreamless sleep.

She wondered if he realized how much she'd learned about him by seeing this room. His bedroom was his weapons keep—which made its own sense, since sometimes a hunter just wanted to fall into bed after battle but also wanted something sharp nearby for anything that could still get through the wards. His bedroom represented the life of a hunter. His living room presented the life of the man—limited though a hunter's could be. All the more reason, she supposed, to have a place so aggressively average, with the occasional luxury that good money could buy. Violet surrounded herself with magic, both natural and supernatural, throughout her waking world. At the same time, her bedroom was largely unadorned so that the visual chaos of the rest of her life didn't reach everywhere.

"I was just about to make dinner." Abel shoved a nondescript tan apron into her arms. "Soup should do fine."

"Excuse me?"

"Don't grouse, Cinderella. I have one cleaner in my employ who cleans my apartments and knows how to get rid of bloodstains, so I'm not going to have you shampooing my carpets or anything." Abel fell back onto his couch and kicked up his bare feet, heavily callused where they rubbed against his boots. "If you can mix a potion, you can stir a soup. There's hamburger or leftover chicken in the fridge — as long as there's some kind of animal protein included. The rest, I'm sure a green-thumbed witch like you can improvise."

"You want me to...make soup." After promising to do almost anything and everything, cooking hadn't been the first thing on her mind.

"You want me to look for your lover, then I need to eat."

He switched on the television to a streaming service and elected to watch old episodes of *M*A*S*H*.

Okay.

She raided his freezer, fridge, and the bookshelf he used as a pantry. He forewent beer, because this was the start of his day, not its end. Instead, he focused on hydrating with what appeared to be a sludgy powder-nutrient-fortified green juice. Important, because a hunter didn't always have the chance to drink during his night and might not even get a chance to eat. He kept all the vegetable, beet, and protein powders in his pantry, which was a glimpse into aspects of his profession — especially given his age and how it made his work harder — that she hadn't needed to consider before. The cannabinoid and melatonin gummies next to the powdered supplements gave her another.

She served him soup in a cereal bowl—because that's what was available—brought over to him on a potholder. She served herself at the counter. Neither of them spoke. He barely acknowledged she was still there except to hold up his bowl for more. She didn't expect politeness from him, and he didn't give it, but he also didn't play stepsister, in that he demanded but didn't torment. The fact he could have had her massaging his feet didn't make things better, but at least the situation could have been worse.

She took the bowl when he finished and washed it out to dry on the dish rack—no dishwasher. Then she portioned out the soup to cool in smaller containers before soaking the pot in the sink while she scrubbed out the pan.

Violet was so focused on the fairly mindless process and listening to the TV behind her that she didn't hear the hunter approach until his heat hit her, right before he pulled himself against her from behind, fingers hooked into her apron strings. She didn't feel anything but the firmer placket of his jeans and the rush of his warm breath against her neck, but she still stiffened, her hands gloved in lather.

"What is that?" His already rough voice graveled deeper. "I can smell it all the way from the other side of the room. You didn't come here with ground feather in your perfume, did you, witch?"

"I burn incense all day, and I dry herbs in my apartment. I couldn't get the scents out even if I wanted to."

He nudged her loose curls away with his nose as he breathed her in, which suggested that, persistent though the lingering fragrance was, it wasn't unwelcome.

Violet squeezed the sponge in her hand, sending a new flood of bubbly water down the pan. She sensed more than felt his cold smile.

He slowly pulled on the apron ties to undo the informal bow. The fabric hissed a warning over the sound of the television until the skirt swung loose. Now, when he slid his hands over her hips and pulled her back, there was something to press against— uninsistent but unmistakable.

She didn't move, at least not on purpose, but he didn't need a hunter's heightened awareness to feel her shaking.

She'd had sex with dangerous people before. She'd had bad sex, hate sex, break-up sex, angry sex, all kinds, but the man had always been her choice. Although she'd agreed to it, this situation felt completely out of her hands, because she wasn't doing it for *her*. All Abel had to do was slide a hand up the valley of her back to her neck, and her imagination did its worst, because he didn't *tell* her what he wanted, so she had to *anticipate* it.

He unsnapped the top of the apron and pulled it away from between her and the counter. "Stealth is out of the question if you can't hide your scent somehow."

"You're not looking for just any demon. You're looking for a specific one. Doesn't that mean flipping over rocks instead of trying to appear like you're one of the things under them?"

"I work best unknown."

"That doesn't mean undercover."

She could kick herself for letting that slip, planting a suggestion that already seemed ready to root, but instead of pressing closer, Abel withdrew entirely. He wrapped the apron into a bundle and stored it on a pantry shelf, still smiling to himself, which as good as insulted her for the anxiety he'd put her through on purpose.

"How about you stick to magic and leave hunting strategy to me?"

He strode into the other room, leaving her with her hands soapy in the sink. When he returned, he was dressed all in black, although he probably still wore the undershirt beneath the sweater and harness mostly covered by his hooded jacket.

"Were you going to join me at some point, or are you trying to slough your macerated flesh off in my sink?"

"Are you sure you don't have laundry for me to do?" Violet shot back. "Or perhaps some freshly cut flowers to arrange in your kitchen window?"

"It seems only fair that, after you invaded my privacy to find my home, I investigate yours. You're driving." He dangled a full keyring from his crooked index finger.

Violet rinsed off her hands, then dried them on the nearest tea towel.

He tossed the keyring to her as soon as her hands were free. "Unless you really wanted that quickie against the kitchen counter."

"Goddamn hunter," she muttered, grabbing her satchel from the other room and heading out that door.

At his urging, she locked both doors, including all their deadbolts. She didn't bother trying to figure out which key went to what, which she was pretty sure he'd intended to make her do. Seeing how easily she manipulated his locks — psychokinesis wasn't her forte, in the same way that cooking wasn't, but that didn't mean she couldn't do it — wiped the smile from his face.

"How did you get here?" Abel asked as she climbed into his truck and adjusted the seat to her slightly shorter legs. "Broomstick?"

"Bus," she replied, cranking the truck on.

If he'd thought she would turn down the volume on the eighties rock that blared from the radio, he was dead wrong.

Chapter Six

They drove into the alley behind Book & Candle to AC/DC's *Highway to Hell,* which seemed anticlimactic, especially when Violet had to shut the truck off in the middle of the chorus. She pocketed his keys, then pulled out her own from the satchel. She, too, had several locks to undo, plus the security system.

She didn't bother inviting Abel in. She lived in a store, which meant she couldn't ward against unwanted guests like he could. She'd set up a few traps of her own before she'd left, but she wordlessly neutralized them as she switched on the lights.

He strode in without a pause, peeked in the back room, then stepped further into the store. "You didn't clean up."

"Store's not open." Before Violet had left to seek him out, she'd put up a handwritten sign on the door in stark Sharpie on printer paper— *Book & Candle closed due to personal matters. Check website or join our newsletter to be notified when we reopen.* "And I had more important things to do with my time."

"No, better that everything's left in its original state. I might be able to find something left behind." Abel crouched within the mess around her religious icons and searched among the strewn beads. "Could any of the things stolen combine into something dangerous or apply to a particularly evil ritual?"

"You know, that question never crossed my mind."

Abel glared at her from his vantage point between aisles.

"No," she answered with her own frustration. "Out here, they took books, potion and spell ingredients, and some knives. They destroyed stakes and crucifixes but left the garlic flowers and bulbs. Sounds vaguely vampiric, but none of the ingredients they took have anything to do with blood or appetite. And vampires just don't usually come in here. I carry limited supplies of certain kinds of blood for ritual use, but they have easier and cheaper ways of getting it. They don't need all these different kinds of magic books, and they certainly don't need anything taken from the storeroom, which includes everything you and the other two hunters brought, plus other incubi and succubi parts, more ingredients, teeth, bone... I've already gone through iterations, common and less common, but once we get into once-in-a-lifetime or never-done spells, there's too many to compare against. And that's not accounting for anything they've stolen to cover their tracks. So why don't you assume I did my magic thing and came to no conclusion, which is why I sought you out, while you stick to your hunter thing?"

Abel sifted a leather-gloved hand through the remnants of where some tumbled stone beads had been crushed to dust. "It's not a vampire. Accounting for burnt incense, I'm not smelling the kind of ash that would accompany contact with religious objects or any items they're averse to. No burning flesh, no brimstone. Even the slightest brush would leave something behind, like a lit match. Do you know exactly what they took?"

From behind the counter, she pulled out the full list of everything she knew had been stolen, plus some of what she suspected they'd taken. She hadn't had time to scour inventory lists to compare more accurately. The minutiae of business could be mind-numbingly comforting, but she wasn't interested in bean-counting right now.

"Show me the storeroom." He took the page from her as they locked step to the back room. Between reading book titles, he looked over the greater chaos of her storeroom, some of it methodical, some of it madness. At the very least, he should have been able to guess that, though her system might be untidy, she'd never make such a mess or mix ingredients so cavalierly.

His nostrils flared as he breathed in. He wasn't as nose-blind to the scents of her store as she was, but at the same time, how could he discern what was normal for her inventory and what was out of place?

Because the only thing different she smelled was him—from the detergent he used to the mustiness of the dresser drawers where he stored his clothes and weapons, down to the leather jacket that didn't just look cool on the street but added a tough layer of hide between him and an attack. She smelled the oil he used to tend to his gun, the oil he used for his jacket. And underneath that was his own scent—neither good nor bad, not sweat nor fear nor anything obtrusive emanating from his pores, but as she had absorbed the scent of her store, he'd absorbed the scent of his profession, each moment combining into something unique in his skin, his hair, his presence. Perhaps that was why they called it essence, and why it evoked memory.

Without looking back, he handed her the sheet.

"You're right. No rhyme or reason to what they took," he said. "If they'd been more specific, it'd be easier to figure out what they want, but it looks and feels like they had only a general idea of what they might need and took as many things as they could, just in case."

"They?" Violet asked.

He nodded. "The store and the back room have heavy foot traffic over the week, I know, but the dust from the stone beads is new, and while I don't get clear footprints, there are multiple tracks here. At least two, a woman and a man, but as many as four, three women and one man. Without more defined footprints, take the gender of the robbers with a grain of salt. Does your security show any unwarranted entry down here?"

She hesitated.

He faced her. "You think your lover was helping them."

"I'm not sure of anything."

"You think your lover was helping them but coerced by the succubus. Blinded by his lust, he let them into the building so that he could fuck her again."

"Thank you. A vivid description was what I was missing."

He stood in front of her inventory as though it was his instead of hers. "And what if he wasn't strung out on some thrall but really did just want good pussy enough to rob you and leave you holding the bag? What if we get to the end of this yellow brick road, Miss Dorothy, and you don't like what you find?"

Violet didn't budge, nor did she look away, although his single-eyed, unblinking stare had become particularly keen. "Then your job will be over, and I'll pay what I owe. I'll deal with him as I see fit. That's not your problem."

"You're going to let him get away with it."

"I didn't say that."

He stepped closer, forcing her to raise her chin to keep meeting his eyes.

"I thought you were mooning over him because you didn't want to see what was right in front of your face," he said. "But you've already come to the right conclusions. You want me to offer alternatives."

"I can come to my own conclusions. I just need your hide-and-seek skills and your ruthless competitive streak." Violet stepped forward to meet him, so that he wasn't the only one in control of their little stand-off. "I told you I already thought of all of this. I need *you* to figure out where they went from here, because I don't track. I don't know where to begin looking. I've given you a scent, bloodhound. You're the hunter. So hunt."

Without a response—unless the lack of response was the response—he strode around her out of the back room and opened the door to the stairs. He was already halfway up before she reached the foot and ran up to follow him. Bringing him into the store uninvited was one thing. Him entering her apartment without asking felt more invasive. He would have had to go up there eventually. She just would have preferred it to be on her terms.

"You're right. That smell is everywhere, isn't it?" He inspected her kitchen, the herbs and flowers hanging from hooks on the ceiling, the living plants that crowded her living room window seat instead of cushions, the vertical sprout garden on the wall next to it, the piles of paperbacks in front of laden bookshelves. "They're going to have to fumigate when you leave, and even that might not help."

More than one person with sensitive olfactory senses had wrinkled their nose when walking into Book & Candle. She knew it wasn't everyone's cup of tea. If he thought he could get under her skin... "I have menthol jelly if you need to block it out."

"It's pervasive, not unpleasant. You said 'his bedroom' before. Separate bedrooms? Trouble in paradise?"

"We've always had separate bedrooms. We have different sleep schedules, and we're friends more than we're lovers. I told you I've known he was seeing someone else for a while. We've never been exclusive. That's easier in different beds."

He hadn't hooded during the drive to Book & Candle nor to search the building. The lines of his worn, scarred face shifted, deepened, contorted in unreadable ways with the passing of thoughts and emotions he chose not to share. A man in as unconventional a life as his had no room to 'young people today' the way she lived or laugh at the consequences of those decisions. Conventional relationships weren't shields against pain.

Abel headed down the short hallway to their bedrooms. Both doors were open, so he could look into each from the hall and make his assessment. If the more muted palette and texture of hers surprised him, he didn't mention it, but he pegged her room as hers over Clive's in a second.

"When was the last time you had someone else in your bed?" he asked.

She'd promised that she would do whatever he asked. She hadn't promised honesty. But she wasn't prone to lie.

"Book & Candle is my business. He's my employee. I'm busier. But I have slept with people other than him since we started living together, if that's what you're asking."

"'When was the last time you had someone else in your bed?' was what I asked."

Violet leaned against the hallway wall with her arms and legs crossed, watching him check the frames and corners the same way she'd checked his. "A little less than a year ago."

"Serious?"

"No."

"When was the last time your lover was your lover?"

"Maybe three, four months ago."

"Is that a long time for you?"

Flames kindled under her cheeks and spread to her ears and neck, then across her lower back like phoenix wings, heat with churning nausea in her stomach. She swallowed against her tightening throat and tried to breathe herself into relaxing enough to seem as normal as she could under the circumstances.

"Not lately," she said, the closest to the truth she could give him in so few words.

The droughts might have been lasting longer now because she was older and didn't have the same impatience as in her twenties, or maybe she didn't have the same tolerance for fools. Or maybe she'd just become complacent in her routine, everything within reach if she needed it. That had been nice for him, too, until what he'd wanted hadn't been within reach anymore. But although he'd wandered, she'd mostly stayed home and waited for him to come back — for something more familiar, reliable, *comfortable*.

Twenty-year-old Violet would never have believed it, but different decades were different seasons, and people changed.

"The spells in your room are unbroken."

"No shit, Sherlock."

"His are in smithereens, or they were until you repaired them."

"The claw marks are succubus. They didn't draw blood last night, didn't draw much before," Violet said, deciding to share information to speed up the investigation. "And there's only been one succubus in that bed."

"How do you figure that, witch?"

"I put myself in her position."

He mirrored her, leaning against Clive's door frame. "Show me."

"I *told* you so we could save time."

"It's relevant."

"She was on her knees, over him. That's how they usually do it when their victims are sleeping, but he was awake. It's not relevant. You're just being an asshole."

"You don't know what's relevant, and we never stipulated I wouldn't be an asshole. I don't need to know the exact position. Just get on the bed and show me how your magic works. And if you want to undo a few buttons while you're up there, I wouldn't mind at all."

Violet pushed past him in the doorway. He didn't smirk, but he also made no effort to make himself smaller for her. Her legs tangled with his, and her chest brushed his crossed arms. He didn't remove that intense gaze from her all the way to the bed, where she crawled to where she'd knelt over the empty space Clive had once filled, arranged her knees where the succubus had straddled him, legs spread. She balanced herself on the headboard, then placed her fingernails on the grooves left by the succubus claws. Already attuned to the bed's previous inhabitants, it was easier to slip back into the memory echo of the succubus.

Ride him hard, make him arch up to keep himself inside you. He needs the movement of your pussy over him, but he also needs to be deep, deep enough for you to drink, even more than he needs to come, even though that's what you drink. Better when they're awake. Better when their dreams become reality and they can never believe how good they have it. They appreciate more because you don't disappear when they awaken. Shivers over your arms, over your scalp, from his cries. Dig deep your predator claws, tear down as your shivers coalesce around his cock and suck the climax from him. You drink and he doesn't die, just keeps giving and giving until he slumps on the bed and begs for you to take him again, craves you like only the living crave death.

Violet pulled herself out of the echo with a shudder, trying to catch her breath against the full-body possession — not as absolute as literally having a demon or another person's soul inside of her, but as palpable as ripples on the surface of a muddy lake. Like psychokinesis, she just didn't do it enough to have as much control as mediums and parapsychologists — the legitimate ones, anyway.

"Any further insight?" Abel asked.

"What else do you think they're doing on the bed?" Violet snapped, more because she couldn't shake the secondhand arousal hopelessly intertwined with her own.

"Witch, I'm going to need you to be more cooperative, or else I can't help you."

"Then you need to be less laconic and ask better questions." She sat back between her bent legs like she had earlier, trying to ignore that if she'd been the succubus, Clive would have been so deep in her then.

Abel sighed, a sharp, gritty exhalation. "Is it the same succubus every time? You said he's been seeing someone else for months. This place is older, with more respect for privacy, good insulation despite the small rooms so close together. Is it possible he's been courted and kept alive by multiple succubi?"

"Fuck. *Fuck.*" Violet leaned back, bracing herself on her hands and fighting the impulse to just fall and lie there among the sheets and blankets and let Clive be gone while she wallowed in the self-pity left behind. "I can't go back very far. The echoes get too soft to feel after a while, and the echoes I do feel tend to overlap. But let me try."

She let her head fall back. If her hair were loose, she might feel it against her sleeves. That distinct sense memory slipped her back into an echo of longer, straighter black hair clinging to bare arms, brushing his thighs beneath as she took him in.

He grasps the bars of the headboard as though desperate for the prison of her thrall, but he can't resist her for long. He grabs her by her hair and rolls them over to bury himself between her legs at his pace, his depth, suffocating her sweetly with his heat and the delicious bruise of his grip, because he can't hold himself back, can't help how hard he thrusts into her. She makes a beast of him and she's an animal beneath him, carving lines into his back as he bites her shoulder and locks his hips as close to hers as he can, grinding with rough jerks through his orgasm.

Violet reemerged in reality on her back, the knot of her hair askew. She wanted to curse again. Instead, she closed her eyes and slipped back into the echoes.

She kisses him as though she's starving, even though she had him last night and two nights before and she tastes another woman on his lips. He's always so needy. He knows what she is, what she can do to him, but he trusts her even though he has no reason to, and she savors that trust like chocolate-covered cherry after cherry. Every time she kisses him, it's as good as the first time, always feels rare, like the last time, the only time, every night a one-night stand, every kiss the kiss of a stranger, and when he slips into her, she's tight for him, hot velvet suffocation to steal his breath, with the glorious way his chest hitches and he moans almost like a sob in the golden canopy of her hair.

"Motherfucker." She pressed her fists to her forehead. When she was this frustrated, she usually got as far away from the feeling as she could, but while she stayed in that bed amid the echoes, they only became stronger, clearer, more intense. She lay right in the middle of at least three people's arousal woven through her own like suture through skin. "There's, um, there's at least two different women. I don't get a lot of physical traits, but they've got different hair from me and from each other, straight black and blonde. And h-he craves both of them as though they're each his only. There's no getting tired of them. Succubus sex is always a novelty, for them and for him. Two, two… I'm only feeling two."

"Roughly my conclusion, at least in this bedroom."

Violet grabbed one of the pillows and threw it at him. Her aim was good, but he grabbed it before it could hit his face — not that it would have hurt.

"If you knew, I didn't have to do that."

"Confirmation doesn't hurt. There's at least two kinds of thralls at work in the room. I've had more experience with sex demons alive. You only know what they feel like in death."

It was a reasonable assumption that sex demons would avoid Book & Candle, given that she trafficked in their parts, but she actually did get a fair number — more than vampires, anyway. They didn't need her for sexual enhancements, but they liked her candle and incense selection as well as her sleep aids, because their circadian rhythms were chaotic at best. The sun forced vampires to be nocturnal, but sex demons could be active day, night, or in between, so they sometimes had issues maintaining a regular sleep schedule that gave them enough hours of rest for the kind of recreational physical exercise their nature demanded. When a bed was as much aphrodisiac as comfort, some sex demons — especially those who nested together — got too distracted to sleep enough.

Did they take offense to what she made of them in her storeroom? Yes. But she didn't hunt them or solicit their parts, only accepted what was offered, and she was equal opportunity in her acquisitions. Demons sometimes brought her hunter weapons to resell, because they could be hard to pawn.

Who knew? Maybe one day, she'd hang that bowie knife Abel had bought back up on her weapons wall, marked as *previously owned*.

She rolled off the bed in a hurry, leaving most of the magic and memories behind as he rounded the bed to the windowsill. He traced her newer carvings refreshing the sex demon wards, then found the more random knife marks that had sliced through the paint and first layer of wood.

"The spells were strong, impenetrable," Abel said. "The man broke the wards and made it look like it had been idly done, maybe in his sleep, probably so he could dismiss it away if you ever said anything. But the corner spells would have prevented somnambulistic manipulation. Your lover is part of this heist, whether you like it or not."

"I already didn't like it. If he's in on this with both eyes open, fine. It'll be easier to get my things back from him than from someone I don't know, and if he's worth a pair of succubi keeping him alive, they'll give back what they took unless they want me to damage what they value more. Now you know as much as I already knew. Do you have a plan?"

"Barring a clearer view of the succubi in question, we'll need to take a page from your book, witch — running around where the sex demons play and threatening them until you find an energy you recognize. Or your boy."

"And why couldn't I do that without you? What exactly am I paying for?"

Abel reached into his jacket and pulled out the beautiful bowie knife. "This."

"I can commit violence all by myself."

He brought the curved tip to her cheek with control and delicacy, not so much as a quiver beyond the slightest vibration of his pulse, which wasn't enough to pierce her skin. "You surround yourself with living things. The dead you dry to keep their soul. You take parts, but you don't carve a heart by your own hand. You *can* kill, but you don't want to."

He slid the blade tip down her neck. He could have thrust forward and pulled back in less than a second, severing carotid and jugular in one slice, and let her bleed out on the bed, but he drew the blade down to the top her plaid shirt, which she'd buttoned all the way up. He clipped the thread of the first button, sending it into the mess of Clive's room.

"You came to me because you want someone to get their hands bloody for you, witch. If the ones bleeding are demons, I ain't going to complain. I'll cut down everything in your path for fifty thousand — and for that look, right there. Not wondering what I'll do to you but how far *you'll* go."

He snicked the second button.

Instead of backing up, she pushed the knife to the side. "Stop getting distracted by succubus trails. The sooner we find my things, the sooner you can air my smell out of your leather."

In the time it would have taken for him to kill her, he flipped the knife back and slid it seamlessly into its sheath. "Hope you got a good night's sleep, because this is the start of my work day. You need to change. When hunting sex demons, you need to be invisible."

"I haven't been invisible all my life. I'm a woman. I'm black. I'm a witch. When I turned thirty, people under twenty-five stopped noticing me as much, but I can't hide any of the rest of those things, even if I try. People recognize me from five blocks away. I'm not the only witch in this city, but I'm the one both sides of the city know."

"You and I, witch, we seem to be talking in different circles." Abel adjusted his coat and backed out of the room to gesture to hers. "I already assumed you had some kind of sightless shield in your possession so you can walk the streets unseen, but you need to change into something more innocuous, because you'll need to fit into the night in a different way than me if someone bumps you or has an all-seeing eye."

"Oh." Violet picked up the cut buttons and tucked them into her pocket. "I don't think I have those kinds of clothes, either. I pretty much wear witch night and day."

"I can go through your clothes myself if you like."

"I'll figure something out."

She stepped into her bedroom door, paused, and looked over her shoulder at him, because she knew what he would tell her to do if she didn't. But he apparently wanted to see her expression more than he wanted to see her naked, because he gestured her to proceed without following her in.

Violet slammed the door behind her.

Chapter Seven

"Mind sharing where we're going?"

Violet walked behind Abel because it was polite not to take up the sidewalk. With some distance between them, she had to raise her voice, but most people didn't pay much attention to their surroundings, just occupied themselves with getting from one place to another with the least amount of grief.

She wasn't exactly hunter chic in a black skirt with a slit up the leg—chosen to give her better range of motion in case of fight or flight—nor in the purple top, frothy in silhouette and sleeve. Altogether, she was a bit more nineties witch than intended, but at least it wasn't completely impractical for moving unseen, and it was less conspicuous in case she was seen.

"Nowhere in particular." He had to speak louder to be heard as well, because he wore the same mask under his hood that he'd worn in her store the other day. "Do you think sex demons have their own bar like hunters?"

"A brothel comes to mind," Violet muttered.

"Some of the young ones get into the business for easy prey, but finding them there is a quick kill for new hunters, too. On the other side, sex demons in strip joints and peepshows are largely harmless. Taking them out is as much a cheap kill as a cheap thrill. I don't waste my time with demons playing safe, and I don't give a damn about prostitutes on principle. But there's a reason why demons and hybrids foolish enough to turn tricks for prey in my motel don't leave again."

"Then where?"

"Vampires and werewolves are social animals. Sex demons are far more selective for their own safety — from law enforcement and from each other more than hunters. They'll rarely nest with more than four of their kind. Tell me you have an all-seeing eye."

"Naturally."

"Look for incubi and succubi hunting in twos and threes. They're more likely to know other nests. I don't mind killing the demons one by one, but then again, one predator is as good as another for me."

Violet wanted to chide him for his reductive view of demons, but most incubi and succubi victims were reduced by the demon that drained them, too. Hunters were cruel, cold, callous, but they occupied an essential position in the strange circle of life and afterlife in a spiritual ecosystem.

Feeding was rarely personal for the sex demons. Hunting often started from an eminently personal place for the hunters, triggered by grief and anger precipitated from loss. After the initial massacre, however, revenge easily transitioned into vocation.

In Book & Candle, Violet was protected from most of these business and pleasure vendettas. Hunters and demons were on their relatively best behavior with her. The part of the supernatural world they were entering now was Abel's domain, where lives were actually at stake.

"Tell me you're good at more than stabbing the nearest demon," Violet said. "That's not hunting. That's Whac-a-Mole."

"I've tracked down solitary demons, duos, trios, whole nests, and not just incubi and succubi. I've even killed two witches. Don't doubt my credentials while I'm still trying to figure out how you, of all witches in Meridian, get immunity."

"Fuck you, brother."

"Please. I didn't gun down a sleepover of exploratory Wiccans. I didn't burn a crunchy mom for wearing patchouli oil and drinking kombucha. I can tell a witch from a pagan. The first one cursed her boyfriend's side piece to spontaneously combust. Prison may have iron bars, but how long do you think concrete walls and steel fences are going to keep someone like that bound?"

"There are other ways."

"There are always other ways, but you've abdicated responsibility for what people and demons do with what they take from your store. I don't have that luxury. While I'm wasting time trying to find another way, the other Broom-hilda decided to pull a Carrie White at the Homecoming Dance by igniting every mum and garter bigger than hers. I don't see you moaning and crying over ninety-six high school freshmen and sophomores overwhelming the burn ward at St. Sebastian's."

That left her quiet for a while, her footsteps matching his, although he had to shorten his stride slightly to allow her to keep up in her sensible platform heels.

It had been a deliberate choice on Violet's part not to have a dog in Meridian's grand fight, but refusing to participate in such a long-standing barbaric tradition didn't mean she didn't contribute.

To be fair, though, online retailers and grocery stores provided many of the same resources, and those resources, in and of themselves, were as neutral as she was. For every terrible thing vampire teeth could do, there were palliative properties as well. A snake's venom had a deleterious effect upon the circulatory or nervous system of a person when injected directly, but the same venom, when broken down and adjusted, could help circulatory and nervous system disorders. Foxglove could stop a heart, but in small doses, it was heart medication. A succubus could be a sexual predator or a sex surrogate.

Most of Meridian was neutral at its core. It was people who decided the sides.

"If incubi and succubi don't like to congregate, are we just hoping we stumble onto one in the middle of their hunt?" Violet asked.

"More or less, but in starting at the outdoor mall rather than apartments, we're more likely to find the demons engaging in a little petty or grand larceny rather than feeding. Let the rent-a-cops protect property. I don't give a fuck. But someone like you might be in a better position to talk to them in a place like this without resorting to violence."

"I heard you killed someone in public in the middle of the day. I doubt that demon was feeding on anyone at the time. Why are these demons different, especially if you know they're probably going to hunt later?"

Not that she wanted to change his mind, but the rules hunters followed were as varied as the hunters themselves, because they all worked outside the law, and they all became hunters for their own reasons. There was no guild, no union, no rules except don't screw over other hunters in their collective and leave humans — at least those unimbued with supernatural power — to the justice system.

"The demon I killed was one I'd tracked over the course of two weeks. He was an avarice demon with a propensity for financial scams on the elderly. He may have never killed someone with his own hands, but a bloodless murder is still murder, and slow death in poverty is still death. He deserved worse." Abel indicated the skyscrapers of the Meridian skyline looming over them, obelisks to new idols. "The green-eyed demons think they're safe from us in their ivory towers. As long as they're just moving their gold hoard around, let them have their Gothic Wall Street. But don't for a moment think they're more harmless just because they're not using teeth and claws. The plain fact, however, is that not all sex demons hunt, at least not to kill, in part so they can avoid hunters' ire. Some hunters don't make the distinction between actively harmful or harmless. I don't always, either, because feeding without killing takes discipline they don't always have. But they're less likely to do it here" — he nodded now at the outdoor mall they approached — "while people are awake. Where do you think you're going?"

As the sidewalk had expanded leading into the Panacea Outdoor Mall, she'd moved beside him, then in front of him toward the arched entrance that reminded her more of a zoo or theme park than a mall.

"I thought we were going to the mall," she said.

"Why? You want a pretzel?"

"Well, yes, but that's not why I'm here."

"Unless you want to interrogate people in the middle of walkways or in the shops themselves, we start where only employees go. The demons sometimes come out the back walls to avoid sensors. No one can see them stealing, of course, but it's easier if the store doesn't even know something's gone."

Abel led her in three laps around the entire outdoor mall under inadequate alley lights, with nary a glimpse of anything except employees taking smoke breaks and the occasional literal mall rat skittering along the wall of the buildings. Abel strode with purpose, as though he could see better in the dark than her, and maybe he could—just another spell he'd inked into his skin.

He didn't slow down, didn't make sure she was following, and if she hadn't been following him, she might have barely noticed him at all. A man of just above average height, lean in his Man in Black dramatic duster, hood, and mask, yet he had the stride of a man fifteen years his junior and blended into the dark as though he was meant to be there. It was uncanny, but it couldn't have been supernatural, because they'd broken through their respective sightless shields so they wouldn't lose each other.

His voice was so distinctive, his face a crumpled, water-damaged, salvaged hardback, but when it was covered and he stayed quiet, he just…faded into the background when he should have stood out. While staving off impatience in this endurance game, she was still trying to figure out how he managed to do that when he raised his hand. The metal of a short blade in it caught one of the golden lights above an employees-only door.

He pointed the knife toward the blank wall of a sporting goods store — not the kind of place from which she'd expect a trio of beautiful young women to pop out, but succubi could wear athleisure and root for football teams sometimes, too.

She immediately knew they weren't the ones who'd been in Clive's bedroom — not unless they'd cut their hair from down to their waists up to their shoulders within the last week. The texture and hues of their hair were different, too. If she came close enough to them to feel their magic and the memories they carried, she doubted they'd feel familiar.

"Make yourself known," Abel muttered, almost incomprehensible through the mask by volume, but he compensated with enunciation. The girls still hadn't noticed either of them by their footsteps, and they didn't pause when Abel spoke below the drone of the many A/C units.

Violet slipped her hand into the pouch on her thigh harness, which held her burner phone, ID, a stiletto, and the sightless shield — things she unequivocally needed to keep with her, although she'd also brought her bag of tricks.

She stroked her finger over the glyph that let her be seen by those she saw, which would keep anyone else from seeing her in the meantime. Then she put her hand in her satchel and grasped the unused itching powder bomb.

Violet walked straight up to the girls. She didn't recognize them, but at least one of them recognized her, and all three jerked away when they realized she could see them.

One of them, a black girl with close-cropped hair, backed into the store, half of her in and half of her out. Violet couldn't walk through walls without spending too much time on a spell, and circumventing the lock on the employee door also would take too much time. They'd be gone by the time she got through.

Violet held up her free hand—ungloved, empty, although that wouldn't reassure them about the hand they couldn't see. Dealing with demons wasn't the same as dealing with hunters. Some demons were indiscriminately violent, and pestilence demons could be vicious if they thought they could get away with it, but by and large, demons worked in secret and shadow. Hunters responded to violence like a dominance game. Demons didn't want to fight when there were far more pleasant ways to spend their time.

"I won't waste your night or mine," Violet said. "You know who I am. Has word spread about what happened?"

The black girl who recognized her shook her head. Violet wasn't surprised. There was no real reason for hunter gossip to reach demon circles.

"Despite the fact Book & Candle and those who work within it are not to be harmed, someone stole from me and abducted my partner," Violet said. "By right, I can use every resource at my disposal to find him and retrieve my product or a compensatory amount. In other words, I'm allowed to annihilate everything in my way. I know he was either taken or conspiring with at least two succubi, probably three. No, I don't think you're those demons, but you might know three succubi who work together and could have done this, or you may have heard whispers about an ill-advised plan to rob me."

111

"It worked, didn't it?" the blonde succubus said. Instead of long hair, hers was short and dyed platinum where it wasn't undercut.

"I take precautions, but I'm easy to rob because no one would dare," Violet replied.

"You don't seem that scary to me." The blonde stepped in front of the girl with longer brown hair—not black and not long enough to be the woman in the echo. "More like a grown woman playing witch. And you're one of ours, aren't you? What if we just drained you right here and left you for the rats, then raided that easily robbable store of yours?"

"Tati, don't." The black girl shook her head, but the blonde was too far for her to reach without also stepping completely out into the alley. The brunette, who was the youngest, squared up behind the blonde protecting her.

The fact that the succubus was protecting one of her own didn't make the magic any less of an assault.

Oh. This wasn't a memory echo or leftover essence. She'd felt succubus feathers on her bare skin, but that was lingering magic, like blood in dead veins.

Violet was unprepared for the way that the girl's magic clutched at her like enchanted tree branches, digging splinters in under the skin. The frustration that had built over the last few days and over the last few months—and to be honest, longer, because before he'd gone looking for sex elsewhere, Clive hadn't really felt there with her for over a year—gave Tati's magic ample energy to grip. The magic was an insidious parasite low in Violet's abdomen, fluttering through her pussy and twitching through her clit, everything flushed and full and heavy and longing. All in a matter of seconds.

She wasn't used to frustration so intense, like she was on the brink of orgasm and would reach it if she could just be touched, skin to skin, if she could brush her bare palm over that close shave of undercut, because she'd always had a weakness for short hair on women.

But she *was* used to frustration and self-denial, so although Tati's fingers on her arm were tantamount to electric current that had her squeezing juices from her pussy with the tightest, most exquisite clench short of climax, Violet knocked her hand away and pulled the bomb out of her bag, thrusting it between them.

Tati grinned a smile of so many teeth, bright between her cherry lips.

"It doesn't look like much because you don't know what it can do," Violet said. "If I can't work, neither can you. Itching powder sounds like a cheap prank, but a good itching spell is so much more than that. How many feasts do you think you'll have to forfeit because you're too busy scratching your private parts raw? When your body is covered in scabs and swelling and pus because not even your succubus claws can dull the itch, you'll only be able to hunt in dreams — if you can keep from twitching and waking them up. It'll be like living in a beehive. Go on, honey. Try me."

"We don't know anything!" the black girl shouted, sinking farther back into the wall until she looked like she'd been cursed into it. "Tati, McKenna, she's off limits. Even if she's on the warpath, she's off limits. It's not worth it to get in her way. Now leave us alone. We don't know anything, and we don't want any trouble."

Violet twirled the vial between her fingers. Miraculously, she didn't drop it from the shaking in her hand. "Any suggestions where to look?"

"Up your cute ass," Tati snapped.

Violet slapped the blonde succubus with her free, bare hand. It was like getting shocked all over again. A cry escaped her lips, but not one of pain.

McKenna, the brunette, darted around Tati and knocked the bomb from Violet's grip before grabbing her bare forearm, wrapping thin warm fingers around the all-seeing eye tattoo. Unlike hunters, Violet had never needed to hide that she could see through charms and glamors.

As soon as McKenna made her move to disarm Violet, Tati brought her body directly against Violet's and slipped her fingers around Violet's neck—thumb pressed in threat against her throat in anticipation of pushing down.

Just as Tati pressed savoring lips against hers and McKenna stepped around her to smooth both hands up her arms, the shrill song of metal whistled through the air. McKenna let her go.

Lush though the kiss was, and as tempting as it was to sink into such sweet arms and finally scratch the unbearable itch she'd tolerated for too long— considering her twenties had been full of her refusing to tolerate it—Violet resisted the temptation and shoved Tati away.

The succubus's widening eyes might have been for that resistance, but then her gaze shifted to behind Violet, and her beautiful face contorted in horror.

Violet whipped around.

McKenna stood there, mouth downturned in an almost comical, open-mouthed frown, with the early stirrings of ugly tears, as she held up the stumps of her hands. Her body, like a human's, would still be shocked. She might not even have more than nominal pain, but that wouldn't last.

Violet jumped out of the way of the blood spurting from the stump. Between strength, aim and the sharpness of the blade, Abel had given both a clean cut, but steel hadn't cauterized the wounds. McKenna could bleed out before she even thought of fighting back.

It was one thing to see a succubus's hands without her body passed over a table in the interest of commerce—and usually that severance was post-mortem. It was another to see her body without hands.

Abel didn't make her suffer. As soon as Violet was out of the way, he plunged the bowie knife into McKenna's heart from behind. It burst through her chest like a bad Halloween effect, stippling Violet with heart-punched spatter. McKenna dropped to her knees, then forward, falling away from the knife as Abel pulled it back.

Screaming, Tati jumped on Violet's back and sank succubus claws into Violet's sodden shirt. The whoosh and flutter of wings filled Violet's head as the demon's magic tore more violently—but no less seductively—through her.

Violet took every inch of frustrated desire and pulsed it far less pleasantly out of her body, sending Tati flying toward the wall. Instead of falling through it, she hit the brick hard enough to knock the air out of her. She gasped on the ground, unseeing, focused only on how to get her next breath.

"Please, stop," the black girl begged, barely visible through the wall now.

Abel strode to Tati while she was still fighting her frozen diaphragm, unable to so much as shift her wings to block him. He buried his blade in her so hard that the tip of the knife sparked against the concrete. He didn't hesitate, nor did he recoil from the splash of blood when he jerked the knife back again. He wiped the blade, both sides, on Tati's pants.

Then he pointed it at the only succubus left. "Don't make me chase you."

The girl shook as though freezing, despite the balmy night, but she didn't sink completely back into the brick. She kept enough of herself out to glance, eyes almost popping out of their sockets, between Abel and Violet, with the same level of fear for both. "I swear I don't know anything."

Abel grabbed her accessible wrist with his gloved hand and yanked her out into the alley, then blocked her way back into the building. "You know who she is. You know the boy she uses. You haven't heard anyone talking about what they want to do with him?"

Violet put herself not necessarily between the hunter and the succubus, but in a better position to get between them. "Anything. Anything at all."

The girl's face shone from her tears in the insufficient light. "You going to kill me if I don't give the answer you want?"

"Only if you're lying," Abel said.

"Don't fight. Don't run. Don't lie. You can leave when we're done," Violet said. "You know something."

"Fine. Fine, all right?" The girl crossed her arms over her chest. "I don't have names or faces. But I might have heard something about your guy. About how someone has him under their thumb and he's going to give them what they need."

"He's going to give who what? What do they need?"

"I don't know, okay? They didn't elaborate. They weren't talking to me."

"How many?" Abel asked.

"Two."

"Where?"

"The historical district, near your shop. I'm not the only succubus who likes the fudge around there. Maybe it's our fucking useless cycles syncing or something, because we end up there at the same time a lot."

Abel hadn't budged his blade from where it pointed straight at the girl for if she answered in a way he didn't find helpful. "What did they look like?"

"I wasn't looking. One of them might have had black hair. I really don't know, I swear. I wasn't even paying attention. It's not like I'm quoting verbatim. Please, please don't kill me. Let me go." She shook her wings out but didn't try to fly, just stood there in tears.

Violet wanted to ask her name, but she couldn't allow herself to get sentimental just because the girl looked young. "Thank you. Spread the word. If you have a text group, a message board, a phone tree, a newsletter, all anyone needs to do is stay out of my way or give me the information I need. If Clive is living, no one has to die, not even the ones who took him. Am I clear?"

The girl nodded.

"Go." Violet stepped in front of Abel now as the girl beat her wings down to take flight away from the mall.

The distant calliope music of a carousel added a layer of surrealness to the blood pools slowly trying to flow to the central groove of the alley.

"Hey!" Heavy footfalls slapping against the pavement headed straight for them — two men.

Abel grabbed her by the arm and pulled her back against him to cover her mouth and nose with his hand, stifling her with the powerful scent of oiled leather and the sharper, meatier odor of fresh succubus blood.

She gripped his arm, but she didn't pull it down. She understood — no matter who was coming, they couldn't see her.

But fuck, he was hard. Not a suggestion. Not a stir. Stiff as the hilt of his knife against her ass. The firmer material of his jeans gave his erection something structured to hold it close to his body as it grew, but there was no mistaking his arousal. His breathing was even and slow in her ear through his mask, but heavy, recalling other pants in her ear in such a steady rhythm, usually accompanied by the creak of bedsprings or groan of wood.

Her arousal was less externally manifested, but it took every bit of her control not to move herself against him, to shift his other leather-bound hand down from her shoulder to her blood-soaked shirt, then beneath.

Because he was right. It didn't matter that he disgusted her, that she sometimes thought she could hate him. Not when she was like this and angrier at someone else. Abel wasn't the reason why blood stung her nose, why two young succubi had died, why a poor young succubus had fled sobbing from a battle she'd never wanted. Abel wasn't the reason she'd needed to hire him in the first place. None of this had needed to happen at all. Things hadn't been great, but before Clive had gone and fucked up, life had at least been peaceful and the blood on her hands from both sides had more or less canceled each other out.

That the two men could see the succubi bleeding out almost certainly meant that they were demonic, too.

The closer they came, the more they confirmed it, because their magic was more directly keyed to her desire than that of the succubi. She could enjoy and had enjoyed women in the past, but she usually preferred men in her bed, and she bit her lip hard behind Abel's hand as the incubi knelt before the bodies. The one looking over Tati could reach out and grab Violet by the skirt.

And that's exactly what he did.

As soon as he touched her, his eyes followed what his hand already knew. "Bitch, you think I couldn't smell you?"

"Shit," Abel muttered.

He let her go just as the incubus jerked her toward him. His wings were massive and spanned the night sky as he clenched fists in her bloody shirt to lift her almost off the concrete.

Once again brought to what seemed like the brink, his power pouring into her through both proximity and contact, Violet let herself sink back into her drowning desire to gather it like wings of her own.

When she opened her eyes, she knew they were glowing again, because her cheeks and her sockets burned and the glow reflected in his dark eyes, against his skin otherwise obscured by the shadow of his wings.

The vial that the succubi had made her drop rose from the ground. She flipped off the lid midair, then called the powder from the jar in a serpent of greenish dust and sent it slithering down the incubus's shirt to spread over his body under his clothes. With a pulse of her own magic in response to his, it absorbed into his skin.

Under other circumstances, maybe it would have been funny, but she wasn't laughing as he jerked and jolted and twitched, still holding on to her and ripping different buttons and the seam of her sleeve in the process. He looked down at himself in confusion, then at her. She saw no recognition, so like the two dead succubi, he wasn't familiar with Book & Candle, but understanding slowly surfaced in his contorting, wincing expression.

"Release me," she said, low and quiet, shaking with the potent combination of fear and lust in his hands.

Those hands cracked as she forced the bones back, forced him to unclasp, forced them open. She wasn't breaking any of the bones — the cracks were just compressed air in the knuckles — but the incubus stared with disbelief at the uneven dance of his fingers before him. He couldn't focus on them for long, though, because the rest of him was doing its own madcap dance trying to escape what made him itch. But it was already under his skin.

She'd never actually seen this potion in action before, and she was a little ashamed at how much she enjoyed witnessing this particular work. The torture of a persistent, full-body itch that couldn't be soothed was one of the most nefarious things she could think of, inspired by certain times of the year when there wasn't a queen mosquito who didn't like to feed from her feet. The itching powder bomb was harmless in and of itself. What the subject did to themselves caused the most damage.

He stumbled back more before finally starting to scratch, because that's just what a person did when they itched this much. He would quickly realize that his impulse, while irresistible, was also futile.

She wanted to see that revelation — that despair.

"Shit. Shit, woman, what did you do to me?" He extended claws to rake at his exposed skin, then under his clothes — revealing the most beautiful dark-skinned abs beneath his shirt. But although he already drew blood, he couldn't stop. He doubled over first, then fell to his knees.

She licked her lips as she approached him. His power wasn't nearly as strong now that he was distracted, but it wasn't gone, so she continued to gather the frustration it inspired around her, burning, burning, until he bared his demon teeth at her in fury, the furrow of his forehead telegraphing a particular kind of agony.

She touched his face to intensify his power in her, almost as addictive as her magic in him was reviled. "Do you want me to make it stop?"

"Please, God, please, make it stop." He tore ribbons from his abdomen, chest, arms, back, probably reaching places he hadn't known he could reach, because he *had* to, *had* to make the itch go away, and couldn't.

"You don't happen to know anything about two or three succubi taking my partner for themselves and stealing from my store in the process, do you?" she asked.

"What the fuck? What the fuck are you talking about? What succubi? What store? *Fuck*." He ripped through his armpit, sending new blood splattering to the ground. "What the fuck is this?"

"That would be my special blend of itching powder. I can render it inert, but I have to be sure that you don't know anything, even something you didn't realize you knew. Two or three succubi, one magic shop employee, loads of magical things taken. You know nothing?"

"I have no idea what you're talking about, lady! You know torture doesn't actually get you information, right? Fuck, fuck, *fuck*, this is…" He flopped onto his back with his wings still open, too distracted to furl them back in as he rubbed his back against the rough pavement and kept scratching wherever he could reach. "Fucking bitch!"

He kicked at her. Her leg snapped back, locking straight, and she lost her balance. When she fell next to him, he pulled himself to her, using her body as handholds until they met in the middle. Still twitching like mad, he crawled over her, straddling her to close his fingers around her neck and squeeze. His hands were much bigger than Tati's. They collared and closed off her air completely.

"Get this off me now, or I swear to God, I'll kill you, and you'll never even know my kiss. Two can play that game."

Despite the wrench and twist of his body, he ratcheted up his magic to as high as it would go, and Violet lost hold of hers. It spilled around and within her like a broken-dam flood of arousal that had her arching beneath him, shrieking at scalpel's edge with everything she'd ever wanted or needed from a man this familiar against her. Even with his hands over her throat, she didn't try to force them off or scratch at his face. The closing of darkness in her vision and the thinning of oxygen in her blood only rushed the lust harder inside her. If he could just squeeze harder, take her deeper into that darkness…

Blood spilled in a curtain from the incubus's neck, pouring over her hot and thick with living incubus

Aurelia T. Evans

magic. When it fell into her mouth, salty, metallic, she gulped it down, bathed in it as the incubus coughed, choked, wrenched one way, then the other, still itching but also drowning with every inhale. Then, with the flash of a blood-coated blade, he slumped heavy over her, his hold loosening on her neck.

She coughed his blood as well, like a consumptive, and gasped for air that cramped in her desperate lungs, but she also moaned from the incubus's heat and weight, because he was still living — for a little longer, and she hadn't been able to regain control of her own magic yet. The incubus was stronger, more desperate, and his magic was a defense mechanism. Her magic needed coherence, and her mind and body were anything but coherent except in their need as the incubus continued attacking her through the last pounding beats of his heart.

The body was hauled off of her by the wings and dropped to the side. Then Abel grabbed her hands and pulled her up.

Although she felt like all taut muscle and no bone, she managed to get her feet solid underneath her, staggering on the slightly uneven alley pavement.

Abel didn't let her keep her feet. He twisted the front of her shirt in his fist, popping another button and wrenching at her rent sleeve seams as he pushed her back to the brick wall. She hit it hard enough to almost lose her breath again, and she nearly slid down the brick, but then he was there against her, his own desire unmistakable from the greater power of the succubi over him. And maybe the incubi got to him, too. But they were also dead, like the succubi, with her incubus a pile on the pavement and the incubus he'd fought somewhere else, no longer a problem.

She lifted her face, bloody mouth and all, up to his, despite his mask, but he turned away. She couldn't see either of his eyes, good or bad, to learn how wide the pupil of the good eye had dilated and whether the bad eye dilated at all.

He stepped back only to roughly spin her around and shove her back against the brick, startling her into a cry. He crowded her from behind, that heavy breathing back in her ear with what heat permeated the mask.

But now his heavy, hot, gloved hand traveled down her spine to squeeze her ass where he pressed his erection. Then he slipped through the slit in the side of the skirt. Her breath shuddered out against the brick.

He stroked over her bare thigh to the garter harness, his thumb finding the crease between thigh and cheek, then further in—*almost.*

She ground back against him now, her breathing just as heavy as his but also harsher, the incubus magic so much fresher inside her, and more weaponized.

He shoved her skirt out of the way, then pulled her black underwear—practical in case of exposure during a fight—down just enough that, after he undid the button and zipper on his jeans, there was nothing in his way as he pressed the tip of his cock to her equally slick entrance. They were both well past foreplay, and she groaned into her arm as her pussy happily accommodated him. It felt like she'd been lonely for longer than a few months—more like ten years.

Abel grabbed her wrists and forced her hands over her head on the wall, pinned them with one of his, pinned the rest of her there as he slid home. He grunted like a beast as he ground into her far more effectively than she had to him, then brought his other hand between her and the wall to cup her mound. He didn't actively rub her clit, but he gave her something to press against as he held her in place to take her.

He was rough, his thick jeans unforgiving, his grasp on her hands and pussy bruising, the friction of her body harsh on the wall, but she pushed back to meet his thrusts as well as she could. It was carnal, physical, animal, a different kind of scratch for a different kind of itch, but it did the trick better than anything the incubus could have done.

Abel stiffened, his forehead cushioned on her hair, locked inside her as he came. "Oh shit. *Fuck.*"

She thought they were just crude exclamations through his climax, and since she wasn't finished yet, she was too distracted to think any differently. He started to withdraw from her, as abruptly as the sex had started, but Violet gathered the magic she'd lost control of and wound it back around her — and him, jerking him inside her with a sound of surprise, keeping his hand holding hers to the wall, his other over her mound. It looked like he still pinned her, but she was the one pinning him now.

"Just stay right there," she murmured. "Don't move."

And he didn't — couldn't, but he also didn't try — just rested his head on the back of hers as she worked herself over his cock but mostly used his hand where his fingers pressed bone and the cluster of nerves just under the surface. She kept him against and inside her until she cried, open-mouthed, into the wall as she finally — *finally* — fucking came.

It would be one thing to endure a dry spell with a few trusty vibrators to deal with it, but three or four months with absolutely nothing would test a nun, and she was no goddamn nun. More than what he felt like inside her — stretching her in all the good ways, briefly making her feel like part of someone else — how he felt holding her from behind after the cascade of climax through her body felt even better. She panted, keeping him there, until the clenching aftershocks had settled into twitches.

Then she released him, which meant she needed the wall to hold her up while she tried to remind her legs that they were still functional limbs.

He pushed himself back, his clothes hissing and whispering as he wiped himself off and tucked himself back into the shadow he'd made of himself, but he was still cursing under his breath — another series of hisses and whispers, but angrier than his clothes.

Only when his seed slithered down her thighs and caught in her underwear did she realize why he'd cursed and was still cursing. To his credit, he wasn't blaming her for it, since he was the one who'd gone and shoved her against the wall to fuck her there.

She was already a bloody mess, so she used the inside of her skirt to grab most of it, then pulled up her panties and put herself in what little order she had left. Then she turned around, and this time she could see his eyes, although not the state of his pupils.

He'd opened a protective case retrieved from one of his many pockets and pulled out a phone, which he proceeded to furiously text with.

"Nice." Violet left the wall to look among the bodies for her satchel.

"They're not getting any fresher, and if we're going to continue searching for specific succubi tonight, I can't stop by a broker. No need to waste good bodies if someone from the collective is in the area." After he finished texting, he lowered his phone. "You're not going to get pregnant."

"Saying it don't make it so. I don't take BC. Can't tolerate the hormones."

Abel sighed. "I mean I snipped twenty years ago. But that doesn't help with other things, does it?"

Well, the first part was a relief, the second part not so much. "Last tests I got, I was clean. You?"

"Same." His phone had neither vibration or a notification tone, but it lit up when he received a text back. "I didn't mean to do that."

"Pretty sure you did. You've been teasing it from the beginning."

"I didn't mean to jump you in the middle of a hunt. I hunt alone and tend to my needs or have them tended to afterward. I don't usually have someone...here when *that* happens." He pointed at the dead sex demons. "It won't happen again."

"I'm pretty sure it will. I wasn't getting a one-and-done vibe from you."

"I meant it won't happen unwrapped."

"Oh." Violet stood from her crouch with her satchel back where it was supposed to be. "You're right. We need to work on our communication. So, I'm kind of blood-covered right now. That going to be an issue?"

"No spells?"

"Not for bloodstains, hon. And this shirt is falling apart as we speak."

"We'll stay in the shadows."

"Does your collective know?" she asked as they proceeded to continue their revolution around the mall as though they'd never stopped.

"Know what?"

"That you're working with the witch?" There were other witches in Meridian, of course, both born and self-identified, but when people talked about 'the witch,' Violet was usually the one they were talking about.

"Of course they do. You nearly blew up a hunter bar to find me."

"It wasn't a foregone conclusion you'd accept."

"I told the collective master how much I'd bring in. They know, and they're doing their own investigating—just not going out of their way. But if they happen to stumble on a sex demon that they can ask before they cut off its head..."

They did another three revolutions around the mall, but the only other people they saw on the way were employees throwing out trash and members of Abel's collective, although she and Abel avoided them, walking near the brick barrier between the mall and the street surrounding it, Violet closest to the wall.

She didn't think Abel was ashamed of her, so it had to be to shield her, although his motivations were likely more practical than chivalrous. She couldn't pay him if someone got trigger-happy and decided to slay a witch while her neutrality was in this strange liminal place. Under normal circumstances, he'd probably switch to her other side if a car drove through a puddle that sprayed battery acid at her face.

"The succubus we let go must have warned the rest," Abel said. "We're not going to get anything more from this place."

"We could try What the Fudge tomorrow when it opens at ten." She shrugged at the glare he leveled at her. "You say they don't tend to congregate. Where else are we guaranteed a regular supply of succubi?"

"Fine. Might as well cut the night short if we need to be awake during the day. We'll crash at your place until then. I have a change of clothes in the truck. Maybe you can grow up and get some real clothes in the morning."

"I don't get pissy that you don't walk through my store in harem pants and gold chains. I dress for what I do."

He gave another brief, violent cough of laughter, so ugly and shocking that it had to be genuine. The thought of what he would look like dressing for a magic shop must have been more amusing than he'd thought it would be.

At the conclusion of their final revolution, they left the same way they came to head back to her home. They went through the alley there rather than the storefront so Abel could pick up his plastic bag of clean clothes.

Once they were upstairs in her apartment, she pointed to the bathroom as she started up the next flight. "You shower first. I'm more of a mess, and I don't want you sitting on my couch until you're clean. The only magic I have for bloodstains is hydrogen peroxide. I'll be up on the roof when you're done."

Chapter Eight

Abel came up smelling like oiled leather, although he wasn't wearing his duster. He'd probably needed to oil the jacket after cleaning it. The man loved his leather jacket. Given its dramatic practicality, she didn't necessarily blame him. If she could fit into it, she'd probably love it, too.

Another white ribbed tank undershirt and pair of jeans. Most hunters didn't seem to have much in the way of varied wardrobe. He probably had a dozen of each article of clothing, with limited palette to blend into the dark or into a crowd, everything chosen for function rather than aesthetic—which created its own aesthetic, as with most professions.

He still wore his weapons harness. The corners of her roof were warded, but they didn't exactly create a forcefield.

She trimmed the dead from the living and watered the plants that preferred to soak overnight. She probably looked like a zombie doing it. Though her neighbors both had taller buildings and windows that looked down into her garden, it was late and those windows were dark, except for the flicker of a television in one. If anything, the plants would enjoy the blood if some flaked into their soil.

Abel watched her maneuvering with her small lantern that allowed her to find the dead detritus in the dark. She knew he was there, but she didn't look up or acknowledge him.

"How do you feel about the demons you killed tonight?" he finally said.

It was a very Abel thing for him to say. There was probably a whole production in his head that ultimately condensed down into the question. It made her wish she could hear the process, but that wasn't how Abel worked. He distilled.

She hadn't killed those demons, but she was responsible for their deaths. Technicalities were for lawyers and referees. This was life, where spirit mattered more than letter.

"I'm upset. But I'd be a hypocrite if I were angry you killed them," she said, tilting the watering pot toward the wolfsbane. "It's what you were there for."

That seemed to satisfy him, although his lack of expression didn't show her how else he felt about her answer. He held up a trash bag. "For your clothes."

Violet emptied out her small watering pot, then set it on the concrete. She was facing away from Abel, toward the street, but the edge of the roof blocked her from view of the street, and the historical district was mostly closed at normal business hours. They only extended them during the Halloween season. This time of night, the square was dead, except for her rooftop.

She unbuttoned what buttons were left on her shirt and peeled it from where sex demon blood had seeped through and stuck the material to her skin—not as effective as living but not nothing. She draped the ruined material over her arm, then pushed her skirt down and bent over to step out of it. The shoes, like the thigh harness, might survive special cleaning, but they would require the same care as his coat. She set the harness on her shoes. She'd get to them another day. Then she unhooked her bra, wincing at the wet, squishy sound of blood not quite dried inside the cups. She pulled off her panties, with stains from both semen and blood.

Barefoot, she carried her clothes to the stairs where he held the trash bag, still folded from the dispenser. She stopped in front of him, completely naked, holding her clothes over her arm. She couldn't read him well, especially in the dark, but the shifting gleam in both his good and bad eye suggested that he took in what he could in the dim light from the lantern in her other hand—blood and ink and so much bare skin. Even Violet wasn't sure exactly what she was doing—challenge, dare, or invitation. But if he could fuck her, he could see her. That was how she was used to doing this kind of thing, anyway.

She stood there, staring up at him, until he met her eyes. Then it was a question of who blinked first.

Abel found the top of the trash bag with his fingertips, then shook out the plastic with a snap. She didn't flinch, just waited until he held the bag open for her. She dumped the damaged clothes into the bag, then stepped around him to pad down to the second story and straight into the shower.

When she stepped out of the bathroom again, he was just a shadow at the end of the hall, limned by light from the kitchen. She smelled tomato sauce, so he must have helped himself to some of the leftover spaghetti, which didn't bother her. She was the one disrupting his usual routine, and she would have offered if he'd asked. Per the spirit of their agreement, everything that was hers might as well be his. She also smelled red wine somewhere, although he didn't have a glass in his hand.

"Itching spell was a nice touch," he said. "You sell that in your store?"

"A much milder version in the practical joke section can be washed off with basic soap or cleaned off clothes with detergent. With the bomb, they have to wait for the potency to fade on its own or negotiate for a counteragent. I sell it sparingly."

She was still naked. She hadn't wanted to touch clean clothes with her dirty hands, and she'd suspected she wouldn't need any tonight. The way he looked at her indicated that she'd anticipated correctly. She could lie to herself and blame the sex demons, the blood she'd scrubbed off her skin, but fucking against the wall had scratched that particular itching spell.

What was left on the other side of that was just as wordless, more physical than emotional, and it left her less certain than she usually was in carnal affairs. Clive had some hand in that lapse of confidence as well.

But Clive wasn't here. Abel was.

Even so, she didn't know what Abel wanted of her. Nor was she sure what a less pheromone-hazed Abel would do or exactly what she'd agreed to — other than anything.

She considered walking down the hall, but she still wasn't positive what he was sizing her up for. "Are you trying to decide if I'm too dangerous to live?"

"Not yet."

"You're not considering it yet, or you don't think I'm dangerous yet?"

"Both." He'd taken off his boots at one point. As he entered the hall, instead of a heavy footfall, he intimidated her with uncanny silence.

"I don't know whether or not to be insulted."

"How you feel doesn't matter to me. You have different tools, but you're no more or less dangerous than a kid with a chemistry set and a raised roof garden so far. At least as far as you've been willing to use your magic. There are nonmagical people who do more damage with less."

Violet tilted her head, letting her curly hair slip down one shoulder. It was hard to fault his logic, at least with the information he had.

Sooner than she realized he could, he reached out and rested his bare, heavy hand on her shoulder. She'd taken a hot shower, but air conditioning had left her cooler than him.

"You realize what you agreed to." His rough voice wouldn't know velvet if he were cocooned it in, but that didn't stop the shiver of something other than cold down her spine, having it so close to her in that particular timbre.

She nodded.

"And you still agree to it?"

"The contract hasn't been fulfilled."

He closed his eyes for a moment. When he opened them again, she was briefly enchanted how the milky one seemed to glow with what little light it could capture.

"What I mean is that I have no interest in a woman crying beneath me. Most of my partners might not always find me to their liking, but unwilling does nothing for me."

"You say the most romantic things."

"This isn't romance."

"I know that. But could you stop pretending this is a chore? You were the one who asked for it. And I agreed, knowing that this was part of what you were asking for."

"Good." He pushed her—not gently or tenderly, but not roughly either—toward her bedroom door. She took his cue and opened it.

He kept his hand on her shoulder as he joined her inside. Although she hadn't planned on turning on a light, he switched on her nightstand lamp. When she turned back toward him, she expected him to grab her with bruising grip and kiss her just as roughly. Instead, he pointed her down onto the bed without a word or additional touch.

And she did as he told her, albeit silently, to do. Because she couldn't get the quick fuck against the wall out of her head, and she wanted to know if the sparks there had all been sex magic or whether there was something more to this silent assassin than point, grunt, come, and make a girl work for it. He wasn't like any other man or woman she'd been with. Then again, most of them had been excited to be with a witch—and all the extra tricks that could entail.

Abel was a different breed. He wasn't intimidated by her power, because he considered himself her equal—perhaps more powerful, given how he was willing to use his weapons to kill rather than temporarily torment. He couldn't know that, at any given moment, she had far more than that in her arsenal, but it did come down to choice, and he was more ruthless.

If there was one thing they seemed to have in common, in their own ways, it was knowing what they wanted and doing whatever it took to get it. She'd forgotten that she used to ask for what she desired, and people didn't used to have a reason to say no to her.

Abel wasn't saying no, he wasn't saying yes, he wasn't telling her what he wanted, he was taking, and she was taking it, and she didn't know what she felt about any of it, except that she wanted to keep exploring to arrive at some kind of answer.

She lay on the bed, propped up on her elbows. She wasn't trying to be sexy for him, wasn't touching herself or shifting her legs to call attention to their length or to what they were trying to hide, because she wasn't hiding anything. If he could plow a field, he could damn well look at it — the privilege of a second try.

It was so strange for her, though, because she usually had such power in a bed. Not a succubus's power, but witchcraft ran deep in her blood, and when that blood pumped harder, like when she exercised, when she fought, when she was afraid, when she fucked, people usually reacted to it — instinctual attraction, if not a rushing of their own blood to certain parts. Some might call it charm. She just knew that a man impassively standing at the foot of her bed wasn't typical.

But it hardly made her feel more pathetic than listening to her best friend and lover fuck someone else while she tried to enjoy it by proxy. So she let Abel work through whatever mysteries unraveled behind his pale eye.

He pulled something off the back of his weapons harness that she was pretty sure hadn't been there before—a roll of duct tape.

"Hold on to the headboard bars." Abel indicated above her with his chin.

Violet settled back on the silk pillow and brought her hands over her head to grip the faux iron.

He rounded one side of the bed and knelt on the bedspread. The roll of duct tape seemed to roar as he pulled a long piece off and ripped the edge. Then he arranged her arms a little wider and taped her wrists to the bars he chose.

"You flexible?" he asked. "You seem flexible."

"Depends." She was almost afraid to ask for clarification.

"Guess we'll see."

Another angry roar of the duct tape. He wrapped it a few times around her ankle, then hauled her whole leg up to bring the ankle near enough to the headboard to wrap the rest around her bound wrist. The process brought the rest of her lower half up with it, which put her other leg at an easier angle for him to force it near her other wrist. She felt bent double and starkly exposed, but it turned out she *was* flexible enough for what he wanted, as long as he didn't expect style points for the straightness of her legs, and that didn't really seem to be what he was going for.

Now that he'd trussed her up, he unbuckled the weapons harness and shrugged out of it, then undid his belt and tugged it from its loops. Not slow enough for a strip tease, but it still gave that impression, despite the fact that his expression hadn't changed from the roof to her bedroom — no smile, no teasing gleam in his eyes, no flirtation. As usual, he was direct with what he did and what he wanted, and he stared directly at her as he pulled his wallet and two condoms from his back pocket. He threw both on the nightstand to his right.

"You realize I don't need hands to kill you," Violet said, "if you try something with me like this."

Abel undid the button and zip of his jeans, then crawled onto the bed between her spread-wide legs. "I don't want to tape your mouth, witch. Don't tempt me."

"Why not? I mean," she amended when he reached for the tape again, "why don't you want to tape my mouth?"

"You want me to?"

"Not particularly."

"I like your lips. And I like the sounds you make with them."

It was the closest he'd come to a compliment, so she was speechless as he crawled closer. The front of his jeans against the backs of her thighs, he leaned over her to stroke her lower lip with his thumb.

She thought he'd kiss her, and she was fully prepared to let him, with the memory of his sounds still fresh, too, even without pulling from echoes. But he drifted his hand down her body instead and did the same with his attention.

He paused at each spell she'd marked on herself. Some she'd hidden within or underneath more innocuous but no less lovely images, but she liked wearing her magic as much as she liked wearing her skin, and it wasn't as though she had to pretend she didn't know what the images and words meant.

However, although her all-seeing eye was in plain view for anyone, other spells were reserved for herself and granted only to those whom she allowed to enjoy those parts of her. She'd done most of the tattooing herself, with the exception of places she couldn't reach. It had taken some real reconnaissance to find someone she could trust not to spread those spells she'd let him see.

Abel traced each spell—some of which were more prayer than demand, like the Numbers 6:24–26 verse that spiraled along the jut of her hip. From her thigh up to under one breast, she'd woven spells to accelerate and smooth out anything that needed healing, then continued the line with a spell of protection, which encouraged the sanctity of her store and herself as diplomat and mercantile mercenary in the midst of a spiritual war. It was designed to be more suggestive than rigid. A stricter spell would be a good way for a playful but hard punch to lead to a missing arm.

The ones that were images were more difficult to untangle without context. The magnification and enhancement of her already potent sexual energy—in both use and deliberate abstinence—was hidden in a series of concentric yonis on the other side of her hip that ranged from abstract at the center to figurative floral in its last ring. No photorealistic vulva, but difficult to mistake once the connection had been made. She also had a mandala designed to center the peace of acceptance, almost her version of the Serenity Prayer. Over her shoulder, she'd used another tattoo artist to ink a serpent for wisdom and a rat for cleverness.

The tattoos could only be in black on her darker skin. Sometimes, when she stared at herself in the mirror, she saw the charm of ancient parchment or newspaper, with ink of another time seeping through or smearing on other pages — a worshipped relic. And what, really, was a witch in these parts but a throwback to another time?

On her back, where he couldn't see, was a call to adventure in the form of a mouse journeying with a walking stick, with letters embedded in the etching style. It had been her first, just a week after leaving home and arriving in Meridian with only a dream and basic business plan, no return ticket home. She also kept a warning there for those who thought she was vulnerable with them at her back.

She felt vulnerable now. She wasn't, not really, but her body seemed to have turned into the largest yoni in her collection, her pussy on display front and center, and with no way to cover herself out of protection or modesty.

He appeared to immediately recognize the suggestive imagery, though, because he drifted his callused fingers from the Numbers prayer to the yoni collection on the other side and stroked over every version of labia. Here, finally, a curious tenderness. There wasn't a direct connection between the tattooed images and her own, but there was certainly an indirect one that he tapped into with his intention.

So when he bent down to stroke that sandpaper palm against her thigh and run his tongue over the inked yonis, following the concentric pattern, Violet twitched. She tried to lift her hips to meet him, but she was bound in such a way that she could really only move from side to side. She had no leverage, no control, at least not physically. All she could do was curl her fingers around the bars and hold on.

A credit to age and perhaps wisdom, he found the inked clit every time, sucked lightly at the skin before moving on. At the top of the final flower, he lingered, and when he lifted his mouth from her, a thread of saliva stuck to the tip of his tongue. He licked his lips to break it.

"It comes as no surprise, I'm sure, that my companions are usually paid, for my need alone," he said, not meeting her eyes, but only because he trailed his touch now to circle her navel, then down to the whispering words just above her mound that wove the images to the source of her power. "Need, but not pleasure usually, and rarely hers."

His lips found her thigh, where healing spells intertwined with fiddleheads, and his fingers found her folds. He traced them as he had the ink.

Now she knew that the grip he'd had on her pussy when he'd shoved her against the wall had been deliberately inadequate until she'd taken control, because he knew how to kiss, knew how to stroke, knew how to breathe in the scent of her soap and skin and what came from her every time she clenched her cunt against the unexpected, languid waves of lust, heady as the red wine emanating from his pores in new sweat.

She tightened her fingers over the metal bars. He'd denied her the opportunity to wrap her legs around his neck, to push and guide his head—which was the whole point. She did know that she could control him here, too, but this wasn't about what she wanted, unless he made it so. And she liked this just fine—almost but not quite a massage more than a caress between her inner and outer folds, stimulating the nerves but also gradually releasing some of the nervous tension in her abdomen and thighs and coiled in her lower back amid slow, aroused heat.

He brought his mouth to her cunt to taste her arousal—a gesture of absolute trust after his hesitation earlier that night, or maybe he'd figured out the connection between the yonis and the healing spells. Then he gathered the saliva of his own hunger in her slit to slip two fingers into her.

She wriggled on the bedspread, bit her lip through the slow slice of his tongue up to her real clit this time. His stubble rasped against her skin, but decades of selfishness hadn't dulled his consideration, because he adjusted his angle when she hissed. She hissed again for a different reason as he flicked his tongue over her clit. He continued to tease her like that, with uneven swipes of wet heat against the sensitive flesh, which twitched to its own uneven rhythm and swelled with heat to match his, although he was a furnace between her thighs.

Then he closed his mouth over her, and cries she couldn't help sighed from her with every exhale. With patience she would not have expected from the same man who'd barely been able to remove her clothes before rutting with her against a mall, Abel applied himself to her pleasure and hers alone, almost as though to prove to her and to himself that he could.

He could, and with his fingers inside her, moving through with increasing ease as her juices trickled lightly down, he knew it. He didn't smile against her, but he sucked her clit with greater intensity, then found the place inside her that conjured the most powerful moans and attacked it with tenderness that melted salted butter inside her from her head down to the juncture of her thighs.

The attention sharpened into assault as his fingers and the pulse of suction quickened. Her lust rose again with it, raising her hips with greater effort, although she always fell back again as Abel kissed down on her clit. Her moans in the small room conjured the memories of Clive in his, back when their experiences overlapped in perpendicular instead of running parallel.

Abel didn't make a sound, unless she counted the wetness around his fingers as he crooked them inside to rub her to completion.

The orgasm burned behind and in her eyes and trailed the lines of ink he'd traced with fingers and tongue. The window steamed with condensation from the inside as their combined heat battled with the A/C. Sweat dripped down her temples, her neck, her lower back, and even though she felt like she should scorch his tongue, he beckoned her pleasure until it finally settled into isolated jerks of lightning sensation. If the lightning entered him — and she thought some of it did — he cradled its conduction like he carried his scars.

He eased off and out of her, then took his fingers into his mouth to suck at the fluids coating them. Then he dipped down to lick at the entrance of her cunt to catch more.

Violet caught her breath, staring at his careful tasting between the forced splay of her legs. "You didn't cover me."

Like the hunter he was, he was suddenly over her, his shadow like a blanket, his hips between her thighs again as he hovered his mouth above hers, then lowered himself to kiss her, her scent coating the lower half of his face.

One hand in her curls to hold her head in place and the other over her breast, he kissed her absolutely thoughtless. This time when his stubble razor-burned her skin, she didn't shy, but sometimes caught it on her tongue as they slid theirs together between their open mouths. His body was a burden, burning, welcome weight, his skin a strange mingling of textures between scars and scabs new and fresh and the odd tiger stripe of unharmed flesh, more pronounced when he relinquished her breast to pull his undershirt over his head.

"I wasn't finished," he murmured against the corner of her mouth as she panted into his. And indeed, his erection had returned, pushing insistently between the open placket of his jeans and damp against her cunt.

"That's not what I meant."

"I know what you meant. And I know what these mean." He touched the relevant tattoos that signified certain protections weren't mandatory. "The women I hire don't let me kiss them, either."

She strained her neck to suck lightly on his lower lip. He deepened the kiss, harder this time, with a tighter fist in her hair and a pinch to her already tight, tender nipple. He ground himself against her through his underwear until he lifted himself away from her to push down the last barrier. He didn't bother removing any more clothes, just got it out of his way so he could bring himself back to her entrance, wrapped in one of the condoms from the nightstand, and push into her.

The man she recognized from earlier that night was back, in that he took what he wanted, holding her head in place and the tape holding the rest. He used her body, moved at his own pace, with his own force. With his other hand bracing him on the bed, the most substantial contact now was his cock inside her, although the angle of her hips meant that he hit the same spot he'd fingered more often than not, and she was already heat-flushed and swollen and sensitive to the push of his lower body against hers, somewhere between a shove and a slap the harder he took her.

Unlike before, she saw so much more of him, from his scars to his own anthology of tattoos — more figurative than literary. The all-seeing eye, of course, but also healing spells of his own, one of which mimicked hers, which was how he'd known what hers meant. The letters had been manipulated into an intricate, Escheresque interlacing Celtic design organic to his skin, like root networks. For every new scar, he had to touch up the design, but he clearly had a trusted tattooist of his own. She wondered if his and hers were the same man.

There was also a date on his chest near his left shoulder in Roman numerals, above a strangely commercial dragon sleeping curled like a cat, which told her it had significance beyond utility. Odd for a practical man like him to display such sentimentality, but he'd had many decades to weave memory echoes of his own into the tapestry of his skin, and one of the strongest echoes was loss. And that wasn't so odd at all. A hunter's origin was usually rooted in graveyard soil, one way or another.

In addition to scars and ink, she saw his age — in the puckering of older scars, in the mottled fish paleness of a nocturnal white man, in the emergence of sun damage from before this life, in the slight slip of less elastic skin. And despite that age, she saw strength, tone of muscle that wasn't centered on bulky strength or brutishness but specific, effective motions. It was gentler on a body, which explained why he'd lasted when other hunters his age would be fighting the consequences of the beatings they took. Over the architecture of his skeleton, he was all jute rope and sawdust held together with twine, and he could still rail a witch in her own bed because she agreed to do it. And she'd fucking do it again, but she wanted more than his hand pulling her hair and his cock hitting the spot that made her clench her own kind of fist around him in return, although hell if she could get a good grip, because he kept moving beautifully inside her and over her, a model of both efficiency and endurance.

Then he thrust as deep as he could, his hips jerking to grind into her once more, and he came, his groans as gritty as his voice, almost grunts as they raked through his throat. He let his head hang, his hair tousled like cobwebs against her forehead, but even when he was finished, he didn't lower himself over her. He pulled out and did away with the condom and its mess with practiced ease. Since he'd licked her without a barrier, the condom had probably been more about practical cleanup, which she appreciated, although she didn't appreciate so much that he'd brought her to an almost wholly physical arousal but left her empty and clenching around nothing.

After tossing the condom into a trash bin by her nightstand, he tucked himself back into his underwear and did up his jeans. Taking his time. Testing or teasing her, she couldn't tell which, because he wasn't smiling. He looked out of the window across from her bed as he stood up to round toward the door.

He slowly closed it, even though they were the only ones there. "You need me to finish that?"

There it was, that smile, cold but not necessarily unkind.

"You son of a bitch."

He laughed, then sat next to her on the bed and slipped not two but three fingers into her until she mewled. Then he resumed his assault inside her and bent down to take her nipple between his teeth, sucking as though it were her clit.

She didn't know how he did it, really, how he took romance — even of the ephemeral, one-night-stand sort — out of the equation entirely, how he plucked arousal in her so physically without peacocking or wooing. The process was as crude as a tone-deaf person plunking on an out-of-tune piano, yet he kept finding strings that struck some kind of chord, dissonant though it initially seemed.

She wasn't used to sex not making her feel closer to another person. He was as far away as ever from her, despite finger-fucking her to another orgasm. Still a mystery, still a man using her to scratch an itch, just a different kind, and even after two climaxes, she couldn't untangle how she *felt* about him, or if she was supposed to feel anything at all. He simply was, he simply touched, and that presence and that touch made her cry out when she came, her whole body rocking with the waves of her orgasm.

He was still smiling when he released her nipple and withdrew his fingers from her cunt to lick at them again. They made a slight pop as he pulled his fingers out.

"Curious," he said. "Can you get out of that without me?"

"If I can't, are you just going to leave me like this till morning?"

"Considering it."

Two hard snaps preceded Violet bringing her legs down from her wrists. She groaned from the release of tension in her hips and back and the stretch in her legs. A second set of snaps meant she could let go of the headboard bars. Abel retrieved his weapons harness and handed her one of his knives so she could get under the adhesive and cut through the rest of the tape.

"Just making sure you could." He accepted his knife back. "If you need to sleep, go ahead. I'm going to stay up for a while longer. Look through a few books. Search your storeroom."

"No arson or thievery." She'd forbid him entirely if this situation were under her control by their agreement, but technically, he could burn the store to the ground if he chose, because it and she belonged to him until the terms of the agreement were met. She couldn't discount that he might take this opportunity to destroy an institution he didn't approve of, no matter what kind of cash it put in his pocket. If he so chose.

"Wasn't planning on it. You have good bookshelves. Might pour another glass of wine. Wake me up in the morning when it's time to leave, if you don't wake me up by getting up." Without so much as another kiss, he left her in her room still naked, still working the duct tape off her skin and pulling some of the fine hairs off her wrists in the process.

The room felt twice as empty without him. If anything, it reminded her of all those nights going to bed alone and listening to Clive. But at least Abel hadn't lain down beside her so that she could feel alone in his company like she had in Clive's bed for too long prior.

She got up to strip her bed, retrieved another quilt from the linen shelf in her closet, then pulled on panties and an oversized T-shirt that she'd stolen from Clive years ago because it was soft from many washings and too pulled out of shape for him to wear it in public. Abel had taken everything of himself except what scent and memory echo lingered. She didn't mind one and let the other go. The night was too fresh on her mind to require a memory.

Violet listened to him moving in the other room. Pacing. It was two in the morning, which might as well have been two in the afternoon for him. Climax didn't exhaust her — and it clearly didn't exhaust Abel, either, at least not enough — but she hadn't stayed up this late in a while, didn't have stamina like she'd had in her twenties.

Just thinking about it made her feel like a crone before her earned time. She had to remind herself that the reason why she was exhausted was because she'd threatened hunters, fought incubi and succubi, had emotionless sex twice, and she was worried about her friend. A woman half her age would be tired.

She wondered whether she could afford to sleep, but the wards in her room, at least, were secure, and she was too tired to stay awake in the dark by herself.

Chapter Nine

By morning, Abel hadn't burned the building down, and despite her anxiety over what had happened to Clive—and because of Clive—Violet had slept well. When she got out of bed, her legs protested the previous night's strain, but after a little movement, they lost most of the stiffness.

Violet chose an outfit that felt more like herself, which would blend in during the daytime more than anything she might use to conceal herself at night or call back to her previous life. Besides, the manager of What the Fudge knew her. They worked on the same square. Marigold was a practicing pagan who knew Violet had real magic in her veins and didn't resent her for it, and she had fudge by the pound for a certain time of the month that no poultice or potion had managed to improve.

Violet knocked around in the bathroom and expected the hunter to be awake when she stepped out, but he was still prone on the sofa, head propped up on a pillow, a paperback tilted onto the floor in his slack hand. He didn't snore, at least not then. He was quiet, his face no less ragged and craggy for relaxation.

It was something she thought few people, particularly of a magical persuasion, had ever seen — a hunter off guard.

Either the scent of cooking eggs or the sizzle of the griddle jolted him from sleep. One minute, he was out like a light. The next, he jerked up into upward dog, one hand on the gun in his harness. She doubted he'd slept in many strange places. She was almost honored that, as she had trusted him not to set fire to the storeroom, he'd trusted her not to cast some kind of spell to kill him in his sleep.

"I'm scrambling." In Violet's experience, everyone who had an egg preference accepted scrambled. "Cinnamon-raisin toast with cinnamon sugar or jam? I also have salsas for the eggs."

"No salsa. Plain pepper and salt," he replied once he'd assessed that her spatula probably wasn't going to impale him. "Butter on the toast, no sugar."

Violet inserted the bread into the toaster now that he was awake and wouldn't become lethal when startled by toast popping up when it was done. She tilted the eggs onto a plate and lightly salted and peppered it in time for him to get his bearings and adjust his clothes into something approaching normal. He shed the harness but left it on the kitchen island within easy reach as he ate.

No frills, no chill, just a steady motion of food to mouth. If he daydreamed, he kept the contents of his thoughts to himself, like everything else.

She liked salsa on her scramble and cinnamon sugar on her toast, and he watched her enjoy every bite of it.

He didn't seem thirsty, but she had his attention. Although her breasts were just sitting there in plain view, framed by the V-neck of the screen-print shirt, the man maintained admirable focus on what was above her neck.

When he finished, he drained the orange juice she'd given him, then went back to the sofa to retrieve the paperback from where he'd left it on the floor.

She left some of her toast behind as she followed him there. He'd sat down before he completely registered that she'd left the kitchen.

He retreated just a fraction — enough for her to tell — when she knelt in front of him, and he jerked his hands away as she reached for the front of his jeans.

It was satisfying to finally see reaction, although reflexive horror wasn't usually the first one men had when she did this.

Violet took her time undoing the button and zip so he could prevent her from continuing, because as direct as he was in taking what he wanted, she expected him to be just as direct to refuse what he didn't.

After his initial surprise, he lowered his hands and rested back against the cushion to let her proceed, stopping only to pull out another condom and hand it to her. She accepted it but cautiously put it behind her on the coffee table, in case his offering was a courtesy for the mess, like the previous night. When he let it lie, she finished opening his jeans and pulled them down his hips. He lifted them just enough to bring the waist of the jeans to his thighs. Then she reached into the front of his briefs without bothering to pull them down.

He wasn't fully hard, but breath harshed through his nose as she gently pulled at his cock, more massage than stroke until he was hard enough to tent the briefs without the help of her fist. Then she folded the fabric back.

This wasn't dark of night or the dreamy light of a single lamp in a dark room. They were well past the influence of demons. They'd both slept, reset. Sunlight was clear and bright through the living room windows, and they were still witch and hunter in the light, yet he responded to her, didn't go soft as he looked into her eyes while she slid her lips down his shaft. She met the curl of her fingers, then drew back up with firm, soft suction, all lips and tongue.

She watched the flutter of his eyelids, the way he struggled not to let his eyes roll back as she stroked two fingers over the wrinkly flesh behind his heavy scrotum, as she rubbed the head over her tongue, paying particular attention to the ridge right under the slit. He failed when he was fully erect and she sank her mouth over his cock to take almost half of it in, swallowing over the head to tighten around him.

He wasn't the only one in the room who could manipulate and take advantage of basic nerve stimulation and increased blood flow. The process didn't take long.

Abel covered the top of her head with the weight of his hand. Although he pushed, he didn't force. When he came, panting accented with subtle groans wrenched from his chest. She swallowed his semen down, taking all his vulnerability and surrender into herself. It wasn't quite the same as wholistic, full-sensory, systemic sex that spoke to mind, body, and spirit in trinity tandem, but it still gave her power that she took but he also gave — the way she had with him the night before, if he knew the first thing about sex magic transaction.

When she pulled off from the head, not a trace of cum was left. He glistened but would otherwise dry clean. She nudged a knuckle against the corner of her mouth, then stood again and went back to the island to finish off her toast and orange juice.

"What was that for?" he finally asked, put back together again, albeit visibly confused, which translated as upset, with knotted furrowing of brows over the bridge of his nose.

"Why does there need to be a reason? You need anything else?"

"I don't need anything else. And I didn't ask for that."

"Just felt like it," Violet said. "Go ahead and stay settled in. What the Fudge doesn't open until ten, and that's just for us to surveil. They probably won't get nocturnal customers until mid-afternoon."

"You 'just felt like it'?"

"Yeah. Like I just felt like cinnamon toast this morning and you felt like duct-tape BDSM last night. Figured you wouldn't mind. Plus, if we're going to be staking out succubi in particular, you could probably use whatever draining your body can stand."

"There's nothing wrong with age, witch. For a hunter, it's a badge of honor."

"Please, you're not even the oldest person I've had sex with, although you've certainly got more battle scars. I'm not saying you're old, hunter. I'm saying you're a man. Without the aid of sex demon magic, I've still come at least eleven times in one night before. How about you?"

He blinked, though not in a comic way. "Something to do with all that ink?"

"They're the reason I did it. They're not the reason I could." She shrugged to work out the morning kinks as she smiled at the memory—no echoes needed, still as vivid as a memory could be.

"They the reason you did me this morning?"

"No. Barely gave me a boost. I really just felt like it." This time she shrugged for his benefit. "Coffee? I can do plain drip or cold press. Some days I take it, some days I leave it, but hunters seem like coffee people to me."

He lifted his coat from the chair near the living room window. "We should go."

"Hon, it's only nine. We can start the stakeout when they open, but do you really think succubi are going to get their chocolate fix before noon? Sit down and read your novel. Take the opportunity to rest. Coffee?"

He draped the coat back over the chair and settled down into the sofa again with an exasperated sigh. "Drip is fine."

"Coming right up." She didn't even mind that he never said 'please' or 'thank you.' That was just the efficiency thing again. Among night people, service workers became more affectionately polite, but the rest lost their filler words. After years of fake niceness as a shop owner, it was almost refreshing to strip down interactions to fundamentals and still remain understood—mostly.

She handed him his cup and put her own on the coaster before plopping down on the other cushion of the loveseat. He side-eyed her for joining him, but he hadn't given her a lot of other options, with the chair taken up by his coat and the dining chairs not particularly comfortable and only used when she was working.

This was the closest she'd gotten to a break from work in over a year, regardless of reason, and this was her sofa, not his.

"No TV?" he asked.

"No."

And that was all they had to say.

* * * *

Just before ten, she pulled on sandals and her satchel of tricks, and he donned his hooded shirt, coat, and boots.

As soon as they were situated on one of the shaded benches outside the historical courthouse that now functioned as city administration, she left her satchel with him and patted his shoulder. "Don't touch. I can control the powder bombs. You'll only get them all over your nice coat, and if you're that foolish, I've half a mind to let you just deal with the aftermath."

She pulled a twenty from her wallet.

"Where are you going?" he asked, looking between the money and her in much clearer confusion than if he'd been wearing his mask. During the day, that would stretch people's credulity much more than the rest of his fit.

"Buying fudge. What kind do you want?"

"Are you fucking serious?"

"I think you mean, 'Are you fudging serious?' We're sitting outside a woman's place of business, taking up real estate, possibly for hours. I'm buying some of her product because it's the right thing to do. What kind of fudge do you want?"

"Okay, when I say I'm not old..."

"If you're old enough for sensitive digestion, you're old enough to keep antacids in your truck."

He frowned at her, but then he peered through the picture window display.

"She's not a witch, at least not like me. She's just a business friend," Violet said. They also commiserated over mothers who'd chosen flower names for their children.

"Fine. Anything raspberry or mint chocolate will do."

"Good. Watch my things."

The bell above the door rang her in—more annoying than her own bell, but Marigold heard it better when she was working in the kitchen. She came out to the counter, where fudge was stacked on marble and wax paper.

"I saw your sign," Marigold said. "I didn't expect you here."

"My personal matters are local," Violet replied. Marigold knew she was a witch, but she didn't quite comprehend the full extent of the supernatural in Meridian. She probably didn't even know she served succubi. She didn't need to know the details. "You didn't happen to see Clive in the last day or so, have you?"

"Sorry, no."

"Can you let me know if you do?"

Marigold tilted her head, then nodded. "Sure. Should I tell him to call you?"

"He knows to call me. He hasn't yet."

"Oh. Okay." Marigold decided not to question further, but that probably wouldn't keep the rumor mill from spilling a little supposition tea. "What can I get you?"

"A half-pound box, half raspberry swirl and half hazelnut chocolate. And two waters."

Marigold packed up the chocolate and accepted her twenty. "Everything okay? I'm asking because it's early, in the day and in the month."

"Just getting in before the crowd," Violet replied. "Thanks."

"No problem."

Back outside, she handed Abel his water and opened the box for his portion of the fudge.

"This is ridiculous," Abel said, but he broke one of the pieces of fudge in half and ate it.

"You're ridiculous," she replied, breaking apart one of her own pieces. "How on earth do you wear all those clothes? We're just at the start of summer, and I'm sweating in sleeveless and sandals in the shade. People are looking at you like you're crazy, not because you're dressed like Blade but because you're in leather and boots when it's going to hit over ninety degrees today."

"Between the two of us, you're the one courting the most danger, with so much skin exposed. It's not about modesty," he added before she could protest. "It's about what sex demons can use. I wear clothes as much to cover my body as to obscure my identity. If I get dizzy, I find a watering hole, recover, and go back out when I can see clearly again. You learn to tolerate adverse conditions, because that's what you need to do to survive."

They ate two squares of fudge before the richness became too much. Violet took the rest back to her apartment—conveniently across the square—so the chocolate wouldn't melt with the rising heat. She returned with a small Thermos of more coffee for both of them, hot and black for him, cold and creamy for her.

She crossed her legs beneath her skirt, and they sat there like a long-married odd couple enjoying an early summer day in a historical district of tourist traps.

Abel's hood obscured some of the severity of his scarring with doubled shade, so few people passing by them did a double-take, but if they did, they often darted their gaze away again, lest they be perceived as staring.

Except for the kids, especially the ones in strollers, who were at the perfect height to see straight under his hood. If the kids seemed curious, he didn't move, didn't change his craggy expression. But if tears welled in wide, cartoonish eyes, or if blood fled from their cheeks, he made funny faces at them to diffuse the possibility of literally making children cry. He'd stick his tongue out, flare his nostrils, and contort his mouth in weird shapes to shift the child's cry into a delighted laugh. Then he would raise his hand in silent greeting to the kids and their parents, signaling himself as even more of a non-threat.

It spoke to experience of being one of the scary things in the dark, but with the intent to scare the other scary things in the dark—not to frighten little kids in the process. He certainly didn't care about frightening her with his resting bitch face.

During Halloween season, when Violet happily strolled through the city for a whole month in more morbid or gory-graphic representations of who she was, she always made sure to lean toward the silly side around children. There were a lot more useful things to grease her broomstick with, after all.

Today, however, she wasn't in a spooky getup, and kids, especially little girls with big acrylic necklaces, loved her accessories. 'Start them early on the sparkly stones' was one of her mottos. It's what sold all those bags of delightful tumbled rocks on a daily basis. She waved, too, when they stared curiously at her tattoos and jewelry.

Jewelry wasn't the most practical thing to wear in battle, but she prayed she wouldn't have to go through last night all over again, especially in broad daylight. Between the hunter and the powder bombs — and being more willing to use both — theoretically she shouldn't have to use her hands this time. She just hoped the succubi here would be more willing to talk rather than fight. Besides, they couldn't buy fudge while invisible.

They could steal it, of course, but What the Fudge would be much worse off financially if all the succubi who frequented it stole product. Chain stores were one thing, but if she caught succubi stealing from a woman-owned small business, Violet might have to have words with them for reasons other than Clive.

The first succubi walked by the fudge shop after noon, two together arm in arm. They entered through the front door, jingling the bell, rather than walking through the windows. Acting like normal people. Because they were, really. Demons, hunters, angels, gargoyles, witches, werewolves… They were all part of the natural world, just not the kind that made sense in the way scientists measured sense.

When they came out again, Violet was there, leaning against the brick column, her satchel on her shoulder and her Thermos under the bench across the street, with Abel watching to know when to intervene.

"Hi." She must have smiled a little too widely, because the succubi stopped snacking on their wax-paper packets of chocolate and froze on the sidewalk. "Do you know who I am?"

"The witch across the way." Both succubi were brunettes, one with pale skin and the other a few shades darker. The one who spoke was taller and in a bandage dress meant for evening. The other was in thin sweatpants and a UTM T-shirt, although she looked like alumna rather than a student.

"Do you know what I'm looking for?" Violet asked.

Both succubi shook their heads.

"Short version?"

They nodded.

"Someone fucked me over, and I'm looking to rectify. Don't fuck with me, and we should be fine. Otherwise, you'll find out just how much I'm capable of. And that gentleman in black over there? He's capable of other things. Make a scene, and he'll make sure it's a violent one. Now, I'm not looking to leave blood pools in front of my friend's shop. Bad for business. And dying is bad for yours. Are we going to have an issue?"

They shook their heads again.

"Good. Succubi, at least two but possibly three, abducted the man I work with. Have you heard anything about who could have done this or why?"

"No. I swear, I have no idea," the one in the bandage dress said.

The student or former student shook her head, holding her packet of fudge like a fan in front of her mouth.

"If you hear anything, you'll tell me." It wasn't a question. "You can go."

The succubi power-walked away, and Violet returned to the bench.

"That's it? That's all you're going to do?" Abel said.

"Most people can't lie to me unless they have a spell that lets them or if they've told a lie long enough that they believe it." Violet crossed her legs once more and settled back. "The interview process is fine until they start acting cagey. Don't tell me hunting isn't sometimes tedious as hell. Besides, what are you complaining about? I'm pretty much paying you to do nothing, not counting the extra your collective made on the demons from last night. You have no emotional stake in the outcome. Take the spa day."

He leaned against the back of the bench with her. "You're a strange woman."

The next succubus who visited the fudge shop was alone. After a quick interception, she didn't have any information, either. Next were three succubi purchasing chocolate on their own, another who slipped in to steal, then two sets of pairs. Violet let the one stealing go, because all the rest quite willingly and happily paid. It was amazing how many succubi had a jones for Marigold's wares. Violet would suspect magic if she didn't know the fudge was simply that good.

Violet had anticipated more opposite-sex couples would nest together than same-sex, but maybe, just maybe, sex demons could have actual friendships. With the power that these women had just by existing, traveling together could have provided the same safety in numbers as among human women. Succubi were far more dangerous than men who tried to predate upon them, but a partner was always better than a black eye.

None of the succubi could tell her anything, although some knew her and some had heard what had happened last night. In the light of day, they were too afraid of her and others to try retribution of their own, reinforcing their preference not to fight when they could run. They were predators, yes, with sharp teeth and claws that they could call out at will, but like most predators, they were shy. Violet was too aware of them to be good prey—and a predator herself, although less obvious than they or the hunters were.

It wasn't until four in the afternoon—when the day was at its hottest and she was melting like one of her candles, didn't know how Abel managed not to, shade or not—that she stopped three more succubi exiting What the Fudge. They weren't the ones who'd taken Clive, but when she asked them if they'd heard what happened, a woman with straight black hair and vitiligo lied when she agreed with the other girls that she knew nothing about the robbery or abduction.

Violet pulled her hand out of the satchel pocket with a vial of a new powder bomb, one that would keep the victim sneezing for a few hours—both debilitating and dehydrating. "Hon, you want to change your story? If you were a puppet, your nose would be more useful."

"You're bluffing. You can't tell if I'm lying," the woman snapped, backing away, nearly putting the woman next to her in front of her as a shield. But those succubi also backed away—in the other direction, leaving her exposed. They didn't have to know the specifics of what was in the vial to not want to get on the bad side of a witch.

"I inherited my inner lie detector from my gran, whose grimoire, by the way, is a prized possession— monetarily and sentimentally—and was stolen along with my friend. I cannot emphasize enough how much I want to get both of those things back. And you know something about where they are. So start talking or start sneezing." She held the vial higher. "It's worse than it sounds."

The lying woman glared at her friends. "You're just going to let her—"

"Hunter across the street," Violet reminded her. "Sneeze bomb in my hand. Is whoever you're protecting worth ruining your day? Or, you know, dying?"

The lying woman tried to keep backing away, but Violet tossed up a temporary barrier. The woman hit it as though it were a slab of granite.

Violet flipped the top off the vial. "I really don't want to hurt anybody, but I *will* use this if you don't tell me what's going on *right now*."

"Fine, fine, fine, okay, okay."

Violet inclined her head to indicate that Abel should join them, which immediately made the other two succubi nervous, too.

"He doesn't attack unless he or I are attacked," Violet said. "Start talking."

"Bitch," the lying woman muttered.

"I don't think anyone in this little circle has a stone to throw. Why was my store robbed and my friend taken?"

"I don't know exactly *why*," the woman replied, cringing from the hunter as he came up behind Violet, his hand on the hilt of something Violet couldn't see. "But I've heard rumors about a group or something of succubi who want a man or three to keep and share among each other for as long as they can. I don't understand why. That many succubi sucking off just a few men would drain too much of them. Even if they didn't die, they'd lose all their energy, which isn't a very good meal. And variety's half the fun, right?" The woman seemed to realize again that a hunter was right there, listening to her every word like it was a confession of crimes. "Anyway, they've gathered, which we don't really do. It's more than a nest. It feels like a cultish reverse harem of some kind."

"Why *don't* succubi gather?" Abel asked.

Violet was surprised he said anything at all to them. She was also a little surprised he didn't know the answer, but if a hunting method was sound, the whys and wherefores didn't matter quite as much.

When else does a hunter have a chance to ask his prey about themselves?

The woman glanced at Violet and decided not to risk Violet cursing her for not answering. "You feel us right now, right? 'Cause we feel you, hunter. Both of you, but especially you. You're feeling it more because there are three of us, even though we're not trying to lure. But we also feel each other, Molly especially." She nodded to the shortest girl of the three. "Now imagine a roomful of us. I don't know of a nest bigger than about five or six sex demons, and I'm not entirely sure how much sleep they get. The number of succubi I heard about... It's a dirty lust bomb for all involved. Sex might be our lives, but we like other things now and then, too. Wherever this is happening, it's probably this supermassive black hole of sucking energy all around it."

"Where is this place that they're gathering?" Abel asked.

"So you can kill them? How long do you think I'm going to last if I tell you, even if I know? Which I don't."

"General area?"

"Either the warehouse or industrial district. Where else can they get all cozy and radioactive without attracting people's attention? Can we go now, or did you have a few more questions for the people you kill and still don't get?"

Abel didn't say anything, so Violet nodded and stepped back into the light, while the succubi went the other direction. When the succubi were a few stores down, she pulled Abel by his jacket with her to the end of the row of buildings and around the corner.

"You good?" Violet asked.

"What? I thought I was practically restrained."

"I mean, are *you* all right?"

Violet opened his jacket a little, dipped her hand into the shadow to obscure what she was doing, then cupped the front of his jeans. The denim contained him to a point—his new pair was of a thicker material than the last—but he was semi-hard again.

He covered her hand over him for a moment, his eyes closing, almost vulnerable. Then he guided her hand away. "I'll be fine. This is typical."

"If we find where we're supposed to be going, it won't be," Violet said, but she let herself be guided. "What do hunters like you do about the whole sex demon magic thing?"

"Get used to functioning with a raging hard-on. It's the same process as when we were young and dealt with spontaneous erections at inconvenient times—just tuck it into the waistband. Keeps it less conspicuous or...protruding." Under the same cover of shadow, he adjusted himself, then straightened, betraying none of his reaction in his face or posture.

Older he might be, but that meant he'd be far more used to killing in less optimal conditions, not just Texas heat. She'd glimpsed sweat stains on his shirt, and she could smell the sweat, but he probably used industrial-grade deodorant, because it lacked the sourness of unwashed body odor, at least from the whiffs she'd received through the open leather.

"This isn't going to be like what you're used to," Violet said. "It certainly won't be like what I'm used to."

"We won't know until we're there. But in my experience, there's a ceiling to the intensity before you come, and that relieves it for a minute."

"In my experience, there's always another level. It just surprises you when you reach it."

He didn't move from the wall, just stared at her, which wasn't new, except his lips were parted as though he wanted to follow up.

He ultimately decided not to ask. "If we're visiting a succubus den, we should go soon, while most of them are likely asleep and their power is weaker, less controlled. If you need to grab something to eat or use the bathroom, this is your opportunity."

* * * *

Abel changed his shirt and undershirt, then put together a turkey sandwich from ingredients in her fridge. He took a cat nap while Violet snagged second shift in the bathroom, then made herself a sandwich as well.

No more coffee, but she'd already screwed with the man's sleep schedule enough.

So she let him crash a little longer while she ate her sandwich and wished there was someone she could talk to or that Clive was down at his work station making something — with the drone of his machines or repetition of carving, reliable breaks in the monotonous stretches between paying customers and browsers.

She drifted a little herself, weary from confronting so many people and walking the fine razor between friend and foe, a balance she didn't enjoy at all. She wasn't quite sleeping, but her thoughts seeped with the nonsense of untethered dreams until the light had changed and she twitched awake.

The clink of her plate on his as she set them in the sink woke him up. He looked like a grumpy cat who'd slept for weeks.

"Just a power nap," Violet said. "Plenty of sun left. And if they're all awake and it's too much, then we leave. We *leave*. You got that, hunter?"

"You were the one who wanted their heads on pikes."

"That doesn't mean I want yours, too. I'm serious. If the sex demons are too powerful, we leave and reassess how we're going to address the situation. Okay? I hired you to help me find them and get my stuff back. Not lose your life trying to kill beings I haven't decided I want dead."

He stood. "Whatever you say…boss."

Chapter Ten

Violet had been to the slightly more fashionable warehouse district before, of course, but here in the industrial district, she was confronted with the reality of block after block of largely unadorned giant concrete or brick buildings, half of them unused or abandoned by business, and each of them with dozens of rooms of their own.

Abel swung them into a parking lot with other cars. His huge truck wasn't even out of place. Working rather than vanity trucks were more common here, with toolboxes, shop vacs, other industrial appliances and wood planks hanging out of beds.

"Are we really searching the entire district?" Violet asked.

"Unless you have a way to narrow it down, sweetheart. Hunting is an endurance game, always has been—even in Meridian, where you practically trip on demons down dark alleys. If we weren't looking for anything, we'd find what we were looking for."

"That makes no sense." She understood what he meant, though. It was a lot easier to hunt demons when it didn't matter which demons you crossed paths with.

"But because we know what we're looking for, I think we'll know it when we feel it," Abel continued, dry and grim.

"If we come across anything else, promise not to get sidetracked?"

"I wasn't sidetracked before. I can always come back and rout a nest."

"But for now we're just 'observe and report,' and the person you're reporting to is me."

"You've made your views quite plain, witch. But this won't be an open-air mall with just a few sex demons. This will be shelter for the degenerate, desecration thick in the air. You do what I tell you, when I tell you. Am I clear?"

"I thought we'd already done that," Violet said, adjusting the strap of her satchel so it was more comfortable among her talismans. She wasn't teasing.

"That was for my fun. This is for your safety. There's a reason I don't hunt with a partner. I don't want you endangering me because you think I'm being petty or prejudiced."

In tacit agreement, Violet gestured for him to take point. To find a succubus harem, a straight man was the better divining rod.

If it weren't for a steady trickle of through-traffic, their determined walk through the industrial district would feel post-apocalyptic, especially as they entered the parts more abandoned than not, although even that abandonment was a misnomer. This was Meridian, where property was prosperity. Here, the buildings were out of sight and out of mind from the financial district and law enforcement, otherwise empty places with which to launder money, make requisite sacrifices, or rent out space for those who did. There were probably more cults and nests here than there were working companies—a feature rather than a bug, which was why none of the infrastructure was crumbling like some of the old neighborhoods untouched by Vega when he got his hands on development.

Sometimes Violet heard other footsteps lock step with theirs, although when she looked over her shoulder, there was no one there. Eventually the footsteps faded or broke away, perhaps deciding that a hunter in full regalia under a Texas sun was not someone to be trifled with.

That it was daytime worked in their favor for now, but once the sun went down, the precarity of her position would become even more tenuous. She might have power, but when it came down to cults, demons, acolytes, and harems, she might not be powerful enough in the right way. Nevertheless, she was more scared for Clive—and for Abel—than she was for herself. She chose to be here, but Abel had to change how he hunted to serve her, and Clive simply may not have known what he was getting into.

At a two-story administrative building, Abel paused, staring hard at the bland, blank exterior, then held up his hand to her. "Stay here."

"Is that an order or a request?"

He glared through the shadow of his hood, but he didn't insist that she remain outside as she followed him to the back.

Abel checked the door—locked. When he pulled out a lock-pick kit, she covered his gloved hand and

Book & Candle

brushed between him and the door. She closed her hand around the lever handle and whispered silently for the lock to yield.

Then she held the door open for him, since she still wanted him to be the first person someone attacked if they woke up cranky and chose violence.

Now that she was inside, she felt what he'd felt—that prickle over and under her skin that told her more subtly than her clit or cunt that she was horny. She wound that feeling through her fingers to use rather than let it use her. However, even with succubi rather than incubi, she didn't think this feeling was powerful enough to be a large group, unless Abel thought they might be in a basement. There weren't many domicile basements on the Austin limestone foundation of most of Texas, but larger buildings sometimes had them.

This time, when Abel held up his hand to warn her to stay slow and quiet, she let him set the pace through the dark hallways in which there was only one visible exit, giving whatever lived in the building the advantage, especially as the magic thickened the deeper they crept.

The hunter didn't open any office doors in the hallways. Aside from trying to keep quiet, she didn't know why until they rounded the corner into a more open office environment. Low-walled cubicles had been pushed against the walls, even arranged as blanket and pillow forts, but the primary part of the room resembled nothing so much as a loft apartment, with secondhand or thrifted sofas and six beds, some with curtains for privacy and some without even headboards.

In these beds lounged three succubi and three incubi. They were watching one of the *Real Housewives*

172

shows on a projector, cuddled two to a bed, a few of them even sleeping.

Violet raised her eyebrows. Abel lowered his bowie knife a fraction.

Together, they backed out of the room under cover of the television program chatter.

Abel swept by her toward the exit. "You've got to be kidding me," he muttered under his breath.

It probably didn't help that once they were back on the street, Violet kept erupting into giggles that she then had to get back under control before he turned around to glower.

"Do you ever think about it?" Violet asked.

"You're going to have to be more specific. And quieter."

"You're dressed like an urban cowboy, and I'm the most recognizable witch in Meridian, both walking out in the middle of these sidewalks. We're not trying to be stealthy out here, are we?"

"Fine. What am I supposed to be thinking about?"

"About how the things you kill are people?"

His jaw tightened and his stride quickened, straining Violet's ability to keep up with him in less practical shoes. "You seem to be under the impression that people should be off limits. People do evil all the time. Humans have systems, however imperfect, for dealing with that. I'm not a cop. I'm not a soldier. I'm not a gangbanger. Killing humans isn't my job. Protecting them is. And if that means killing non-human people doing bad things — because cops don't know what they're dealing with and prisons can't hold them — then I'll kill them.

"You think because we saw a bunch of sex demons *not* killing people that they aren't responsible for fistfuls of obituaries? You think because an avarice demon wears a suit and doesn't get his hands dirty, he can't destroy thousands of lives with one digital signature? Yes, they're people, they're intelligent, social, and they're often camouflaged to look like us. And on a normal day or night, I wouldn't walk into a nest. No one's doing anything they shouldn't in a nest. I'd rather disrupt a cult sacrifice. But don't think that just because they're suckers for reality shows that they're safe."

Abel slowed down enough for her to catch up to him, but he still walked more quickly than before, forcing her to struggle to stay next to him on the sidewalk, because he kept glancing over at her as though to see her reaction.

"You're a witch," he finally continued. "You're human, which means you're like acolytes. You can go either way. And you *do* go either way. It's only because you're more useful alive than dead that both sides agreed to leave you alone. But that doesn't let you off the hook."

"I don't need you to let me off the hook," Violet replied. "And you're not exactly a shining white knight, so don't give me that moralistic bullshit. A hunter doesn't get the reputation you have because he's just doing his job, thank you, ma'am. You're called 'Willing and Abel' because you like it a little too much, go a little too far. You're more useful alive than dead, too. And all this pissed-offness about working with a morally ambiguous witch, you're still willing to do it for a price, even suspending your own work."

Now she was the one speedwalking, soles striking the pavement so hard that her footsteps echoed among the buildings.

"So don't saunter there like some spaghetti-western sheriff and pretend you're better than me because you kill demons and I sometimes help them. You're helping me right now because both of us are useful to the other, and although you kill succubi who turn tricks in your motel, you don't mind fucking me as part of this transaction, or compelling me to agree to something I don't even know I'm agreeing to, just because you figured you *could*."

Both of their steps set the brick walls to drum beats all around for a few blocks.

Then Abel said, "I'm not better. You're just the kind of woman I'd kill if you stepped across the wrong line."

"I wouldn't kill you. You'd only wish you were dead."

Abel's thick eyebrows quirked under the hood in subtle acceptance of the terms.

"Are we there yet?" she asked.

That, at least, granted her the briefest of smiles. "You got somewhere else to be?"

* * * *

Once the sun crossed the roofline of the tallest building in the district, Abel glanced over at Violet to check whether they should keep going. The search would become more dangerous, but at the very least, Violet wanted to *find* the nest so they could come back to it tomorrow. She nodded them on.

"Oh." It was such a soft exclamation and muffled under his mask, which he'd raised as the sun set. He stopped on the sidewalk, turning his head like a satellite dish. "That. You feel that?"

"You're going to need to be more specific." She was hot, sweaty, aching from the power-walking, and her feet hurt. Her shoes could get her through a day-long shopping trip, but they weren't really built for pounding the pavement so hard.

"In this concentration, you should—"

"*Oh.*" Her exclamation was more emphatic. She'd been tingling and prickling ever since the first nest, and it had grown more and less pronounced as they'd passed different buildings. She hadn't immediately processed this particular uptick in the sensation, and her legs ached so much that she hadn't recognized the heaviness between her legs as arousal. But now that she'd stopped walking and he'd called attention to it, she couldn't deny how her physical awareness of sex demons had intensified. "Where?"

Abel led her to a white-brick building. White brick was a terrible idea outside of single-family homes, because of the upkeep against exhaust and other elements. However, one whole wall of the building had been cluttered with graffiti like a tattooed lady, but only that alley-side wall, which suggested a specific, concerted effort, and most passers-by might not recognize the sigils and symbols painted among the rest of the images.

Violet hovered her palm over some of the spells lower on the walls.

"All of this was done by just one succubus. Quite the artist, too," she said. "I might even recognize her if I see her, because that"—she pointed to a complicated symbol at the corner, sigils rounding a double-circle—"is custom. I remember thinking it was an odd request."

"Why?"

"It's a fertility charm for the infertile. But succubi don't..."

"Breed," Abel finished for her. "And you didn't think to question it?"

"It was like someone with a hysterectomy coming in and begging me to help them get pregnant. Of course I questioned it. I just figured she knew an incubus who was looking to cuckoo in someone else's nest, or maybe a friend who *was* capable of producing offspring. I don't ask why a person wants a spell unless I need those details to create it. I certainly didn't have a reason to refuse her."

Even if she'd thought the spell had been for the succubus in question, a fertile succubus wouldn't be appreciably more dangerous. If it worked, the woman would get her baby. If it didn't, no one got hurt.

But she'd already given the woman what she'd wanted. If Clive had been taken for this reason, destroying Violet's shop and stealing from her made no sense.

"No reason not to give it to her except that it's unnatural. They already propagate by nefarious means through one gender. You wanted to give them both?" Abel said.

"It still wouldn't work. They have uteruses, but they're completely incapable of getting pregnant by incubus or human man. Their body is inhospitable to it. And no need to hate on parasitic propagation — cuckoos have to eat, too, and at least sex demons don't starve their siblings. Besides, if you think about it, sex demons born and raised by sex demons sounds like a much better idea than planting seeds in someone else's garden." She stayed practical, because it kept her distant from emotions that threatened to burst from her like blood blisters if she lingered too long where they hurt.

"None of this sounds like a good idea. You and your partner are quite a pair. Don't even realize you're being taken advantage of, like every other demon mark."

"Sympathy for the devil isn't being taken advantage of. It's being broad-minded."

"So broad-minded that your brain's going to spill out of your brainpan. I'm certainly not going to catch it," Abel said. "You want to go in and actually see what your meddling's wrought?"

She couldn't manage to convince her throat to speak, so she nodded.

The white-brick building—closer to coffee-stained ivory these days—was four stories high and ostensibly abandoned, with broken windows, but there were three locks on the door in the shaded alley. Still, there wasn't a lock that Violet couldn't open, one way or another.

"*Fuck.*" Abel adjusted himself under all his layers as he stepped inside the building.

"Need a hand job outside?" she whispered.

"Won't help. Find stairs. Even winged creatures tend not to look up."

The back of the white-brick building was all enclosed offices, but she understood what he meant when she peered down the dark hall to the light at the end of it, which indicated that the corridor opened into a much larger, possibly high-ceilinged room, like the last nest.

With his nocturnal eyes, he found the stairs first, and she unlocked the door so that they could ascend to the fourth floor.

The dense cluster of offices on the fourth floor terminated at what looked like a communal break room. It boasted enough dust-free surfaces and lingering savory odors that Violet guessed it still had a working kitchen, but at that moment, the room was unoccupied. Other scents drew her and Abel to the railing separating the open break room from the larger room below that comprised the other half of the building.

If Violet had to narrow down the industry, she thought it might once have been a printing company of some kind, but most of the smaller machines had been removed, nothing left but the more saturated color on the carpet where they'd once stood. As in the last nest, all irrelevant pieces that could be moved lined the edges of the room like a barricade. Although some windows at the front of the building had appeared broken from the outside, they were all repaired on the inside, which was explained by one of the many spells that had been artfully graffitied onto the side of the building—a glamor that made the building appear uninhabited, uninhabitable.

But the HVAC was functional, air conditioning blasting on full to combat a heated cauldron of bodies in the gathered beds. No pretense of separation or domesticity here, and no distractions.

Impossible to know if sunset had intensified their activity or whether they never slept. As the succubus at the fudge shop had suggested, this might be how it always was—heaven and hell in one orgiastic package. Now that Violet was here, gently wreathed in their heat and unintentionally but violently invaded by their sex magic, she couldn't tell if what she saw and felt was wonderful or terrible, which she knew in the back of her mind meant it was more terrible than wonderful — like the scent lure of a pitcher plant.

On her knees, she peered over the middle railing, grasping the metal to anchor herself there so she wouldn't crawl to the stairs to join their mass of bodies. Abel knelt next to her, fighting for breath like a bull behind his mask as he, too, stared down into the perfumed writhe.

There had to be two dozen or more succubi alone, which seemed unthinkable when the one she'd spoken to suggested they rarely went above five. A few of them had made an effort at clothing, but it had eventually fallen or ripped away from certain areas, left to drape over them in annoyingly attractive disarray as they rubbed their bodies against each other to stimulate — almost as an afterthought, to scratch the whole-body itch that didn't seem too distressing.

Among the roiling, sighing, moaning tangle of varied but perfect feminine bodies, four men had been bound to headboards by soft but sturdy silk — one man for each cardinal direction. They'd been stripped entirely, and all of them were ridden at a slow, excruciatingly exquisite pace, if their torturous expressions were to be believed.

Their eyes were rolled back, eyelids fluttering, mouths open as though struggling to breathe, but their gasps sometimes curved into smiles, laughter cut short as another succubus bit his nipple or dipped her tongue in his navel or slithered up his body to kiss him or straddle his face. He would then oblige with worship of his own, the way they seemed to worship at the obelisk of his cock. When one woman finished with him, however many times they made him come, another would climb on. There was little fighting between them to be next, because they seemed to understand that they'd eventually get their turn.

It took a minute to recognize him, which was telling in and of itself, but Clive was the man marking north.

Violet couldn't discern individual sexual magic energies amid so many, but two of the women around him included a long-haired blonde and long-haired brunette, so they might have been the ones who'd been in her home, in her place of business, touching things they had no business touching. They had their hands on him now, stroking the coarse hair on his chest and abdomen as he raised his weary hips to meet those of the woman taking his erection into her.

He had several days of scruff, which was to be expected. What wasn't was how gaunt he appeared after just a few days. He'd always taken care of himself, but work was also his only workout, so he'd carried some softness on his frame. All that softness was gone, revealing definition to his jawline, cheekbones, and ribcage that she wasn't accustomed to seeing. One of the men was a person of some girth, but Violet had to wonder, based on some of the loose, easily moving skin, how big he'd started out.

Abel covered her with shadow. She bit her lip against every brush of his leather jacket against her bare arms.

"One of them yours?"

God, when he speaks like that *in my ear...* But Violet pointed to Clive.

"Worse for the wear," Abel muttered.

She was honestly surprised they hadn't worn Clive's erection down to the size of a pencil with all the friction, or macerated flesh with all their juices. None of this could be healthy, although sex demons did have antiseptic and antibiotic properties in their magic to help minimize the trace they left and to neutralize any venereal disease that came into contact with them.

"But alive," she said. "They want them alive."

For how much longer?

The succubi wouldn't be getting a proper feed, not with the nominal amount they took from these men in their present state, and the men might have forgotten about real food entirely with so many tastier things on the menu. The sex drive wasn't an actual drive for humans, but under the influence of sex demons, people lost all perspective about what they needed. This kind of obsession was dangerous for everyone involved.

Abel didn't move from where he'd overlapped her with his body, didn't move his mask-covered mouth from her ear. He subsumed her grip on the railing, hurting her knuckles as he squeezed.

The succubus riding Clive clutched at the jut of his lower ribs, wings shaking out of her shoulders as she approached her climax. All over the bed, the other succubi responded to her and to him as she dragged him to the edge of the waterfall with her. The other three men let out their own broken moans to join his, hers, all the women around them. Hands and mouths and cunts and cocks and wings all moved more quickly and insistently. Holds tightened, awakening new bruises, reawakening old ones.

"Oh yes, oh yes, oh fuck, oh yes..." Clive chanted as he used the binding around his hands to pull himself up, to push himself deeper into her. "*Ohhh...*"

The succubi riding the men all shouted their climax almost in unison, and the men joined them in a discordant chorus of pleasure. The others rubbed harder against their companions in envy and softer climax.

Violet's eyelids fluttered closed as she fought the same rise in her own arousal, skating just at the edge without the stimulation to push her over that waterfall with the rest.

But Abel brought himself closer, his hips jerking against her ass as he came against his will. He tightened his fist over hers so hard that she muffled her mouth against his coat to keep from being heard.

"Hurts," she muttered, trying to stretch her fingers out from under his.

"I don't— I can't do this. Can't do this right now. Fuck. *Fuck*." He pushed himself off the railing, off her, but he hauled her up with him as he stood.

She nearly fell as he pulled her back with him. They both stumbled through the dark, risking the tender melee below hearing them if they knocked into things, even though another succubus had replaced the briefly satiated on each cock, and they continued to be otherwise occupied and much less on alert than a more sustainable nest.

When Violet couldn't keep up walking backward, he dragged her to the stairwell and forced her hand on the handle so that she could unlock it, because it had automatically locked behind them. She levered the handle until they were alone in the darkened stairwell. Glass-block windows would generally let in more light, but the sun had almost set and the windows only had a view of another building, which blocked most of what light remained. She could barely see Abel's eyes at all as he let her go only to crowd her against the plaster wall.

He pulled off his gloves, then undid his jeans and advanced upon her without a word. His erection pressed against her hip—wet, yet as hard as though he hadn't come at all. He slipped his bare hands under her shirt, skin to skin, the same way that the succubus bodies had needed touch, *contact*, with each other as much as the men. He pushed under the shirt, shoved under her bra, groaned under his mask, which pressed hot against her neck. Her nipples tightened under his squeezing fingers—still too hard, but he wasn't doing this for her, and she didn't expect him to.

She trembled, caught between fear and arousal like a hare considering whether to kick.

Then he gathered her skirt on either side of her hips, bunched it up until he could reach under and yank her panties down past her knees. They fell to her ankles. She managed to step out of half. The other caught on her shoe. But he jerked her thigh up and brought his cock to her pussy, which was wet, but she wasn't ready, wasn't *ready*...

Her magic shoved him back before she could even stitch a word, much less form a coherent spell.

"They don't hit me as strong as they do with you. It's not the same, not without touch," she finally managed to say.

Abel panted at her from arm's reach—without her arms holding him there. Finally, he stopped fighting against it, and she slowly released him.

He didn't accuse her of not keeping her promise, just brushed her hands away from her thighs, where she'd formed an almost demure shield—a gesture she hadn't used often in her life. This was different, this was fast, this was promised, this was *anything*, and he kept himself so contained and concealed, maybe even from himself.

Shaking for different reasons, he brought his fingers to her pussy instead of his cock. He didn't ease in, but he used two fingers instead of three, pressing his thumb just above her clit, then immediately found the spot inside her that made her moan—more physical than mental arousal, but he knew it would do its job because it already had. And when he smothered her mouth with his mask, she let him press her to the wall again and fingerfuck her until her moans rose higher in her head with her arousal playing off the succubi magic and what he was doing to her, the way he smelled in leather, the way he felt, the way he gave exactly one fuck and no other, but that was the one fuck she needed at that moment.

Then she grabbed the leather lapels and bit his lip through the mask. "Now," she whispered.

He didn't bother with a condom, probably didn't have the discipline or coordination for it. His breathing only harshened as he positioned his cock at her entrance again, and this time he received no resistance as he thrust in. Then he just held her in place, shoulder and hip, as he screwed her. Their breath hissed hot as steam from an iron pan against the fabric of his mask, but he couldn't kiss her like this.

Pleasure grated through his throat as he came again, buried deep inside her and crushing her against the wall. He kept grinding into her, even as his cum trickled out in a sudden wash down her thigh. He was still hard.

"*Fuck*. It's not enough. It's not…done. This is fucking ridiculous." He looked away from her, not embarrassed but frustrated by his own loss of control.

"They may intend to keep those boys alive, but how are they still? I can't... Goddamn it, I can barely *think*."

"Thinking isn't exactly high on their priority list. Can you walk and chew gum at the same time?"

He gritted his teeth, eyes narrowing, but he nodded.

"Okay. We know where they are. We have an idea what they're doing. We need to leave. We need to clear your head...our heads..."

He pulled a handkerchief out from one of his many jacket pockets and wiped it up her thigh, then between her folds to catch the rest of his seed, pressing the heel of his hand against her clit in the process. Her head hit the wall. Now that all her desirous nerve clusters were properly awake and unsatisfied, she was more easily distracted by contact, by proximity, by scent, by the magic still weaving through them like suture needles.

"Downstairs," she managed to say.

He put the handkerchief back in its place, then grabbed his gloves. She pulled her underwear back on before adjusting the position of her bra. Neither could let the nest know they'd been here, if they ever came up for air.

Violet and Abel ran down the four flights of stairs as quietly as they could, then crept back through the hall. Violet closed the door behind them before releasing the handle to minimize the click.

When she turned around, Abel already had his knives out at a pestilence demon who'd slimed through the alley and apparently waited for them at the exit. He was half naked and clearly turned on by the same sex magic, but that was less of a concern for a pair of humans than the open boils and sores on his exposed body.

The only reason Violet could think of why a guard wouldn't work too hard to stop them from going in was because the succubi, especially in their numbers, could take care of themselves. The pestilence demon was there to keep anything from escaping.

"They don't give me much," the demon rasped from a mouth filled with too many teeth and too much saliva. "But what they call is sweet enough. What do you have for me tonight?"

Violet rested a hand on Abel's arm for him to lower it, then slid down to take the smaller of the two knives from him. "Amnesty, if you step aside."

"I'm not letting a hunter walk out of here unscathed, Magic Mystery Woman. Oh yes, I smell it on you, all over you, inside. I think I'll leave you with only a bite, just to see what grows from it. But the man has to die."

"I'm untouchable, so he's untouchable in my employ," Violet said. "You don't have to die tonight, but you will if you try to take us."

"I have my orders and a craving for hot blood meat, my love," the demon replied. "You're not going anywhere."

Violet sent the entire swirl of her frustration and fear into the demon's repulsive body, ripping every ligament and tendon she could find, snapping it like a knife to gristle. It wasn't among her more natural skills. She swayed from the sudden drop in energy.

The pestilence demon collapsed like a discarded ventriloquist dummy. Even its jaw was loose, although its tongue retained prehensility.

She came up behind the demon, each step shaky but steady, without him able to stop her or do anything but strain to see where she was and try to lick her vulnerable skin. But she cut at the tongue to make it whip away, then stabbed the knife into the demon's neck, quickly severing the relevant blood vessels.

The demon's black blood gushed down the alley to the nearest drain until there was nothing left but a trickle.

Abel straightened, sliding his bowie knife back in its sheath. "That's my job."

"Thought it would be good for you to see I can, in fact, fight back," Violet said, panting and fighting the urge to vomit and moan in the same motion. "The same thing I did to the duct tape, I can do to organic material, too. Just because I don't want to hurt anyone doesn't mean I'm weak, hunter. *That's* why they leave me be. I'm not as complacent as you think."

She handed him the knife, which he wiped on his jeans. He'd need to sterilize the blade before using it again, but he had others.

"Good," he said. "Truck."

Chapter Eleven

All the way to where they started, he didn't say a word. If she hadn't known how much lust he was in, she would have guessed from his gait only that he'd been injured in action or an old wound was acting up.

When they reached the truck, he gave her the keys. "You. Drive. My apartment, not yours."

Once she turned on the truck, she blasted the A/C as high as she could, not just to cool the oven of the cab quicker but to cool Abel, between his hunter ensemble and his ardor.

As soon as he was in the passenger seat, Abel pushed back the hood and yanked down his mask, ran his hands through his hair. Then he slammed his fists on the dash, startling her into a slight swerve.

At a red light, she glanced over. "You can rub one off, you know. I thought that was why you wanted me to drive. Road head is distracting, no matter how disciplined you are."

"Just...stop talking." He released the clenched fists from his jeans to hold up a hand at her, as though to block her entirely from his sight.

She switched on his radio. He didn't seem to mind that, although it also didn't seem to make anything better, considering the nature of a good number of classic rock and metal songs.

When Violet pulled into the motel parking lot, he didn't even wait for her to stop the car before unbuckling his seatbelt and opening the door. She shoved her foot on the brake so he could stride relatively smoothly from the car to a room not his own. She practically heard the slices of his blade and didn't look too closely as he dragged two trash bags from the room to his office, where she wouldn't have been surprised to find a freezer or three.

Violet took her time getting out of the car, mostly because she wasn't sure what he'd wanted her to do other than drive. She suspected, however, that there would be more to the story tonight, so she let him exorcise his frustrations on whatever sex demon had been foolish enough to choose his no-tell motel to feed in.

Abel strode up the stairs to the second floor of his open-air motel walkway and entered another room. Ten minutes later, he left with another two trash bags. The overhead lights over the walkway and sidewalk were only intermittently working, so he remained a baleful shadow, although he hadn't replaced his hood or mask.

She waited between his two adjoining rooms, growing increasingly tense, the flow of fear and lust rocking together within her, but she sat in her discomfort and frustration. In her terror.

Of the many succubi to their few male victims, of what they wanted and what they were willing to sacrifice to get it.

Of what Mr. Willing and Abel would be willing to do to get rid of succubus sex magic greater than even he had ever encountered, such that the vaunted veteran hunter had scurried from a nest with his tail firmly jutting out between his legs.

Of herself, because she'd always been able, but how far was she willing to go for both of these problems?

Finally, Abel returned to his rooms. He took the keys from her to unlock the door to his more impersonal bedroom, then pulled her in by the wrist. He slammed the door behind them, locked it with one hand, then pulled her to him, hand familiar and almost gentle over her ass to press her against him.

He'd made his adjustments, but he was still completely hard. She licked, then bit her lip as she pressed back. But then she pushed at his chest, distancing herself as much as him.

She unbuckled her shoes and kicked them away, then removed her shirt. It had some bloodstains on it, transfer from Abel's jacket, but not as bad as her last outfit. It could be salvaged. She threw her shirt on the weapons dresser, then unzipped her skirt.

Abel shed his jacket, which would need to be cleaned again. Both of their hands were bloodstained, hers from the pestilence demon, his from the demons he'd killed in his rooms. She held out her hands to indicate the problem, then strode past him to the bathroom sink, where she scrubbed herself all the way up to her elbows. More than any other demon, pestilence demon blood wasn't the kind one wanted to swap through open wound or sexual contact, and

Violet wasn't sure which one of them had to worry about that more.

Abel yanked her skirt and underwear down while she washed her hands, impatiently unhooked her bra, then wound his fist into her hair before she could dry her hands. Still mostly clothed, he drew her back with him into the bedroom.

"Which bed won't kill me?" she asked.

He dragged her to the one on the right, then shoved her onto the comforter, where she undid the fastenings of his jeans while he kicked off his shoes. She pulled off his shirt when he had to bend down to remove his socks, but he shrugged out of his undershirt himself as he climbed onto the bed over her.

She thought he would cover her like that, but he flipped her over instead before kissing down her spine, this time without gentleness or tenderness. If there had been something for his teeth to hold, she thought he would have left bitemarks, like he did on her hip where one of her health spells spiraled over her skin.

He shoved her thighs apart and jerked her hips up to lick her pussy and through her folds, tasting her, tasting himself, tasting sweat and skin and unclean need, burying his tongue in her as though to gauge just how wet she already was for him by more intimate means than fingers.

Unlike her, he hadn't bothered to wash his hands. He smeared sex demon bloodstains up her back as he licked her—again, not tenderly. She hadn't thought anything so intimate could be so hot and cold at the same time, but they were both helpless to the magic. She was pretty sure some of the blood on his hands had come from an incubus, because she gathered fistfuls of the comforter as she ground back against his mouth and wished for that impassive passion to shift down to her clit, or that maybe he'd use those rough, bloody fingers again.

Now he crawled over her, holding her down with dead weight that rattled the weapons concealed in and near this bed as well as the other. She knew she was at least safe from a mattress bear trap, but she didn't feel safe with him over her like this, where she couldn't see his face.

It was different than at the mall. This was his space—impersonal and, more importantly, private. Although he'd just killed two demons in his motel, no one had so much as stepped outside to see what the commotion was about. Screams might not be enough to rouse someone from whatever kind of slumber they chose for the night.

He could do *anything* to her. No one here would care, she had no one at home to notice, and no one in her family would know anything had happened. Protection charms on her body were supposed to prevent her from getting into situations like this against her will, but she'd knocked on his door, she'd employed him, and she'd stayed when she could have called a rideshare home. Pentecostals weren't the only ones who rolled with serpents. She'd put herself in the viper's mouth of her own accord.

Her chest tightened and air got harder to breathe because of it, but also because of his hands on her back, compressing her ribs as he held her down. He didn't grab her hair to smother her in the comforter, but it was hard for her to hold her head up, and once he'd slid into her, he closed his hands on either side of her neck. He used her to pump in and out of her pussy, clenching just a little with every thrust. He didn't choke her for more than fractions of seconds. She could still breathe. That's what she kept telling herself as he throttled her with his rough working hands and she throttled him much more softly with her cunt.

Her arms were dying spider legs on the covers, her thighs spread too far to get leverage. She was a soft place for him to land and all bent limbs for herself. She breathed between squeezes, told herself that she was alive, tightened around him every time she thought her vision was about to gray out.

She cried out when he came, because it felt like it had almost no build up for him except for the sharper slap of his hips against her ass, but he didn't stop, just kept fucking her as his cum splattered out from the force of his thrusts. Then she did gray out as she came, despite the fact that he wasn't stroking anything inside or outside, just using her to scratch that itch as unbearable as anything she'd stirred up in a spell bomb — an itch he couldn't satisfy with a demon, dead or alive, but he'd decided a witch would do.

But only because she knew what he was and he could do to her what he might not be able to do to someone more professional. Because he squeezed a little harder now — still not a sustained strangle, but she couldn't know whether her next breath, or the next, or the next, would be cut off by the press of his powerful hands on either side of her windpipe.

He could crush it, if he chose. Or snap her neck. And then how would her magic save her?

Tears leaked onto the comforter, smearing rather than absorbing in the polyester. She jerked against the punch of her latest orgasm, against the shift in his cock's angle, against the fight for unreliable breath, as though she would pass out any moment. Even so, her eyes rolled back and her toes curled, her legs on the edge of cramp from the tension.

She scrabbled at the comforter with her nails, striving for purchase when there was none to be had, and he tightened his hold as he finally locked his hips against her and came again, groaning from the relief of more fulfilling release.

As soon as his hips and his cock stopped twitching, he loosened his grip on her neck. The tension in her body released as well. Magic — hers — rushed and heated through her blood, muscle, burning behind her tight-shut eyes, in the treasure chest of her head. Abel groaned like he'd been struck in the stomach and snapped his hips against her ass again, then again — in dry orgasm this time, because his cock spasmed but no additional seed slithered out of her to join the rest of the mess on her thighs and the bed beneath her.

The magic wrapped around her and him, not binding like his fingers nor like she'd held him to hold her against the brick wall. She felt him beneath her as much as behind and over her, and held them like that, feeding far more benignly on the energy released than anything an incubus or succubus could do to them. Her pussy continued to clench around him, and she bit the covers to less literally bite her tongue.

Finally, Abel held himself up from her by the bed instead of her body, giving her upper half room to move. But she didn't, not at first.

When he ran his hands over the smeared canvas he'd made of her back, he was still neither gentle nor tender, but the push of his fingers into her muscles was more deliberate — the pain of a deep-tissue massage, the roughest admiration she'd ever received. Whether it was intended as apology or not, she relaxed her jaw to relieve the comforter of her teeth.

She arched up from the bed, and those sandpaper hands dug under her ribs, into her hips, down to her thighs, and still he stayed inside her, not quite as hard as he'd been but not softening any more. He leaned into her against her back, his breath hot on her neck and disturbing her loose hair. Just when she thought he might kiss her, he closed his teeth over the base of her neck, sucking where he'd smeared demonic blood over her, until all that was left was her skin.

His firm massage shifted back up her thighs, then between. She hitched and shied away from the firmness, especially when she was already sensitive from her orgasms, but the stimulation hadn't been to these particular nerves. All too quickly, she was moaning again, almost angry that he seemed to have figured out reaction to a science rather than the art she was used to. But she was just as susceptible to it as she was to sex demon magic.

If she could have used her own wiles to even the score, she would have, but the succubi had handled that side of the equation. It wasn't a position she was used to being in, a proxy party in a sexual arrangement, the agreed-upon fleshlight who whimpered on command, just the right amount of autonomy to add novelty.

Except he hadn't let her go yet, and although he stroked his cock with her body, he finally seemed more interested in that body than his cock.

He bit without drawing blood up the length of her neck as he made her squirm — too hard, too rough, yet the very nerves he overstimulated didn't seem to care about the 'over' part. She grabbed his forearms but couldn't quite convince herself to push those hands away, not until they'd deep-tissue massaged her into a violent climax that had her gasping and her nails digging into his scarred skin.

Then she shrugged him off her neck and shifted herself up away from his hands, which were still stroking too deeply into her, pushing her into a whine until he gave one of his short, harsh laughs and bit at a place on her shoulder where it stung when his tongue pressed against her. He must have broken through at least a little.

Violet reached behind her to take his hair the same way he so cavalierly kept grabbing hers. She pulled until he grunted and released her. Then she adjusted her grip closer to the roots so that it wouldn't hurt anymore, but her hold was more implacable, more controlling, as she guided him around her — which also drew him out of her and away from the heavy pelvic bruise that he'd made of her flesh between her legs.

She tugged his head back until he was flat on the comforter beneath her. His Adam's apple jerked under the stubble of the day as he stared a dagger at her with his good eye. It wasn't quite a violent dagger yet, but the smooth temper of a blade cold and flat against her skin rather than on the honed edge. She stroked his cock, which rested slightly to the side on his abdomen, then lowered herself to slide the shaft through her folds. Between their several orgasms, neither of them needed anything to slick their way in the slightest, but she teased the head with her fingertip and threat of her nail.

"How many of these do you think you have in you?" she asked.

"Surprise me."

But he surprised her instead, brushing the wispier hair at her temples, then sliding his fingers into the more substantial curls without grabbing her.

She tucked his erection back inside her, squeezing more deliberately all the way down. "Now, who do you think can get there first?"

"I thought you were a marathoner."

Violet tilted her head, then ground down over his erection, squeezing again. "Oh, you'd like this to be a marathon?"

He pushed himself up onto his elbow to smooth his spread fingers over her lower back. He closed his mouth over her breast before narrowing the suction until it was painful at the peak, yet still shot little lightning bolts directly to her clit, which throbbed in response.

She cried out, shaking her head. She'd had plenty of rough sex in her time, but this was different—more deliberate. This was someone knowing every pressure point that somehow aroused her at the same time. His need was keen, but he wasn't mindless or thoughtless. He wasn't hurting her by accident.

She was curious, with all his experience, whether anything less potent than a sex demon nest could surprise him. It wasn't even the sex magic that had thrown him—just the sheer amount of it that they'd hit him with, and not even on purpose.

Violet curled her nails into his chest like cat's paws and pushed him back down. "That's not what I meant. I mean I'm going to have *my* fun with you now. Who do you think I'll get there first?"

"What are the stakes?"

"There are enough stakes in our lives as it is," Violet said, still rocking herself over him, searching for that perfect angle. It was easier with fingers, but if she could just... *Yes, right there.* She had to lean back, holding herself up by his thighs, but he seemed quite content with the view, bracing himself on both elbows now. "Try this. Breathe with me."

She slowed her breathing and the dancing of her hips over him, showed him and made him feel the rhythm until he inhaled when she inhaled, exhaled when she exhaled, although sometimes one gasped or groaned when the other didn't.

Not everyone had a good sense of rhythm, and sex didn't always need it at every stage, but people trained in fighting often learned the same eight-count as dancers, and if you could eight-count, you could breathe in tandem. Focusing on breath instead of just pleasure allowed it to build like the tide to a dock. Every time pleasure threatened to move them instead of their own will, Violet would stroke her fingernails through the coarse-soft hair on his thighs and slow until they'd returned to rhythm.

There was a curious quietness in Abel's face around his eyes and in his forehead. Sometimes he stared intently as though she were a stripper moving to his favorite stroke song, but sometimes he just closed his eyes, and the lines in his face smoothed like drought soil under new rain. There was no power on Earth — at least within a humble witch's hands — to make him look young, but it definitely made him look younger, without the ravages of the world, physical and emotional, upon him.

She was the one who quickened the pace, both in how she fucked him and how they breathed. By then, they were more in tandem than not, and when she moved faster, harder, her breathing harsher with effort, his arousal rose to meet her. All he had to do was lie there, hold on, and breathe with her, and when she used his erection to stroke that spot in her, the angle also increased pressure against the head, and their quickening breath made the pleasure headier — the same principle as his hands around her throat, but a lot less likely to hurt if she slipped.

Which wasn't to say that what she was doing wasn't dangerous. With each inhale, she drew on the power of the yoni spell at her hip, used it to make threads of their air, stitching in and out between them with the motion of her hips and the way his cock moved in and out of her. With those threads and the needle of her magic, and as her arousal intensified, she could do all manner of things to him, and he wouldn't have the first clue how much power she commanded.

Maybe, if she could gather enough threads for this one masterpiece…

She went even faster, panting now, forcing him to shorter breaths and a return of the tension in his face, in the beautiful lines of his neck and torso as he canted his hips — not quite pushing or thrusting, but as though dancing with her.

As she whimpered, he gritted his teeth against what raked through his throat. Their rhythm threatened to fling off the track she'd set at any moment, but she wrapped her magic around them, gathered the strings like hay into a sheaf, bound their climaxes inexorably together. Usually, shooting for synced orgasms was both a fool's errand and not worth the effort, but her magic ensured mutually assured destruction.

She drew it out as long as she could, posting against the spot over and over and over, torturing herself, until she squeezed their pleasure like sun-ripened grapes.

She clamped her knees on either side of his hips and with every burst cried out as though no one and everyone could hear her.

Abel live-wire-arched under her, twitched more than thrust, as he came with her, and because she'd tied their lust together in an exquisite bow, his orgasm lasted longer than it ever should have. He planted his heels on the bed, his strangled groans finally rising to a moan like a plaintive howl, but she didn't relent as long as that coming cock kept her coming. Her magic burned hot again behind her eyes and at her hip, where she stored what the magic harvested — nothing that wasn't freely given.

Finally, her climax reached its end, shifting into aftershocks, and Abel collapsed back on the bed with an extended groan like the creaking open of a haunted-house door. His chest rose and fell as he fought for his own breath, his own rhythm.

They'd been so in sync that breathing on their own seemed wrong, but it certainly cleared her mind. She released his thighs to stroke the scars over his abdomen and chest, up to the knot on his chin that extended up to the cloudy eye. She only made it as far as his lip before he hooked his arms behind her shoulders and flipped them over, heedless of the mess they'd made from his unnaturally extended orgasm.

Abel cushioned her head with his arm under her hair as he kissed her like he wanted to crawl inside and consume her from the inside out, rolled her nipple between his fingers so hard that it triggered her hips to rise and meet his.

He'd softened since she'd wrung him almost dry, but still not completely. He seemed to stimulate himself with her whole body, which she slowly curled around him as though he'd killed her. Because he'd bound her the last time, she hadn't been sure how much he really wanted to be touched, to be held, but he just moaned so low in his chest it was almost like distant thunder, and he continued to stiffen against the mess he'd made of her thigh.

Then he was inside her, and he lowered his hand from her breast to her clit again, but he didn't dig the point of pain, which told her that his counterintuitively effective technique had been deliberate. He bookended her swollen, sensitive clit with his fingers and stroked, *pressed*, but didn't dig, and just screwed her.

How he luxuriated as he used her suggested at least a measure of affection, and she thought the way he stroked her clit was for her, for the first time—a lantern for her to follow him in the dimly lit room and dark of the night, an acknowledgment that her pleasure had value in and of itself, even if it didn't serve him.

She traversed the parchment map of scarring on his back, slipped her fingers through his sweat-greased, shaggy hair, moved to his rhythm instead of her own, and told him in whimpers that he was bringing her close again. She scratched at his scalp, at the give of his shoulder, as he moved his consumption from her mouth to her neck, no longer muffling her as he increased his pace both in her pussy and over her clit. She crossed her legs around him and shuddered as he brought her to climax.

His breath hitched in her ear when she settled, muscles loose and relaxed, back in his arms. He shifted his hand from her clit to slip under her thigh, holding her closer as he took her deeper and kissed her again, expiating his hunger until he rolled his hips and locked himself inside her with his climax.

Even so, Abel didn't immediately stop kissing her but settled almost into a somnambulistic feast that felt like worship. Violet couldn't even remember how long it had been since she'd been kissed like this, with someone present with her instead of her wondering who he saw in her place when he closed his eyes.

Romantic he was not, and this wasn't love so much as an excess of lust, but as his erection finally subsided without any sign of stirring again, she had nothing to blame for these languid sauna kisses except his choice. Even if it was just because they felt nice, he still chose to do it, and with her, rather than finding milder company for the night. That was more than she could say for Clive. She could only see that clearly while a proper sloppy mess in another man's bed. And she didn't fucking mind.

She ran her palms and sensitive fingertips over the textured patchwork of his skin and held his heat against her until he withdrew his lips from hers and stared, as inscrutable in his clear eye as the milky one.

She finally traced the scar from his mouth up to the dip of his socket, skipped the eye to the interrupted eyebrow. Then she kissed the jut of cheekbone above his stubble and adjusted them both upright.

"You keep messing with my hair. You better have a good conditioner in that bathroom. And I do not have a change of clothes."

"I'll find something, although I doubt it would be anything you'd choose." He looked down at himself, at both of them, at the bed. He sighed like a motel owner. "I'll finish showering before you do. Hungry?"

"You're joking, right?"

He grinned. Between sweat and other fluids, plus all the walking and fucking—and sex demon magic to smother the signals of other needs — both of them were in desperate need of hydration and substantial fare, even if it hadn't hit them yet how much.

There was no pretending that her lower half wasn't slathered in seed mingled with the juices of her arousal, so she stood up without trying to cover herself or wipe it away. He slapped her ass lightly before pulling the covers off the bed with him as he stood, to throw in a heap next to the front door.

Chapter Twelve

Violet showered in the bedroom, while Abel crossed into his living space to use that bathroom instead. He did not, as she'd hoped, have a good selection of hair products, but at least they were slightly better quality than the kind usually provided in a motel — when any were provided at all. After this adventure, she would have to do a deep conditioning sooner rather than later.

When she finally emerged in the misty bathroom, some clothes had been set on the counter for her. His lotion selection was better than his hair care, probably to help facilitate healing after potions had done what they could — and she did see a few of those potion containers from her store there under his sink, as well.

The undershirt tank top was looser on her than on him, but this wasn't the first time she'd worn one, nor borrowed a clean pair of boxer shorts to sleep in.

The door to his other room was open, so she stepped through. It smelled like the cheapest, greasiest pizza bites were cooking in the toaster oven, which suited her just fine, as did the Thermos of water he'd put out for her. He sat on his couch, bare heels up on his coffee table as he read a library book, reading glasses low on his nose. He raised his gaze to acknowledge her, but otherwise said nothing, just watched her drink the Thermos empty, possibly distracted by the fact that she wasn't wearing a bra under his shirt.

After finishing her water, she raided his fridge — two could play at that game — and pulled out a beer, although she preferred wine. When she held up another bottle, he nodded, and she used the magnetic bottle opener to remove both caps. It was decent beer, sweeter, which made it more tolerable for her.

"I expected you to hitch back home when you finished," Abel said as he accepted the beer.

She sat on the coffee table. "Why?"

"Just because it's harder to see bruises on you doesn't mean you don't have them."

She shrugged. "You weren't the only one hit by the sex demon magic."

"That's like saying I only get a certain way when I'm drunk." He punctuated the point with a deep swallow.

"I can kill you with a thought if I have to. I didn't."

He leaned forward, his elbows braced on his knees and the beer held between his legs. He'd changed into long sweatpants and a lighter hooded shirt and cranked the air conditioning up to counteract the summer night and their hot showers. "Why did you trust me? Why *do* you trust me?"

"I *don't* trust you. I already guessed you might want to do things with me that you thought you couldn't do with other women. I shook on it, anticipated it, and you trod the line because you warned me and I didn't run. Giving you chances isn't the same thing as trust." She shrugged. "I came looking for *you*, Abel. If I'd wanted a politician or a prince, I would have looked elsewhere. The succubi made me a victim of robbery. Clive made me a victim of betrayal, though he might be a victim himself. I may be younger than you by a few decades, but you didn't victimize me. As I've demonstrated, I can stop you at any time. I can end this arrangement and leave *at any time*. So can you. I didn't leave. You didn't kick me out. And that's where we are."

She took another swig from her beer, and he did the same, discomfort making his glance away furtive, but he deliberately returned his attention to her.

"So what are we going to do about that nest?" she asked.

"I think it goes without saying that, if I return, we need another plan other than walking straight in. But you found the succubi, found your boy and your things. What do *you* want to do now that you have an idea of what they're up to?"

"If we hadn't agreed I would decide what would happen to them, what would you do?" Violet asked. "Were they just sex demons in the nest, we'd have less hands-on options, but there are people in there. Actual victims."

Abel's scars accentuated his sneer. "Yeah, they looked real tortured."

"All it took was a few minutes above the burning coals of succubus magic before you couldn't think about anything but sex, sex, and more sex. You think they're going to do better after a few days of being bound, held, and ridden? They're slowly dying and don't even care," Violet said. "That's why y'all hunt sex demons — because the influence they have is so insidious, it leads perfectly reasonable people to do things they would never have done otherwise. I don't think we can assume the men are there of their own will. Even if they agreed, they might not have *understood* what they agreed to. A pretty succubus could have just said, 'Hey, I have these friends, and they think you're really hot. Want to come home with me?'"

"I can't speak to the others, but I still think your boy stepped into that demon den of his own accord. He knew exactly what he was doing when he cut through those protective spells of yours," Abel said.

The toaster oven beeped. Abel stood to remove the pizza bites to cool on a plate. He brought them to the coffee table, but neither of them wanted to burn their mouths yet, although after the shower, her stomach had finally realized it was famished.

"We can't assume they're self-sacrificing," she said, "and we can't just launch a rocket at the building if there are potential innocents inside."

"What difference does it make to you?" Abel snapped. "You sold the demons the charms they used to protect their nest. You've given them and so many others the means to hunt more effectively."

"I gave so many of your kind the same," Violet said. "Look, we're not going to agree on each other's ethics. But you have no stone to throw if you're willing to do business with me at the same time you're mad I'm doing business with demons, who get mad that I do business with hunters. It just never ends. So unless you think my magic shop could survive if I only stocked harmless, useless New Age tourist crap, stop riding me about my profession and I won't point out the problems with yours. I hired you for one problem. If you're too busy judging me and my partner to save a few people, then I *will* walk out of here, and you can go back to your riveting night life."

"Then you would be right back where you started, alone in the same home where your boy cheated the hell out of you with creatures he should have known better about."

"Not right back where I started," Violet said, pretending none of what he'd said stung. "I know where Clive is, I know where they're keeping him, and I have at least part of an idea why. I could leave right now and figure out a way in, because although they ransacked my supplies, they certainly didn't take everything. Besides, I can't use a man who can't control himself around that many succubi."

"And once they got their hands on you, you think you'd do much better? I'm more susceptible, but you're not immune. They'll sink you under their morass just as much as me." He bit into one of the pizza bites, winced with a hiss, then let it sit in his hand, steaming.

She leaned forward, too, not necessarily mirroring him, but she ended up in a similar position anyway as she drank from her beer. Without food in her stomach, the sweet beer hit harder, which did nothing to quicken the mechanical turning of her thoughts, but at least they were moving. "What if there were a way? To make you immune, I mean. Not perfectly immune. There's never perfect immunity. Whatever created this particular conflict would never let there be pure immunity, or else there would be no conflict at all, and where's the fun in that?"

He handed her a pizza bite, which meant she must have been slurring more than she thought. Taking his cue, she bit the corner to let it cool, but it was already better than when Abel had started. They gradually worked on the plate.

"Well, there *is* immunity," she amended. "But I don't think you'd like pure immunity, even for your work."

"What is it?"

"A complete lack of interest in sex. Metaphysical castration, you might say, for those not born into it. I can do it, if you find your particular desires... inconvenient. Most men would never agree to it, though."

He shook his head, but he didn't appear disgusted. "It's not a matter of vitality. I'm just used to it. Nests like *that* aren't supposed to exist, and I wouldn't have been looking for it in the first place if not for you, because while they're feeding on the willing, they're not feeding through people's dreams. It would be useful to control my reactions better, but I'd be lying if I said it didn't make me feel alive. It's...something."

"So, no cutting off your balls, metaphysically or otherwise," Violet agreed. "Maybe there's a way to lessen the effect of the magic. Does an incubus make you feel anything when you're hunting them?"

"Not nothing. But not much."

"Then you probably don't need a blanket shield," she muttered, staring now at the couch weave as the cogs started properly turning, even though they still needed better lubrication than the beer. "As part of your agreement, you said you wanted one of my protection tattoos — not just a small charm but a full-on spell. What if I made one specifically to dull the effects of succubus sex magic?"

"So you can use yours with impunity?"

"So I can find the incubus who looks like Oded Fehr and sic him on you."

His harsh laugh wasn't attractive in the slightest, which was why she liked it. It meant she'd surprised him.

"The more specific the spell, the more effective it can be. If I weave it in with a protection spell — or prayer, however you prefer to view it — you might be able to walk into a succubus infestation without your dick trying to drill a hole through your jeans. The only downside is that you'll have a new tattoo, and all the requisite aftercare, to contend with while actively hunting. I don't recommend that, because it leaves you open to other complications."

"I'll do it," he said.

"Wow. No hesitation."

"Already wanted it. Adding the provision for succubus-specific magic is more than I asked for. I'd be a fool not to take advantage of the opportunity. Don't concern yourself with complications. Our collective works with a doctor who liberally writes prescriptions for antibiotics — important when fighting pestilence demons in particular — and there's always the healing ointment when I can get my hands on the good stuff." He set his empty beer bottle down. "Do you have a particular spell in mind?"

"There's one in my grimoire, which the goddamn demons took." She swigged the rest of her beer, then left her bottle next to his. "I have a general sense of how it goes. The exact words aren't important so much as the sentiment. And I can adjust the design to add the provision. I can't promise anything, because I've never tried something this specific for a tattoo before. Sightless and all-seeing eye are specific spells, but they're old and they're simple. You try to etch in something more complicated, the result can end up complicated, too. But if it works right and you're willing to risk that it won't, the protection spell should tamp the succubi's effect down so at least one of us can be level-headed."

"Can you tattoo while drunk?" Abel pointedly held the pizza plate in front of her.

"I'll sober up. You drive."

* * * *

Standing at her backroom table, Violet scribbled out the spell as she remembered it, but she could tell as she wrote it that it wasn't quite right. She played with words and placement until the magic in her head rang as true as champagne glasses at midnight. Then she considered the wording for the spell's addendum, doodling spirals on the printer paper until she cobbled together what to tack on to the rest. While she worked, Abel did some basic cleaning and tidying to make plenty of space for the refurbished vinyl dentist chair she used for more extensive tattooing.

After she'd set up her tray of tattooing tools, she paused, still holding the ink, her eyes closed.

"Tired?" he asked.

She nodded.

"Coffee?"

"I'll get it myself. You should strip down." She handed him a spare blanket to protect the dentist chair, which she'd reclined to its furthest extent. "On your stomach. Protection spells like this go better on your back, but for the full effect, it needs to traverse as much of you as possible. You can cover your lower half with your clothes or another blanket until I need it, if you want. Be right back."

When she returned with a tumbler of cold-press coffee, he'd covered the chair with the blanket, as she'd wanted, but hadn't bothered to conceal himself. He'd probably thought it was useless to try to unring that bell.

She was done for the night as far as doing anything about her arousal — aches had settled into her muscles like sunburn, and bruises were in full unseen bloom — but she licked her lips nonetheless, admiring the tone and the shape that such disciplined, cultivated strength created.

"You still willing to do this? It'll take a few hours," she said.

"Of the two of us, you're the one who can wield the tattoo gun," Abel said. "I'm more worried about you dozing off in the middle."

"I'll take a break if I need it, but that's not usually my problem. Sometimes I forget to blink."

"You tattoo freehand?" he asked as she settled in her own chair and started mixing the ink to include some powdered herbs and spices that bolstered the properties that the words encouraged.

"For symbols and sigils, I'll trace first, but word spells prefer freehand. Don't worry. I've done this before."

He rested his head on his crossed arms and only twitched from the first few stabs of the needle. He'd done this before, too.

For a while, the world was just the dim storeroom and the bright light she shone down on his pale body. She'd have to work around his existing tattoos as well as some of the more prominent scars, but her word spell tattoos tended to wind and wend, like ambling through the woods. As long as the spell crossed certain parts of his body, it didn't matter how she got there, although spellcasting in ink inspired her to spiral.

"Now that I've got you pinned down like a beetle in a shadow box," she said, "do you mind my asking?"

"You'd have to ask for me to know if I mind."

"Why'd you become a hunter? Most people aren't born knowing about the supernatural world like I was."

"You think there must be a tearful reason why I'm an asshole?" he asked, faced away but somehow reading between her lines.

"The hunters I know tend to have some tragic origin story of losing someone they loved to a demon."

"I stumbled into this world," Abel said shortly. "It doesn't really let you go once you're in."

"What did you stumble on, then?"

She'd already resolved not to push the subject any further when he sighed and turned his face back toward where she sat, although he didn't look directly at her.

"I lost my family, my life, but not to a demon."

Violet lifted the tattoo gun away for a moment, then resumed her work. The only thing that might be worse than her knowing was if she showed pity.

"I stumbled into the supernatural world after the death of my son. Childhood leukemia. The prognosis was worse then. His mother and I were by his side twenty-four-seven. We decimated our savings, went deep into debt so that we wouldn't abandon him for something as unimportant to us at the time as money. He died anyway. Two o'clock in the morning, while his mother slept and I held his hand. A month from his sixth birthday."

She spiraled the first line of her spell over his heart, but she noted again the curled dragon on his arm and the date, which seemed to roughly match his account.

"Middle of the night, a hospital is quiet. A dead boy's bed is quieter. I didn't tell anyone, not the night nurses or my wife, just switched off the monitor and unplugged it. I wandered the halls. When you don't know where you're going, the halls are labyrinthine. Some people go up, striving for stars. I went down to the basement, to the morgue.

"Hospitals here all have sewer access. Ease for public works, they say, but it's so the coroner and morgue attendants have somewhere to dump inconvenient bodies, the kinds they don't want record of. Pestilence demons already swarm hospitals, but at the access grates, it's easier for them to smell the diseased, the susceptible, the vulnerable, like carrion to flies.

"I didn't know what I was seeing through the bars. I raised the grate. Two pestilence demons leaped to the opening. I'd never seen a monster before, except for what had ravaged my son. I was just a family man who only had his nine-to-five by a thread — and that because of a sympathetic manager who couldn't afford to offer much more good will. I'd just lost the heart of my family. I was scared. But I was also angry, angrier than I'd ever been in my life, with nothing upon which to unleash it — until the demons came at me."

She slowly crossed from the spiral over his heart across his spine. He winced in discomfort as she moved the tattoo gun over vertebra, but turned his head again as she continued the spell in a winding path down his back.

"I pushed the bodies back into the hole and closed it. I washed my hands. I stole scrubs from the closet. Then I went back up to my dead son and my wife, who had already begun mourning and had no interest in joining her grief with mine. The love that had created our son wasn't enough to keep us going after. She didn't die, but I lost her just the same. Though the split wasn't acrimonious, I wouldn't call it amicable. We never speak. We never meet at his grave. She has another life, other kids, and the man I was might as well have died in that morgue.

"I didn't jump straight into hunting. My wife and I split our debts as equitably as we could, because they were debts incurred for our son—for nothing, in the end. We sold our house. I lost my job. I drank too much. I was lost. I was nothing. I was dead."

His back raised through an extended sigh, like steam from an engine. He sounded neither sad nor angry still. There was no emotion in his voice or on his face.

"I found hunting when I interrupted another hunter by beating a cult demon to a useless pulp for no reason other than something to do. I wasn't even all that drunk, because it hadn't numbed me up as much as I'd wanted it to. Just made me angrier, meaner. Because I *was* angrier and meaner then. Maybe you wouldn't believe that."

Violet believed it. Spirits, for some, were a magnifying glass. She believed him well capable of worse with nothing to lose.

"I'd robbed him of his income, but he saw my potential. Cold showers and cold turkey woke my nerves, woke me to a world I hadn't wanted to acknowledge and its crueler underbelly. As soon as I started making some money by honing my anger into something more productive, I crawled to my feet, squinting at the sun and moon like a revenant. I didn't like the world I'd become a part of, but it was something to do, and turned out I was good at it." He shifted as she spiraled over the flat of his lower back, to harness his sexual energy as she had his heart energy and to link the spell through his spine. "Think you understand me now? Am I just misunderstood?"

"You're nothing special for what you lost. That doesn't mean what you lost wasn't special," she replied. "It makes sense of some things, but it doesn't explain or excuse the kind of hunter you became. That was already in you. It usually is. I was just curious."

"You think I need an excuse?"

"I think you've done things you're not proud of, and you justify them to yourself. Just maybe accept that these things came from you and not your tragic backstory."

"You could have stopped what I did," Abel said, angled too far away now for her to see what iron burned in his eyes like her magic behind hers.

"Yes, I could have. But letting you do it to me didn't challenge who *I* was."

"How do *you* justify it?"

"I don't justify it. It simply is what it is. You're not a sociopath. You keep your emotions tightly bound and you don't show them, but that doesn't mean you don't have them waiting inside you like landmines. You know exactly what your violence means, what its consequences are. You care, but you choose it anyway. Before, you were aimless, but you latched onto a profession that allows you to kill with impunity, no oversight or regulation. You're not out of control. You're a violent man, Abel, and you like it. You're the one judging yourself for it, and it'll help you not to cross the very last lines. But I'm not judging. One of the advantages, I suppose, of joining forces with a witch like me. Which was why I came to you and why you agreed to do it, too."

He twitched irritably as she made a small spiral over his right buttock. "Really?"

"I have to get to your thigh somehow. Otherwise tolerable?"

"I *have* done this before."

Violet finished off the rest of the tattoo in silence, and she suspected he dozed off soon after he stopped talking, either because he needed to ruminate or because he was simply done.

She wasn't here to be his conscience or provide him absolution. That was between him and his priest, if he had one. If he'd hoped to scare her off, he'd have to try harder. She'd been friendly with too many things that went bump in the night for a dangerous lay to frighten her back to her burrow.

She wiped off the excess blood and ink and rubbed her own antibiotic ointment into the spell lines. The narrow length of the spell made it difficult to cover, but she had enough plastic and gauze tape to protect the whole thing. He'd only have to wear it for half a day or so. The ointment included a milder healing potion to speed up the process. It was essential to offset her additives to the ink, which could cause additional irritation or infection without magical aid.

When she was finished, Violet hovered her hand over the spell to confirm that her power had infused it and seeped into his skin. The magic whispered to her in her own words.

As the ring around the moon,
Shield the soul of the man
And the skin he holds it in.
May roads lead where he seeks
And bones never crack on concrete.
Under the gazing eyes of stars,
Watch over the hunter,
Give him stealth and generous wealth,
And wherever he shoots his arrows,
Let him not become an easier target
Than what he pursues.
When seductive succubus song
Insinuates too sweetly,
Eradicate the poison of pleasure
With resistance rather than insistence,
To recognize lust that hides its lies.

She covered him with another blanket and let him sleep in the dentist chair, leaving a bottle of water near him for when he awoke. They both still needed to hydrate.

Violet returned to her own room, mildly surprised that she wasn't looking forward to an empty bed, but her sheets were cool and she was tired and even more achy from leaning over him for so long. Nevertheless, she struggled to fall asleep, not least because of the coffee that had gotten her through the spell and the confession.

She kept seeing Clive on that massive bed, bound with silk rather than silver handcuffs, begging for his cock's release but not his own, claw marks on his chest and abdomen in a pattern that reminded her of the scratches on his window frame. She hadn't seen any of the things they'd stolen, but she and Abel also hadn't been able to get closer than four stories up while breathing in their magic like steam.

She couldn't stop seeing Clive come. Had it been his twentieth time? His sixtieth? Had he been tortured, soft and delirious, or had he held his hands to the headboard while the succubi who'd seduced him in his own bed tied him down? When they surfaced to breathe, did they laugh at the witch whose trust they'd broken worse than anything Abel had done to her?

And when she and Abel returned, when Clive met her eyes for the first time after his betrayal, could she do what needed to be done?

Chapter Thirteen

Violet woke up around her usual time, but she didn't feel rested at all, which meant tea would have to be that morning's sponsor instead of coffee. She sighed, opened her eyes, then rolled out of bed when she couldn't figure out where the twisted covers started and she began. She was still in Abel's clothes, so she pulled them off and changed into her own.

Once she was finished in the bathroom, she found Abel in her living room, eating again. He'd redressed in the same clothes he'd left his motel room in the night before, ready to hunt. He'd already set out a water bottle for her to drink from, which she downed before she poured some black tea and lemonade together for a dark Arnold Palmer. Abel sneered with revulsion at the combination but didn't comment. She put some cinnamon-raisin bread into her toaster and pulled out some chunky peanut butter while Abel ate the eggs he'd cooked. She shook her head when he offered to make her some.

"How are the tattoos?" she finally asked, halfway through her toast.

"No complications. Have you decided what to do about the nest?"

"Visit again. Now we don't have to waste time trying to find it. We'll learn if they're always like that, and we'll learn whether the spell works to alleviate the effect of their magic. If it does, we can confront them."

"And by confront..." Abel slid his bowie knife halfway out of its sheath.

She shook her head.

He slid it back in.

"Not right away. Seriously, I just want my stuff back. If they give what they haven't used back and let Clive go, we don't have to do anything."

"What if they don't do what you want?"

"Then you can stab anything that gets between me and my things." She sipped her dark Arnold Palmer and winced. It didn't really go with peanut butter.

"And your boy and the other 'victims'?"

"Play that by ear. No grenades. I know it's disappointing, but even if they're there of their own free will, that doesn't mean we get to go blowing up people just to get the demons with them."

"We going?" He sounded anxious to be on their way, itching for a fight.

"After I finish my toast. Open-faced peanut butter doesn't travel well."

* * * *

They parked closer to the nest this time.

Somehow, knowing exactly what they were heading into made it worse, because she'd given Abel protection but not herself. How Violet had reacted to such intense succubus magic from a distance hadn't been insurmountable, but that had been when they hadn't known intruders were there. She didn't know if she could trust herself enough with stronger and more deliberate succubus magic, nor that she could trust Abel's tattoo spell when they hadn't tested it first.

If it were just a matter of the succubi, they'd have all the time in the world, but the sex demons were slowly draining the men they kept, and Violet wasn't entirely sure that was their intention. Sperm donors for succubi probably weren't in short supply, and men were far from a necessity after that point when it came to pregnancy or child-rearing, but a spiritual commitment to fertility suggested a desire for a certain level of permanence, and the bindings had been silk, the men otherwise unharmed.

If succubi had been working Clive for as long as Violet suspected, they'd either done so to guarantee access to the store or they were truly interested in keeping their men for a longer haul. There wasn't really a *point* for succubi to build a long-term relationship — however illusory — with a man just to kill him.

No, regardless of Abel's opinion on the matter, Violet didn't think there was malice in what the succubi were doing. That didn't mean people hadn't and wouldn't get hurt.

Part of her just wanted to turn around and go home. She didn't have insurance, but she'd survive, even with what she'd promised to pay Abel. She'd started over with nothing before.

Clive had known what he was doing, influenced or not. They couldn't *make* him break the wards. They couldn't get into his dreams to trick him into doing it, because the wards prevented that. They could entice him with beauty, seduce him with pleasure, but he'd still had to accept it. Pleasure was a lure, but it wasn't necessarily a hook.

What Violet couldn't stop thinking about was that Abel, too, had been overwhelmed with succubus pleasure, and he had turned to *her*.

Clive had had so many moments to say no, to go to Violet for the pleasure inspired instead, but he'd chosen a small harem of succubi slowly sucking him dry, leaving her with a store of broken glass. She prayed that they'd held some kind of blackmail or other intimidation over his head, threatened to hurt her if he didn't do what they wanted. But she couldn't assume that was the only reason why Clive was there.

"Already their magic feels different," Abel said from where they stood outside the white-brick building, out of view of the windows. "Like noon in early spring instead of noon midsummer. Good spell-work."

He was so stingy with praise or positive comment of any kind that the compliment warmed her more than the late morning sun, more than the succubus magic that she, too, could feel, although of course it hit her no differently than before.

Until they rounded the building toward the side door and magic hit her like a brick torn from the wall and planted between her eyes.

She staggered. Abel caught her before she could scrape her knees on the concrete. She already knew what she'd see when she stood again.

The succubus nest had upgraded its guardian from a pestilence demon to an incubus. Which meant they'd already guessed that a human woman had been there. Maybe one or two members of the nest had come up for air long enough to hear that Violet was looking for them and taking names along the way.

The incubus perched on the stair railing leading from the door. He was shirtless, his wings on full display. Even from twenty feet away, she wanted to lick from his treasure trail all the way up to his trimmed goatee, imagined rubbing her body all over him. Some of that reaction was his magic, which he'd throttled up to ten, but sex demons were also just that pretty.

The incubus slid down the railing in a way that made her whimper.

Abel's expression was somewhere between highly amused and concerned, as though she was delirious on anesthesia.

"So you're the little witch causing such big trouble," the incubus said. "Suffice it to say, you're not allowed in. Even with a hunter at your side, you're not going to get very far. Hunters depend on the element of surprise. Both of you left a pheromone trail as intense as cologne yesterday. Especially you, brother." The incubus turned his attention to Abel. "To be fair, there are lots of pretty ladies in there. I'm impressed you managed to leave at all."

"I don't know who you are to these women, good friends or they just pulled you in off the street," Violet managed to say, proud she could even compose a coherent sentence. "I don't know if you know who I am —"

"You're that witch on the square with the fun smooth stones. I have a whole collection of those in my nest. They're nice to hold in your hand."

"Then you know I'm off limits. My shop, me, and my employee are off limits. Your friends — or these total strangers — they seduced my employee, which was bad enough, but then they stole him and stole from my store in the process. They broke good faith. I am the consequence. Now, if I were you, I'd let me through. I've been dying to use my sneeze bomb."

She pulled the vial out of her satchel. The incubus looked like he'd break into hysterical laughter any moment.

"What's the most you've ever sneezed at once?" Violet asked.

"Thirty-six times. I think I had pepper in my nose. Why?"

"Thirty-six sneezes take, what? Three to five minutes? Now imagine what it's like if you can't stop for three hours. We'll see how sexy even an incubus can be with snot dripping out of his nose in ribbons and tears gumming up his eyes."

The incubus's grin slowly faded. "I could still send out my magic. You'd be the one wanting to fuck me like that."

"You won't be able to think about anything but sneezing. It kind of takes over your whole consciousness, doesn't it? Then the hunter here can decide if he wants to kill you while you're down or just point and laugh."

The incubus spread his wings, his cock pressing against his tighter pants. "I think I'm going to have fun with you. You're inventive."

He ratcheted up the intensity of his magic even higher, weakening her knees again and startling a moan from her, but even as she hit the ground at a kneel, she opened the bomb and, through the shudder of an almost-orgasm, sent the powder swirling out of the glass toward him.

He wrenched back like he'd stepped on a wasp nest, but the powder invaded his mouth and nostrils no matter how he turned his head or batted at it.

Within seconds, he faltered, jerking, face contorting in new and exciting ways. The gale-force strength of his incubus magic faded to background noise as he worked up to a sneeze. Then another. Then another.

"Oh, you bitch," he managed between his eleventh and twelfth sneeze.

"Can't say I don't warn 'em," she muttered.

At the incubus's twentieth sneeze, Abel did laugh, more than just the single harsh cough of surprise but a sustained bark of genuine schadenfreude delight.

With each successive sneeze and the tears in his eyes messing with his vision, the incubus gradually replaced Violet on the alley ground, bracing his hands on the concrete with each convulsion—the perfect position to be slaughtered.

After the hunter stopped laughing, he contemplated the incubus with narrowed eyes. Then he took out a small switchblade and stuck him straight in his carotid. The demon would bleed out in less than a minute while still sneezing.

"Last thing we need is someone coming at us from behind because we assumed we were safe," Abel explained.

Once in the dark office part of the building, where the succubus magic was stronger, she turned back to Abel. He nodded that he could still endure it, and they found the stairwell again.

There was still no one in the fourth-floor break room, although things had been moved. There were several boxes of store-brand cookies on the tables, and plates were soaking in the sink, so there was some feeding going on in the traditional way — hopefully for the men, too.

Violet and Abel were able to crawl to the railing uninterrupted. She checked with him again. He nodded and didn't feel the spontaneous need to mount her, so she peered over into the collective bed. She had to press her thighs together, but her reaction was also otherwise manageable, even after the incubus. The only difference so far this time was that she might not have minded if Abel had decided to climb over her.

Very little in the orgy below had changed. The succubi still writhed and rode slow, like a dream, but even they looked tired. Some appeared to be sleeping even as they mounted thighs and mouthed over lightly sweating skin.

Just half a day later, though, the men appeared more than exhausted, the bags under their eyes like bruises, some areas of their bodies macerated from too much moisture, which didn't seem to be a problem on the succubi. The men's skin was loose, slipping for reasons other than age. Clive appeared to have lost more weight, so even if the succubi had given the men a chance to eat, it wasn't enough to counteract the literal consumptive effect of constant feeding.

Violet couldn't stand to see him like that. Amid the low simmer of succubus magic working its will inside her, she was more distracted by distress — a literal pang in her chest of fear and urgency to *stop* what was destroying him, whether that destruction was intentional or not.

"Cover me," she whispered under Abel's hood. "With guns."

She crawled away from the railing so she wouldn't call attention to Abel, who didn't need the extra force of succubus magic. Then she stood, brushed dust from her skirt, and started down the stairs, no longer hiding.

"Hello, ladies."

Descending a spiral staircase down four flights of stairs took longer than she would have liked, but it gave the succubi time to climb off each other and the men and for Violet to assess their feelings about her. Their magic ramped to another level, but not as intense as the single incubus emanating at her with everything he had, so even if they considered her a threat, it wasn't a considerable one. Safety, however, in numbers.

Two of the three succubi who crawled off the bed were immediately recognizable by their energy and their long, long hair — the blonde woman who looked like a wind-swept Midwestern Venus and the black-haired Desi woman. The third was a bottle redhead — there was no person in the world whose ginger hair was that flame-vivid without chemical help. It had been cropped short and spiky and made wilder by grasping hands pulling.

The redhead was familiar by the remnants of her magic in Book & Candle but also because she'd been in the store before, although nothing immediately stood out in Violet's memory. She was more naked than the other two, who could at least partially cover themselves with their hair. Nudity in itself was certainly not vulnerability for a succubus, but neither did it seem to be overt threat so much as her own version of armor.

"Hello, Violet." The redhead took a position in front of the other two succubi who'd put themselves between Violet and Clive, but there was no animosity in the redhead's expression or stance. Clive strained in his binding to look over his shoulder, eyes wide — seeming wider still because his face was so sunken.

"We knew you came here yesterday. You think we, of all people, can't smell a virile man with all his strength still in him?" the redhead said. "Considering you left without confrontation, we thought you would be smart enough not to return."

"I'm not here for a massacre."

"Could have fooled me."

Violet was almost to the ground floor now. Her legs were a little shaky, and the demons were increasingly wary, but she kept her pace, despite her clit practically begging her to stroke it to ease the heavier and heavier ache.

"May I ask your name?" Violet said.

"Hilary."

"None of them had to die, Hilary," Violet replied. "The only reason — and I cannot stress this enough — the *only* reason they died was because they got in my way to retrieve what is *mine*. You and your girls are why they're dead. You firebombed a demilitarized zone, ensuring that I couldn't stay neutral. Not wanting to fight doesn't mean I won't. You did what more powerful demons wouldn't, and that was your mistake, not mine."

"We didn't exactly plan to shoot first," Hilary said. "But we won't just sit back and let you take what's ours now."

Violet raised her eyebrows. "You think it's yours because you took it while I slept? It was never yours. You don't have the first idea how to use what you have, or even whether you can."

At that, Hilary finally looked uncomfortable. "What makes you think —"

"Because the men you're using are wasting away. Or was that part of the plan? Really, you can tell me. Was the whole point to just milk them as long as you could before picking up new models and throwing out the old?"

"Don't be ridiculous." Clive's voice was charred from dehydration, but the irritation was plain. "Does it look like they're trying to kill us?"

"Yes! And if you had a mirror over your bed like a proper succubus nest, you'd see how well you aren't."

Hilary tried not to smile at the mirror comment, but she looked over her shoulder at Clive, worry unmistakable in the set of her eyebrows.

"You're concerned, too," Violet said, slowly removing her hand from the satchel. "May I go to him?"

Hilary shared a look with the other two succubi, then the others who had stopped as well, leaving their bed sparse and their men uncovered by a blanket of women and straining against their bindings because of it.

But Clive slipped right out of his. "I thought leaving was the hint, Vi."

"Leaving would have been a hint if that had been all you'd done." She couldn't conceal the quaver to her reply and hated herself because of it. "Can I come see you for a minute?"

"Yeah. Yeah, sure. Okay."

Which told her he was concerned about his health, too, and that he had most of his wits, despite the continued, alarming rigidity of his cock. He wasn't resisting the succubus magic, but he also wasn't taken over by it, a wordless mass of nerves who couldn't think, much less fight.

The other men slipped from their bindings just as easily.

Shit.

If the men weren't actually bound, if they could leave at any time and the silk was just to hold them in place for everyone's enjoyment, that took the captive theory off the table. They could still be influenced by succubus magic, but they certainly weren't trapped. Just the absence of human waste indicated that they could get up to use the bathroom whenever they pleased. They could get far enough to come to their senses instead of coming themselves sick. But all four of them had made their choice, and it wasn't walking out on a bunch of hot women fucking them senseless.

The succubi reluctantly allowed Violet to pass.

She grimaced at the bed, which didn't have human waste but had plenty of biologicals all over it, and she didn't know how stringent these people were about changing their sheets every few rounds when they were just going to make everything filthy again, fornicating even in their sleep.

Violet sat on the less soaked edge next to the headboard propping Clive upright. She was almost prim, with her legs together under her skirt, staring at her naked lover, boyfriend, best friend, employee — sometimes all these things, sometimes one at a time. They'd never really discussed it beyond employee contract and emergency contact numbers, but maybe they should have discussed it, or discussed *something*.

He clenched his jaw, accentuating how hollow his cheeks and sockets had become, but although he jutted his chin, he didn't seem angry so much as upset. He stared up at the skylights instead of meeting her gaze.

"Clive, look at me. The least you can do is look at me."

He rolled his eyes, but he looked down, first at the bed, then at her.

"What is this?" Violet said. "You need to actually talk to me now, not just get all silent and distant and have your sex demons steal shit for you. Because I have curse bombs, and you know I'm not afraid to use them."

"What was I supposed to do?" Clive snapped.

"Oh, I don't know, told me that you wanted to leave, then taken *your* crap and left like a normal person?"

"And you would have just let me go? Really? And when I came to you for spells for *us*, you would have just given me what I wanted?"

"Yes, you asshole! I'm a witch, and I'm occasionally wicked, but I didn't freak out when you saw other women, did I? I knew you were with someone else these last few months and didn't say anything. I knew you were growing more distant, but I didn't cling harder. What made you think I was going to put you in my goddamn oven if you left me?"

"Because I know what you make when the store is closed," he replied, "and you just said I know you're not afraid to use them. Because I make the weapons, but you know where they all are and how to wield them, too. Because I know the kind of people you associate with. Because if you knew what I was leaving to do, I knew you'd do exactly what you're doing now."

"I've been doing this because I thought you were *kidnapped*, you son of a bitch. I figured out succubi had been visiting, and I thought they'd ensnared you, ensorcelled you into breaking the wards and letting them in, then stole you away with my things. My grimoires, Clive. You *let* them take my grandmother's Book of Shadows?"

Clive had the slightest decency to finally look ashamed. "We didn't know if what we needed would be in the books. We thought the grimoires would help, since they're more experimental than anything in print."

"You could have just asked. You've been my best friend for nearly ten years, and you'd thought I'd be jealous because I lost someone I sometimes slept with, someone with whom I thought I had good chemistry? We were friends first, and I'm here now not as a jealous lover but a very fucking pissed-off friend," she said through clenched teeth. She tried not to cry, but arousal had a funny way of whittling down that particular dam, too. "And as a friend, look what you've done to yourself. You've been gone only a few days, and you've lost about thirty pounds, only ten of which you could afford to lose."

"We're fine," Clive said.

Violet dug through her satchel until she found her compact mirror. She opened it and held it in front of his face. "Tell me you're fine one more time."

Clive squinted, as though he couldn't recognize the reflection.

"Now, I'm asking you again, what the hell was all this about?" she said. "And don't anyone dare lie to me."

Hilary tentatively stepped forward. "We're not trying to hurt them."

Violet held up a finger to stop her from getting any closer. She didn't want to be blocked into the bed. "Was all of this because you want to be mothers?" she asked, more gently than she felt her expression was giving. She was still so furious that her magic burned behind her eyes, only bolstered by the same distracting arousal the incubus had started and the succubi continued.

Hilary and the other two succubi behind her retreated slightly in surprise. "Yes," Hilary replied.

"Succubi can't have children," Violet said.

Clive snapped the mirror closed and shoved it back at her. "Why do you think we turned to magic?"

"What are you mad at *me* for? *I* wasn't an absolute prick. What did you tell them about me? Did you tell them I was a nightmare, that I cling too tightly, that I'd never let you be happy together? That I had my whole life planned with you penned into it with permanent ink? That I'd lose my shit and attack everybody until I had my plaything back?"

The way the three succubi who hovered over him glanced down and fidgeted with their fingers suggested she wasn't too far off the mark. Violet's throat seemed to swell too much to swallow. For a moment, she couldn't see for the swimming blind rage threatening to latch onto her still-welling magic and do some real damage—like a laser instead of a bomb.

"When did this happen? When did I become your villain? I knew you were distant. I knew you were drifting. I didn't know you hated me. Hated me so much that you made me evil to justify what you were doing to me. Was I wrong from the start?"

Clive wouldn't look at her again. "It's been bad for a while, Vi."

"How long is a while? I've been aware of something wrong for about six months. Maybe a year."

"Try three."

Violet abruptly stood, her hand flying just short of her mouth. "Three y— You mean a whole third of all the time we've been together, you thought I'd imprisoned you in…what? Some business transaction? Sex for money, room, board, and your life? Clive, you entered into our situationship of your own free will, the only contract signed a boilerplate employee agreement as easy to tear as the paper it was printed on. You were more than welcome to leave it at any time."

Violet looked around her at all the stunningly pretty young women, some probably not as young as they looked. They stared back with wide innocent eyes, most probably not nearly as innocent as they looked. But although she knew succubi to be thieves and dream-feeders, she sensed no outright malice — only chagrin and secondhand embarrassment.

Being judged pitiful by a crowd of prom queens was doing nothing for her self-esteem that wasn't usually so crumbly.

"I'm sorry, everyone. I'm sorry this happened. I'm sorry about the ones who died. If he'd just walked out, I would have had an ice cream and horror movie marathon like a normal person. And if you'd asked me to help you figure out how to have children beyond those fertility symbols spraypainted outside, I would have helped. I believe you when you say you don't want to hurt these men. Maybe you even like them? Or love them?"

She passed her gaze over the whole succubi crowd. They all nodded or shrugged. So some were ambivalent and just wanted to be mothers, but most, like Clive's succubi, genuinely appeared to care.

"Yes, Vi. I love them. Okay?" Clive said. "I love them. I love the way they make me feel. I love the sex. I love the passion. I love the excitement. I love the dreams. And I want to give them children. I was willing to steal from you to do it. Are you satisfied?"

Violet raised a hand. Red ribbon appeared out of nowhere — technically, from her accessory drawer — and sewed itself into his mouth before tying itself off with a pretty bow. "If you could keep silent for three years after you tired of me and found my company so utterly inadequate, you can stay quiet a little longer. And because I really, really, *really* want to smash your face into one of these headboard posts, I suggest you sit there and think about the lies you told to the people you love and to yourself. In the meantime, me and the grownups are going to talk."

She firmly turned away from Clive and faced Hilary, who seemed happy to speak for everyone. The nest had probably even been her idea.

"There's nothing in my grimoire that can help," Violet said, "and there's nothing in my grandmother's grimoire about how to create fertility from nothing."

"But we have periods. Most of us start late, well after puberty does...*this* to us." She gestured to her body with a light flush to her pale cheeks, as though she just realized she was naked and how much Violet wasn't. "But we do have human-like cycles. And we wouldn't have cycles if we didn't have eggs."

"You're immortal," Violet replied. "There's almost always a check on immortal fertility."

"It makes no sense that the check is on us but not the incubi," Hilary said. "They're just as horny. They have just as much sex. But they don't have to raise the child. They just plant their seed and leave. Having something else we need to take care of would be a win for us and for you, if you think about it."

"For the amount of sex they have, even incubi aren't exceptionally fertile, though. They might father one or two children in a human lifetime."

"That's the point of this." Hilary waved to the bed and all the other women. "Maybe we're not actually infertile. Maybe it's that our window is so narrow. There have been stories of children born to succubi. Just not many, like vampire children. And we're not even undead. There's no reason in the world why we can't have children, under the right circumstances."

"Okay." Violet crossed her arms—not defensively but to hold herself in while she considered the problems and solutions without knowing enough about sex demon biology to make definitive statements on reproductive realities.

Hilary made some excellent points based on basic knowledge, but the only ones getting familiar with sex demons' insides were hunters. Cryptozoologists were too distracted by Sasquatch to look in a demonic direction, and the bodies hunters left behind were either broken apart or taken by pestilence demons to dispose of. She supposed a coroner or two might know something about their anatomy. She could always talk to her morgue contact to see if she could do some proper dissections to study how succubus bodies differed from human. Hilary probably wouldn't donate anyone's body to science, so they'd have to wait for subjects to drop into their lap or pay a hunter for an unblemished specimen. She wasn't sure how Hilary would feel about Violet using hunted bodies, but if they were already dead…

It was really difficult to think objectively while surrounded by naked women who seduced by their very nature—not to mention with her ex-lover behind her back, where he'd stabbed her.

"If it's okay with you," Violet said slowly, "we can talk further about this, just you and me, or maybe a few of you at a time. I'd like to help. I don't know if you want me to or if you'll like how, but it'll be better than you trying to figure out what to do with what you stole. If you throw the wrong ingredients together, you'll only make things worse. You could accidentally summon a wholly unsympathetic demon. Or you could just end up with a weird-smelling mess."

She looked around at all the women. The magic directed at her had already gone down, and she thought she saw... Was it hope? Then she made herself look at the men, although she deliberately avoided putting Clive in her field of vision.

"But if you care about these men, you've got to stop this," she said. "Because even if you don't want to, you're still killing them."

"What difference does it make to you?" Clive asked through the half of his mouth that he'd managed to untie. "You're talking about 'helping' them and our 'safety', but you're the one who brought that old wolf of a hunter into the den."

"He's covering me. That's all. I didn't know what I was walking into," Violet said. "And a good thing, too, because if I'd gone looking to save you alone, I would have died at least twice. But I guess I'm such an awful person that you don't even care about that."

"But now he knows where we are!" Clive shot back.

"We can't let the hunter live," Hilary said. "Maybe he can't take us all out at once, but he can take us one by one or two by two, and if he has other hunters he can work with, all he has to do is call them in."

The other succubi seemed to agree, because the hum of arousal over and under her skin intensified once more. Gazes lifted from her to the fourth floor, to the shadow hovering over the railing and the black glint of metal from the guns she'd told him to use instead of his knives, to minimize close combat.

"And one of the first things I was going to suggest was leaving this particular nest," Violet said. "True, he's now the only woman-oriented hunter who can enter this place without completely losing his head — again, something I wouldn't have had to do if your lover had just broken up with me like a normal person. And true, although he doesn't hunt demons who aren't actively hunting, I did lead the wolf right to the coyote den. But if he were there or not, it's still in your best interest to leave. Girls, I swear to the devil and baby Jesus that if you fly up and try to take him, I'll rip your wings off myself," she snapped at several succubi who had shaken out their feathers and looked like they were going to launch. "The condition of him working with me was that he'd help me find you and protect me in the process. But what he does with y'all is up to *me*."

"For now," Hilary said grimly.

"He could say the same of you, and there are a lot more of you than there are of him. You don't touch him, he doesn't hurt you, at least while he's in my employ. The grievance here is between you and me." Violet touched Hilary's cheek to turn it toward her, away from Abel — a different kind of distraction.

For a moment, her breathing quickening and shallow, Violet wasn't sure whether she'd be able to break direct contact. Hilary felt it, too, her mild blue eyes deepening, brighter against her flaming hair. She stroked along Violet's forearm, using her nails rather than claws.

With a deep breath, Violet deliberately stepped back.

"His employment will soon be over," she said. "What you do with each other then will be up to you, although I'd recommend you each avoid the other, because I can't honestly tell which side would do the most damage, and that's not particularly conducive to procreation. If you're devoted to having children, set your sights on that. This kind of building might be good for a cult, but it's not going to work for so many succubi, and I think you've begun to realize that. Clive lost twenty to thirty pounds in three days. It's a unique weight-loss spa idea, but it's not sustainable long-term."

The succubi around the bed slowly crept closer. A few of them kept their wings, but Violet couldn't see any sharp teeth or claws, and really, they looked more curious than cautious now. Maybe because she was taking their concerns seriously, and because she was saying things they'd already been thinking but hadn't been able to rub two brain cells together to reach a solution any more than the men.

"You need to split up, either different rooms or different buildings entirely. Even if you're all into sharing each other's men to increase the likelihood of implantation, you need to do it in shifts. There needs to be few enough of you that you come up for air. No one's sleeping enough, and for an Olympic-level orgy, there are not nearly enough plates in the sink for how much you all need to be eating to keep up. All of you here together will wear them into cardiac arrest, and the rest of you aren't looking so great health-wise. I'm talking Michael Phelps's swim-training meal regimen, three or four refrigerators' worth of accessible food. And *everyone* needs sleep — a solid eight hours. Which means *separate* beds or bedrooms from the men so they don't feel compelled to crawl between your thighs instead of between sheets."

"Sounds reasonable to me." Hilary checked with the blonde and black-haired succubi. They were nodding, too.

"If you haven't already, then you need to decide if, once one or more of you are pregnant, these men you like or love are going to act as fathers or if they're just for stud. Because if you want fathers, y'all need to start talking more than fucking so you know more than that his ex is a bitch. For instance, does he want your child christened, for whatever reason? Does he want to bring you home to Mother? Private or public school? I'm not saying you didn't think things through, but right now, I'm not sure how much thinking is going on, much less talking, and children need more than parents with good chemistry in the bedroom."

"How would you know?" Clive asked. To be fair, his mouth was still bleeding and probably stung like hell, but to be fairer, he knew how sensitive she was to the fact that children didn't seem to be in her cards, albeit by ambivalent choice.

"Witches don't spring from the foreheads of their fathers," she said. "I had parents and aunties and uncles and grandparents. I got to see the good and bad firsthand. And I may not have known what was going on between us, but I think we can both agree that *not* talking contributed to the problem. You never lied to me, but you haven't been telling me the truth. By the time I realized something was off, I just hoped it would get better on its own, and now... Now I don't even recognize you, and it's not because of the weight loss and the fact you're covered in goo. I'm so fucking angry at you right now, so don't you dare get up, don't you *dare*..."

Clive climbed out of bed, although he was still hard as a post from proximity and shaking from hunger he clearly didn't even know he felt. "You somehow manage to get your hands into everything, don't you? I burn the bridges behind me, and you just float over and insinuate yourself into the lives of my lovers. I can't even cheat on you without your two cents on how they can use me better."

"If you wanted to be rid of me, you should have left Meridian, because I'm part of its tapestry. You stole *my magic* to experiment and thought I wouldn't follow you. Even if I hadn't found you, *I* would have been the reason why your women had your children, if they hadn't fucking killed you first. So you're fucking welcome, Clive."

"Yes, thank you. Thank you so much for luring me in with the novelty of magic, then becoming just like everyone else, but with a spice rack instead of a cubicle—same thing every damn day. As though because you have a little magic, that made you exciting."

"Oh my God, Clive, you could have *left*! At any time. You didn't even have to put in two weeks' notice."

"If I could have just left, what are you doing here?"

"Have you been listening with your dick? Making sure you weren't taken against your will. Making sure you're not dead or dying. Since you *are* dying, you're welcome again! I'm sorry a life of business and neutrality wasn't the bacchanal you thought it was going to be, but all you ever needed to say was 'it's over'. You never had any trouble telling me you needed to take a break or you wanted to go out with another girl for a while. It wasn't as though I locked you into your bedroom at night. I don't know how you managed to convince yourself that boring little me was keeping you in a dungeon when you were fucking three succubi in your very own room with wards that you broke all by your damn self for months, but now you know that's not true. You don't ever have to deal with me again. And since I'm taking back what y'all stole from me, you won't have to deal with the taint of my magic either. I'll leave a few things behind," Violet added to Hilary, "things you can actually use. If you still want me to help with anything else, you need to compensate me like everyone else in this city. Understood?"

"No. You can take your grimoires. We've already gone through them anyway," Clive said. "Consider the rest hazard pay."

"I *paid* you, you bastard," Violet snapped. "You had an hourly salary, and you didn't even have to pay a full half of the rent, while I leased both the store and the apartment. I paid you in money, spells, flexibility…"

Clive scoffed.

"Relationship flexibility," she amended, although once again, he'd found the sore spot and dug his thumb in. Most of the time she was so confident in herself as a witch, as a woman, but it was hard to compare against succubi. That was just a fundamental, biological fact. "Anything I leave is a gift, not compensation. Where are my things?" she asked Hilary.

Hilary pointed at the smaller first-floor break room — just two tables, a microwave, and a small fridge in comparison to the full-service kitchen above.

Violet beckoned Abel to come down.

He holstered one gun but kept the other trained on the nest as he descended the spiral stairs.

"How is he doing that?" Hilary swayed toward him with curiosity that edged on the carnal, the cant of her hips almost invitation. "I can feel him, and he's reacting, but he should be—"

"Incoherent? Humping everything that moves? Yeah, we couldn't come back until I fixed that," Violet said. "Anyway, it's been real swell, but we're going to get my things, and you can go back to having fun trying to get pregnant. And you can keep my ex, if you still want him—if you think he won't frame you as a pile of harpies as soon as he gets bored."

Hilary shrugged. "Boredom doesn't really happen with us. And most people remember their exes poorly. You started well, I assume."

"You'd think that would earn a woman some courtesy—the good years, the wild, magical years, the experimental years. I'm not immortal like you, you know. How the fuck am I supposed to compete?"

Hilary slowly brought her hand back to Violet's arm, gauging whether Violet would allow it. Violet's inhale was shaky, but she managed to keep some composure as her skin heated, and as that heat dripped down to pool between her legs.

"You're not," Hilary said gently. "That's the point of us. But just because they were good years doesn't mean they were the best. Trust me. I'm older than I look."

"And you still like him?" Violet asked.

"Goddamn it..." Clive advanced, clenching his hand into a fist.

She wasn't afraid he would hit her—the fist was his left, and he was right-handed—but she raised her hand toward him, because she could use magic with both of hers.

Hilary spread her wings.

Violet didn't know why she expected them to be just as flaming as her hair, since feathers didn't always match the curtains or drapes, but the pitch black was stunning nevertheless—the absolute blackout of fainting or suffocation.

The succubus pushed Clive back with her wings and blocked his sight of Violet in the process.

Violet bit her lip and swallowed back a sigh as Hilary's magic pulsed out to send Clive reeling onto the bed, clutching his cock like a handhold, while Violet still had skin contact with her.

"There are some things I like," Hilary said. "Probably the same things that attracted him to you and you to him in the beginning. As for the errors in his judgment and perception, well…he's young."

"Only a little younger than me."

"You're young, too. He has so many things to learn and a predilection for the supernatural. And yes, I'd like to keep him around for a good long while, for reasons both obvious and less so."

"You realize I can't leave the theft unpunished," Violet said, although Hilary had somehow drawn her close enough to cup her elbow instead of holding her wrist.

"You do what you have to do." Hilary pressed her lips to the corner of Violet's mouth. "I can't say we're too upset about it, but I understand how you might be."

"No, this isn't about my feelings. And this isn't about breaking the law, which I understand you don't care about. You broke the unwritten rule. Of the three dozen succubi here, not to mention Clive, someone should have made it clear that Book & Candle is to remain untouched. If I were more vengeful and didn't care about motive, I could technically kill everyone here, and no one would be allowed to reciprocate."

"How would you kill all of us?" Hilary asked. "I mean, I'm sure you're capable of killing a few. But that's one of the benefits to so many of us in one place — too many to kill quickly before we overwhelm them."

"Why does everyone underestimate me just because I don't walk into the room with a flamethrower? You dug through a witch's magic shop, and you think I can't simply immolate all of you with a delayed incendiary charm?"

Violet forced herself to step back again, although under Hilary's influence, those beds looked awfully inviting and her shirt seemed too tight and her skirt too long and, really, why did anyone who dealt with sex demons in any capacity bother with underwear when they were so uncomfortably damp so quickly?

To her credit, Hilary seemed to view her in a slightly different light the more steps back Violet took. She didn't show fear so much as possibly the respect that Clive had long since lost.

"I'm already pissed off enough that blood was shed because my ex-boyfriend didn't have the balls to speak up," Violet said. "I have no interest in killing anyone else, so if you could just give the hunter room, darlings, and not threaten him, we can avoid bullets. I wouldn't bet against him if he feels like his life is in imminent danger."

Hilary quickly waved the other women back. Some succubi climbed on the bed with their men. Others increased the intensity of their magic, searching for Abel's weakness, but he didn't so much as stumble as he backed toward the smaller breakroom.

"Excuse me." Violet gave a slight bow, then followed Abel into the breakroom.

"Do you know what you're doing?" he asked.

"Not in the slightest. Still holding up?"

He nodded. "You could sell this spell for a fortune."

"I gave you this spell strictly for your service to me. You may see my reluctance to mass-produce it as a matter of morals — or my lack of them — but really, it's a matter of escalation. I start helping sex demon hunters resist their demons, the demons start employing me to break my own spells. I already make money off of this war. There's no need to make it worse — the spiritual version of antibiotic-resistant infection."

"Fair enough." Just two words, but an unexpected concession. "What do you want to take here?"

Violet collected her grimoires before anything else. There were boxes on the edges of the room, which is how they must have transported what they'd stolen. It was too much for the two of them to carry and for Abel to protect himself at the same time. So, a box apiece, if that.

Some of it had already been used to adorn altars set up on three sides of the beds — including some of her more expensive and dangerous pieces — for the purposes of improving their unconventional fertility. It also looked like the succubi had stolen most of her sex demon inventory just because they took that personally, which was understandable. The wings were too big for her to prioritize, but *all* the severed anatomy was too expensive for her to just leave on principle. She left most of what they'd taken from main store itself and packed instead as many things from the storeroom as she could fit into two moving boxes.

It wouldn't make her whole or recoup her losses, but it would make them less painful — where the theft was concerned, anyway. And the grimoires were the only things she couldn't stand to lose.

She took a box and the grimoires. Abel left first, gun up, the second box hooked against his hip. Before Violet left through the first-floor hallway, she set the box and books down and opened her satchel.

"Let me just say that this punishment isn't personal, and you *will* live through it — even if, at some points, you won't want to. Please, tell your friends, so they don't think they can do what you did without consequence. And if you still want to after this, Hilary, do call me if you need help with those fertility issues."

"Oh shit." Clive vaulted awkwardly from the bed, still erect as hell, and started for the other hallway off the breakroom.

Violet opened the first bomb and sent the powder in his direction. Immediately, he let loose an explosive sneeze — the kind that always used to drive her bonkers during cold season, because they'd make her jump if she didn't know they were about to happen. The succubi around him also sniffled and contorted their faces to fight the sneezes that the powder triggered.

"You've got to be kidding me," Hilary muttered. She retreated, preparing her wings for flight like some of the others who hadn't yet breathed in the bomb. But the movement of their wings spread it around faster, and Violet was the only one who could create a shield against the powder to protect herself and Abel behind her.

Violet pulled out the second bomb. "This one manufactures a third nostril, so you'll have a faucet of mucus from a new and exciting place. It's temporary. I'm sure that's small consolation."

She popped it open and sent the powder out into the room.

"And this one is my favorite. It's like a skunk bomb, but congratulations, the only ones that can smell it are flies, and what they smell will be utterly irresistible. Which seems appropriate. For the next day or two, you'll experience your own personal plague. At the very least, you might get a break from fucking."

She sent all the powders into a whirlwind to catch the demons before they could fly out through the walls or ceiling.

"If anyone attempts to retaliate against my retaliation, I won't resort to mere prank-store curses. All of you are incredibly useful to me dead. So don't be foolish, darlings, and don't *ever* steal from me again. But you can keep the man. I'll leave his things out in the alley."

Violet stayed long enough to get the singular bitter joy of watching her ex-lover sneezing strings of mucus onto his pretty lovers, getting it caught in their hair, while they, too, sneezed over and over again, with barely enough time to breathe before the next— certainly not enough time to wipe their eyes or noses or turn away from each other. In such a large nest of succubi, these potion bombs wouldn't diminish their sexual power, but they'd probably have a difficult time feeding for a while, and once the sneezing stopped, Clive was guaranteed a mouthful of flies every time he ate for a few days.

She kind of felt sorry for them, but they weren't her problem anymore. Maybe they'd think better of choosing Clive. Maybe he'd grow as a person. Maybe the shared trauma would bond them even closer and they'd all continue to call her a bitch behind her back.

Whatever the outcome, she was done, and she needed to leave before the flies arrived en masse. Really, if she'd been particularly malicious, she would have just sent out the itching powder and called it a day.

Chapter Fourteen

Abel continued to keep his gun trained toward the building, although they were well out of sight. As long as they could hear sneezing, he stayed on guard.

"Why *do* you only seem to have prank-store curses in that bag of yours?"

"I have more malevolent curses, both potion and spoken," she replied, "but no one's earned them from me yet. People tend to be their own curse, and life is hard enough without me making things more difficult."

"And when others ask for them?"

"I don't sell the really bad ones. The inconvenient ones are more in keeping with rage that tends to cool. Less to regret once they feel better. If someone really wants to put a dangerous or debilitating curse on someone, they'll find someone who'll help them or a book with what they're looking for. But they won't get it from me, and if they get it from one of my books, they have to work for it. The work usually takes too long, takes too much effort, or takes too much money, but if they commit to the violence, they also deal with the price. The same could be said for a gun. I can't change people. I sell rocks, candles, and incense more than anything else."

"But you're capable of more."

"Of course I'm capable of more. What do you think I use the demon parts for when I don't sell them?"

"You realize you just offered to help sex demons double their population, right?"

"There's not exactly going to be a population boom, Abel. Meridian only has a disproportionate number of demons because this place calls to them. The best way to avoid succubi is to simply not live in a hotspot. You could try Galveston."

"You're funny," he said dryly.

They stored the boxes in the truck bed, but Violet carried her grimoires with her to the front. He didn't throw her the keys. Although she suspected he did have an erection—more difficult to be sure when he wasn't jamming it against her ass—he was in control of himself enough to drive, and that suited her just fine.

She was still reexamining every interaction she'd ever had with Clive, viewing it through the lens of his irritation, hatred, even fear of her, trying to determine if it had ever been good or if she'd misinterpreted everything. Over eight whole years became ugly in an instant. The veininess of her hands, the way skin gathered at the knuckles of her fingers, the slighter scars and tattoos on her arms—touched by a succubus and still singing with the contact—seemed just as ugly to her as her memories. And that was...new.

She hugged her grandmother's Book of Shadows against her chest as she stared out of the passenger-side window. She didn't understand how he could have gotten so tangled in her life if he hadn't wanted to be, didn't know if she was the one who'd tangled him in there, couldn't say whether or not she was actually the monster in all this. Clive wasn't the only one who thought she was. The hunter driving her home thought the same thing. In a city full of monsters, had she just gotten so used to being one of them that she couldn't see it anymore?

Once in her alley, Abel helped her carry the boxes in and set them down in her storeroom. Then he crossed his arms and leaned in the storeroom doorway. He hadn't even removed his mask, and he didn't say a word as she unpacked her things, then grabbed her cashbox. At least they hadn't been able to steal anything from that.

She handed him five stacks of ten thousand dollars each.

"You sure you're not selling curses, that much cash?" he said.

"I keep cash for hunters like you, and I make it by using or selling what you sell to me. Why? Itching for something else to kill?"

"Did you think this would end with me slapping your ass and calling you pretty?"

Violet sighed. She'd known from the beginning that he'd been with her for a job and an outlet. But she could have used that, yes, even just as a fond farewell.

Still, he'd earned his money, and their transaction was complete. He checked the stacks of bills, then stored them in his jacket before backing out of the storeroom. "Pleasure doing business with you, witch."

Fuck you, too, Abel Simmons.

* * * *

Violet spent the afternoon putting her store back in order.

She opened a bottle of wine, turned her music on high and drank three-quarters of the bottle while she swept, vacuumed, rearranged, then did inventory, because she might as well while the store was still closed.

She also prepared a job description and considered requesting a roommate. It would take some work finding someone who both knew about Meridian's dark little secrets and wouldn't be thrown by the accoutrements and attendant smells that accompanied being a witch, but she could really use the extra money coming in to cover the lease. And she could use the company.

While she waited for dinner delivery to arrive, she cleared out Clive's things from his bedroom, at least what he hadn't already taken. She nearly stumbled down the stairs more than once, because she hadn't eaten anything with the wine, but she didn't want to stop until all his things were outside in the alley. Violet didn't care what happened to them now, as long as his stuff no longer took up her space and she didn't have to see it ever again.

When the delivery guy arrived with her white pizza with mushrooms, she suddenly couldn't stand being alone in her empty store or apartment. She carried the box with her to the outdoor patio a few blocks away that screened black-and-white movies in the evening. That night was a double bill between *Casablanca* and one of the Thin Man flicks. She bought a drink to justify her being there with an outside dinner, then claimed a picnic table for herself.

Many people doubled up with other groups, but she must have put out a vibe that suggested very strongly that she wanted to be alone. No one tried to sit with her, which made her feel even more lonely. The movies made her feel a little better than the food, though, while the food at least settled her stomach and counteracted the effect of the wine.

She bought a chocolate soft-serve ice cream cone, then stayed for the last bit of the Thin Man movie before slowly walking home and back upstairs to her empty apartment. More than anything, she just wanted to sleep, and when she couldn't sleep anymore, then she wanted to do a proper conditioning of her hair before even thinking about opening things back up.

She supposed she could burn some incense for old times' sake. And as a witch, maybe it was about time she got a cat. At the very least, she needed to put the new job listing up at the front of the store and online.

Even so, Violet had come to Meridian alone. There was no reason why she couldn't be alone again. It had just been a while.

She stripped down to her underwear and pulled on a sleep tank top to crawl between her sheets in the cool darkness. She wasn't afraid. She had a baseball bat under the bed, a ritual knife in her nightstand, and she had herself, more dangerous than anything else she owned to protect her.

* * * *

The quality of the morning light was different. At first, she thought the day was overcast, but the light was still golden, not gray—just blocked.

Violet rubbed sleep from her eyes and unwrapped herself from the sheets.

Someone was standing on her fire escape.

At first, she panicked, fearing that Clive had led the succubi to her to take an eye for an eye until everyone was blind, but she sensed no magic emanating from the shadowed figure. When she woke up enough for a clearer look, she saw the hood he wore, the familiar silhouette of his jacket. He was facing away from her, watching the sunrise.

She got out of bed and tiptoed to the sill, then knocked on the window. He jumped only slightly before turning around. He wasn't wearing his mask under his hood, but backlit by the low sun, he might as well have been.

"Forget something?" She hadn't seen anything while purging Clive from her apartment, but she hadn't been looking for Abel's things at the time.

He indicated for her to open the window.

Well, with him standing in full beam of sunrise, she knew he hadn't been turned into a vampire. She pushed the window open. "I was planning to send your clothes back after I cleaned them. Or did I leave something at your place?"

He grabbed her by the front of her rumpled tank top and pulled her upper body through the window and against him, angling his hood to let her in so he could kiss her. She gave a muffled cry of surprise, but as soon as she registered what was happening, she sank into his scent of leather and sweat from working during the night. She smelled blood on him, too, but not a gush or spray, nothing that stained her shirt as he hooked his arm around her, which pressed her hips against the windowsill. She smoothed her palms down his jacket, then dipped her hand beneath the waistband of his jeans.

He groaned into her mouth as she squeezed over the length of his hard cock, tucked into the waist of his briefs.

"I thought I took care of this," she muttered between each time he captured her mouth, as though he didn't even want her to breathe without him.

"Conquest cultists tonight. No sex demons. This has nothing to do with that. Through the whole unloading of the bodies, I've been fighting this goddamn erection, and I didn't have anything to blame it on except you, you fucking witch. Now, invite me in."

She dragged him through the window. He landed gracelessly on the floor, boots slamming onto the floorboards. He almost fell onto her rather than against her, not that she would have minded him collapsing them both into her bed. As he shed his jacket, which crumpled like a dead body on the floor, she drew him back with her to the mess of blankets. When she tried to pull his hoodie over his head, he got briefly caught inside, but she used that opportunity to push him onto her bed and straddle him as she shoved up his undershirt, then pulled all of it off at once.

As soon as he was free, Abel flipped her underneath him and bit his way from her knee to the top of her thigh, pressing his teeth harder and harder into her the farther up he went, until she shouted from what would probably bruise in the shape of his bite.

But she thought she'd absolutely melt when he laughed against her pussy through her underwear, then licked through the material for as long as he could stand before jerking them down her thighs to lick her more directly. Her panties caught around his wrist and stayed there as he worked open his jeans and pushed them and his briefs off his legs. Then he used her underwear to masturbate as he settled between her legs to lick at her, occasionally startling her with his teeth over her folds — albeit much gentler, the suction more violent than his bite.

"Mmm, *fuck...*" He tossed her panties aside, then threw himself fully into the task of making her toes curl against his back, where the same strips of plastic she'd applied still covered the new tattoo. With the healing potion, he'd probably healed already, just hadn't had a chance to remove them.

When her thighs clenched on either side of his head, his stubble bristled against her skin. She arched to meet him anyway, grasping her headboard of her own accord and just letting him take her for a smooth, smooth ride as he worshipped her in his sandpapery, ragged way, all hot breath and drowning himself in her while he canted his hips against the foot of her bed.

She shuddered and moaned, first muffling herself against her arm but then just letting herself cry, despite her open window, because who the hell cared anymore? This was her home, and hers alone, and if her lover was making her feel good this early in the morning, expressing that was her prerogative.

Especially since it had been way too fucking long since she'd had someone in her bed who wanted to be in it, who'd craved her so hard that he'd climbed her fire escape to be right there when she woke up. He hadn't pounded on the window to make her awaken before she was ready and serve his pleasure alone. He'd waited for her to wake up on her own, waited for who knew how long.

And even after she came, he stayed between her thighs, alternating between her cunt and her clit, tasting her juices then torturing her again with slow, hot suction, just to smile every time she twitched.

Finally, she grabbed him by the hair and drew him up her body. Between his nature, summer, and how long he'd been wearing thick, heavy clothes, he almost burned as he covered her. He cupped her breasts, left tooth impressions on them as well, sucked each nipple, the right so hard that her legs curled up and she punched him with her knees. He laughed all the way back to her mouth, where she made him shout from how hard she bit his lip to get back at him.

Sometime between crawling back between her thighs and climbing up her body, he'd put a condom on, and she kind of loved him a little as he pressed against her entrance and let her swallow him up in her body's own time, all while looking like he was being strangled with piano wire. She hummed as she drew him down on top of her, then held him as he lost himself in her. He grabbed the headboard with one hand, using it to pull himself hard into her, then kissed her senseless, stopping only to press his forehead against hers, breathing her in, as he finally let himself come, as deep inside her as he could go.

After pulling out and slipping off the condom, he arranged himself over her again and brought his fingers to her cunt. He wasn't gentle, wasn't lost. He knew exactly where he was going and where he wanted to go with her.

"God and his devils, that is so fucking unfair," she groaned when he found the place that had her gasping and shouting and wild beneath him, rendered carnal alone. It was utter bliss not to think, not to *need* to think. He fingerfucked her into a mess of defensive limbs until she bore down and came so hard that the room went dark again, and not just from her vision bursting with gray clouds.

She shoved him off and out of her, pushed him back down onto the covers to kiss him while he memorized her body with his big, gritty hands, now that all urgency had been removed. Sweat cooled on their skin.

When they finally came up for air, he spanked her ass. "Hey, beautiful, grab me something cold to drink."

Violet huffed as she pushed herself upright and slapped his rough cheek almost as loudly as he'd spanked her, but she rolled off him and off the bed with a grin. The hunter was insufferable when he knew he'd get what he wanted.

Epilogue

Violet glanced up from the lathe when bells rang in a late customer. The working stakes were easy enough to create, because she'd occasionally joined Clive on that, but the ornamental ones had required a steep learning curve.

The fact that she turned stakes three or four days a week didn't seem to bother her new employee, who had been as up front about being a vampire as Violet had been about the fact that stakes comprised a significant portion of their revenue.

Hannah had nodded and just declared that she wouldn't make them, but Violet wouldn't have dreamed of requiring her to do that. The arrangement worked in Hannah's favor, too, since she was part of an alliance between hybrids and a large number of hunter collectives, but that didn't always save the hybrids from independent mercenaries the way that working for Book & Candle would. However, the fact that Hannah was part of the Alliance meant she didn't necessarily piss off every hunter when they came in and were served by a vampire.

It wasn't common for a vampire to keep such diurnal hours, but one of the benefits of working with a witch was that the hunters started bringing more demon blood and even vials of their own for a discount on their purchases, or an extra twenty or fifty added to their sale, depending on the donor. As long as Hannah's werewolf friend drove her to the perpetually shaded alley every morning and she had her own shelf in the new blood fridge, she didn't mind wearing sunglasses in store during the brighter hours.

With someone to cover the counter, Violet could take on a more creative role in addition to what she did afterhours with her potions and bombs, which was a welcome change. She was learning metal-etching to customize her own knives, she made more jewelry with the soldering techniques used on the custom stakes, and she wanted to learn how to do some resin work. There was always room for growth and change.

She still hadn't found a roommate, but now that she'd added a few more people into her life and went out more often than not after closing up the store, she'd converted the extra room into a laboratory, where she could experiment in a little more space than the cluttered storeroom. It meant that her apartment smelled more like herbs and spices than ever, but that wasn't such a terrible thing, and it offset the occasionally less pleasant scents she brought into the house, like viscera or sulfur.

This early in the morning, Violet wasn't surprised by the hunter who entered with a pair of wings mounted on the harness over his long leather jacket, a squint of effort over his mask. He slammed a shatterproof pint bottle of blood on the counter.

Hannah grinned. "My favorite." She had no problem day-drinking in the store. If clueless humans bothered to ask, she lied that it was pomegranate-blueberry.

"Fresh," Abel said gruffly.

Hannah had learned not to take his brusqueness personally. "Boss, you've got some business."

If she implied air quotes around 'business', neither Violet nor Abel acknowledged it.

Violet climbed off her stool and nodded for Abel to go ahead to the storeroom. "Cover the front?" she said as she passed Hannah.

Hannah drank deeply from the bottle. "Shame to waste this high. Maybe someone will come in who I can neck — in a completely consensual, non-bitey way, naturally."

In the back room, Abel had already undone the wings from the harness and set them out on the table and was now going through his backpack, pulling out piece after piece of the incubus he'd killed. When hunting to kill, he had a good grasp on how to minimize damage, and after field-dressing it, he had the strength to carry as much of the body as possible, including the massive wings. Ever since making her his primary broker, he cleaned her out on a regular basis, but then she could turn right around and sell what he'd sold her, and the right buyers put even more back in. He was so good for her business, and she was now no longer out of his way, no matter where the hunt went down.

"Twelve thousand for the lot," she said. He'd brought her enough nearly full collections that they rarely bothered haggling. "Even though that blood's going to leave Hannah flirting with everyone who comes through the door for the rest of the day. And probably you when you leave."

"You're too generous." It wasn't a compliment, nor was it completely honest. He would have preferred fifteen thousand and could sometimes get closer to thirteen elsewhere, but there was no beating the perks of bringing them to her.

She lifted the wings from the table to carry them to the coatrack. She felt covered with lust dust by the time she hung them under the vent. Abel didn't help while she arranged things in storage. He'd done his work by getting it to her. He just leaned against the wall and glared darkly as she put all the pieces where they belonged, the swish of her skirt becoming more and more unbearable as the incubus feathers did their work on her.

While she retrieved the cashbox, Abel slowly closed the storeroom. When doing business, she never closed the door. She didn't trust hunters or demons alone with her, and any battle could threaten the inventory.

But with the door closed, Abel pulled down his mask and shed his jacket, which he hung on the corner of a shelving unit rather than bothering with the coatrack.

When she opened the cashbox, he stepped around the table and crowded behind her, finally pinning her against the edge.

"Ever since that spell you inked on me, witch, incubus magic hits stronger than it used to, as though to compensate for the immunity you gave me for my original preference. I react almost the same to both. You were right. That magic doesn't seem to like such a specific protection spell. Still better than it was, but if I have to suffer, you have to suffer more."

Sometimes he tantalized her with blood, which made her irresistible to Hannah for a disorienting day. Sometimes he used hair or claws. But most often, he pulled feathers from where he'd stored them in his sleeve—designed to torment himself all the way to the store more than even the weight and brush of wings, the effect of which was more muffled through his thick layers.

The angle at which he pinned her to the table had her grinding her mound against the edge as he ran the feather from her cheek down her neck. Her gasps were almost moans until he covered her mouth with his gloved hand. Hannah might know what they were doing in here, but customers could come into the store at any time, and trying to keep quiet was half the thrill.

He followed the path of the feathers with his lips, not quite kissing her but breathing her in, breathing in what happened when incubus feather mingled with her skin, like the chemical reaction of perfume.

Then he shoved his hand rudely down her shirt to cup her through the lace bralette. The lace meant that the feather teased bare skin between the filigree, and when he brought the feather to her nipple, she cried out into his hand, grinding down harder against the table until she nudged it too far for her to use. The hardened nub of her nipple pressed uncomfortably against the lace by the time he let up. Jerking her around to take the lace and her flesh in his mouth didn't make it any better. He continued to stifle her with his gloved fingers as he sucked her tight and flushed and tortured the other nipple with the feather. She squirmed, pushing ineffectually at his arms until she abandoned all attempts to stop him and instead pulled her skirt up to stroke over herself as roughly as he'd taught her to crave.

"Oh no, you don't get to do that, witch." Abel slapped her hands, then bit her nipple until she withdrew.

He pulled her skirt down to pool in a liquid puddle at her feet. Her panties caught at her ankles, but he didn't give her the opportunity or the balance to step out of them. He spun her back around toward the table. Then, standing, he shoved her against it, scooting it across the floor until it hit the doorframe.

"You know, you could stand to be a little less rough on my furniture and the structural integrity of my building." But Violet grinned as she said it, especially as she felt him undoing his pants as well as he could while still smashing her against the table.

"You tell me to be less rough on your hair, your clothes, your furniture, your building… I'm beginning to think you'd prefer a gentleman." After a crinkle of foil, as he rolled the condom down, he used his other hand, fingers spread wide, to slowly push her forward onto the table, her disheveled front flat against the polished grain. "I can do gentle."

Then the feather slithered through her folds, and she stuffed her own hand in her mouth to bite down on her knuckles. When he tickled it over her clit, the tip was wet.

She drew blood with her teeth. "Oh God…"

With just the feather, he brought her over the edge. She nearly broke the table herself, pounding it with her free fist as the climax jolted through her as powerful and painful as electric shock, all while he *laughed* at her.

"For fuck's sake, just fuck me already. Don't be so damn soft…yes, fuck, please, just like that…" Then she let out a long, sustained moan turned rhythmic with his forceful thrusts, banging the table against the wall.

Really, there was a reason why Hannah barely bothered pretending that these little visits were just business transactions.

He held her by her neck but kept the incubus feather between them so that it brushed against them both. Though he squeezed her throat, it was he who sounded strangled as he thrust into her as hard and fast as he wanted, as she wanted. Under the influence of incubus magic that affected them both, all too soon she was shouting her second climax, and he fell over her as he jerked his hips and came, her cunt still clutching at his erection.

"You realize," he panted in her ear, "we might have used most of the magic of that feather, but there are over ten thousand feathers in a sex demon's wings?"

"Only so many minutes in a day." But she stretched luxuriously under his weight, flattening her palms against the door.

"Ever the practical witch." He pressed a kiss to her shoulder, then her hair. That, at least, he'd taken direction on. She didn't mind a little hair-pulling now and then, but she didn't like him getting too much of a mess in it. She was less serious about her clothes and her furniture. Clothes could be mended or replaced. Furniture was made to be used. And although she didn't bruise easily, she liked the ones he gave her.

He hauled her up with him, pinched her taut nipple again, then eased his cock from her and cleaned up after himself while she put herself back in order as best as she could.

As he pulled his jacket on, Violet arranged the table back where it should be. "Dinner tonight? H2Overlook has a horror movie on the roof with a panini food-truck-type thing and ice cream cocktails. Think you can relax before going out?"

He'd be heading back to his motel to sleep, and she had a whole day left to work, but where they had crepuscular overlap, they managed to enjoy each other's company, one way or another.

When Violet opened the door, Abel trapped her in the frame, pinning her there with his body, even though anyone who might have been in the store could see him. He leaned in and kissed her as she worked his mask up his neck and chin, then broke away to let her cover his mouth.

"I could spare the time."

Sign up for our newsletter and find out about all our romance book releases, eBook sales and promotions, sneak peeks and FREE romance books!

Want to see more from this author? Here's a taster for you to enjoy!

Meridian: Tattered & Torn
Aurelia T. Evans

Excerpt

On an unseasonably cool evening in September — a Tuesday — a meteor entered Earth's atmosphere, scorched the dimming sky with a blue glow for fifteen seconds, then burned out over Meridian, Texas, before it could hit the ground.

This, in itself, was not unusual.

Objects from space enter Earth's atmosphere all the time without anyone seeing them, especially during the day. However, this celestial event occurred when the sky was dark enough and the meteor itself large enough to last long enough to notice. A number of security cameras also caught the event.

In this case, only a handful of people actually noticed it, and because it didn't last long enough to capture on their phones, most of them promptly forgot. No one posted asking about whether someone else had seen that flash in the sky or some UFO. No one reported it to news outlets. No meteorologist thought it was important enough to mention during the evening news. The event lasted fifteen seconds, in a brilliant bright sapphire, and died without fanfare.

* * * *

The head librarian of Archimedes Public Library — three stories of books, a rare book collection, several rows of DVDs that echoed Blockbusters of old, and a children's section that doubled as a play-date space, a mix of the magical and modern that made her proud to be a book bearer — switched off the last light in her office. She folded her jacket and scarf over her arm in case the false fall weather was too chilly for her from the building to her car.

After locking the grand wooden double doors behind her, Beth gripped the railing to descend the two dozen stairs down to the street. On wet days, the stairs were a bit more difficult and she would use the zigzagging accessibility ramp to ease her way down, but tonight she was feeling particularly lively, and she was looking forward to a date with an older gentleman at one of her favorite restaurants.

He'd texted her to let her know that he was already at the restaurant and was ordering some wine for when she arrived. This was their third date, and although she hadn't been looking forward to returning to the dating world, she was quite enjoying being courted. Her apartment still smelled good from the roses he'd bought for her last time. And since this was their third date, she might just let him try to kiss her.

Young people usually thought the third date was the sex date, but she and Gerard weren't going that fast — although she certainly wasn't planning to wait six months like with her first boyfriend, back before texting and golden-age dating apps. There was something exhausting and exhilarating about trying again, though, in the new world, with its new ways.

Beth had lived in Meridian all her life. A few years ago, she'd transferred from the old public library to the Archimedes, which the notoriously solitary Mr. Vega had built for the city. She'd watched Meridian turn from a nothing waystation on the way to Fort Worth to a bustling city to rival Dallas. She hadn't known whether she'd like it as buildings stole the horizon and it began its inevitable sprawl into suburbs, but she was still here, her family was here, and it wasn't terrible at all.

Her shoe hit an uneven place on a concrete stair. Beth clung to the brass railing to keep from falling.

The Archimedes was such a new build, even by Meridian's standards, that there was no reason why concrete should already have been so uneven from the annual freeze and melt—which seemed to destroy streets and sidewalks solely for the devil to laugh at the inevitable skinned knees, black eyes, and tire blowouts.

Streetlights hadn't quite caught up to the earlier evening darkness, and Beth's eyes weren't so good at night anymore. She found her flashlight app and switched it on to see what that dark blob in the slightly darker blob on the stairs could possibly be. No one had run in to tell her that something terrible happened during open hours. And she might have bad night eyes and needed to wear special glasses to drive, but she would have noticed if there had been an earthquake, even a minor one.

The flashlight switched on—blinding at first, but her eyes eventually adjusted.

Beth stumbled back a few steps with a gasp. A shriek strangled in her throat behind the hand she brought to her freshly lipsticked mouth.

"Oh my God, you poor dear. Oh my."

She fumbled to get to the actual phone part of her phone to call emergency services.

"Hello? Hello? Yes, I'm at the Archimedes Public Library. My name is Beth Holding. I'm the head librarian. There's an unconscious woman on the front steps. The concrete is all broken around her, and it looks like she's knocked out and bleeding. No, she's not dead. I may not be a doctor, young man, but I can see her breathing. No, I haven't touched her. I don't want to hurt her any more than she already is. Oh, she looks like she's been beaten pretty badly, or maybe it was a fall? I can't imagine how or why. Just get paramedics down here quickly. Oh, dear. Can I cover her with my jacket? She's not wearing a stitch. Okay, I can hear sirens."

Beth crept carefully down the steps and unfolded her jacket to shake it out like a blanket and cover the poor girl's nakedness. She was bleeding from multiple places on her bare body, but not terribly. Just by eye under the flashlight, Beth couldn't tell if she had any broken bones.

"Just hold on, sweetheart," Beth whispered to the girl. "Just hold on. See? Help is on the way. I'll pray for your healing."

Red and blue lights flashed against the looming hulk of the library above. Beth ran down to meet the paramedics, who pulled out a gurney but rushed with a spine board up to where the woman lay halfway up the stairs.

When Beth turned back to watch them, shining her light where they were working, she thought it was such a curious thing. Where the concrete damage spread from a central point under the girl, the cracks looked just like wings.

About the Author

Aurelia T. Evans is an up-and-coming erotica author with a penchant for horror and the supernatural.

She's the twisted mind behind the werewolf/shifter Sanctuary trilogy, demonic circus series Arcanium, and vampire serial Bloodbound. She's also had short stories featured in various erotic anthologies.

Aurelia presently lives in Dallas, Texas (although she doesn't ride horses or wear hats). She loves cats and enjoys baking as much as she dislikes cooking. She's a walker, not a runner, and she writes outside as often as possible.

Aurelia loves to hear from readers. You can find her contact information, website details and author profile page at https://www.firstforromance.com

ENTWINED PUBLISHING

www.ingramcontent.com/pod-product-compliance
Lightning Source LLC
Chambersburg PA
CBHW020818260626
47169CB00003B/723